Celia Brayfield is also the ~~author~~ ... ~~Getting~~
Home published by Warn... ... ~~The~~
Prince, *White Ice* and *Bestsel...* ... ~~book about writing.~~
As a journalist she has written for a wide range of publications, including *The Times*, where she was a television critic for five years, and London's *Evening Standard*. She was born in London and educated at St Paul's Girls' School and at university in France. She now lives in West London with her daughter.

Praise for *Celia Brayfield*

SUNSET

'Told with great skill and masterful timing' *Good Housekeeping*

'A complex and cleverly written book' *Image*

GETTING HOME

'Deliciously comic – lightning flashes of wit and scalpel-sharp observation' *Daily Mail*

'With a sharp wit and snappy dialogue Brayfield has produced a very funny, cleverly plotted novel that displays Fay Weldon's understanding of the pleasure to be derived from seeing the bad get their just desserts' *Daily Telegraph*

HARVEST

'Sophisticated, well-plotted and cannily conversant with the mechanics of betrayal, duplicity and, ultimately, revenge, this is a deliciously satisfying read' *Sunday Times*

PEARLS

'Ms Brayfield knows what she is doing, and what she does, she does well' *Anthony Burgess*

9/21

For Sarah and John

Acknowledgements

I am deeply grateful to Jackie Bragg for her knowledge of Canarian history, geography and culture, and for tracing the text on which the journal of the Cura Rosario is based. I am always grateful for Willow and Tony Schulte for following their dreams and this time for enhancing my Spanish on the way. While this book struggled from an image into reality, Imogen Taylor and the Little, Brown team have been a delight and an inspiration, and Jonathan Lloyd has been a hero who always called back.

CHAPTER 1

Beach Bar

Only certain people come here. The sign at the end of the row of white houses says PLACIDO'S BEACH BAR, with a kinked arrow below to tell you to walk around the back. The sign is old and hard to read, the street looks like the places where people get shot in spaghetti westerns. Square white buildings turn blind walls to the space. It's empty and it promises to lead nowhere.

There is no beach here. This is the rocky end of the bay; the bar overlooks long spits of black basalt reaching into the sea. The rocks could be the fossil backbones of dinosaurs; they look as if they lived once.

The sign is not a joke. In spirit, Placido's is a beach bar. Whatever it is that draws people to a beach, it's here. When you've spent time at Placido's, it will be the only beach bar you'll ever think deserves the name.

The beach at La Quemada is the other way, a shining field of sand running a couple of kilometres to the black cliffs. The sea is always rough, the waves are huge; this is the Atlantic, after all. At low tide, because there is almost no slope on the beach, the sea boils over itself halfway to the skyline, angry and silent. When the tide rises, the waves come roaring in over the sand faster than you can run. Boys are drowned every year.

The wind is always from the north, raging down from Africa. Quemada is a great surf beach but deadly to the innocent. There is never a lifeguard, nobody runs up flags. The island lets people take their chances. I used to think this was callous; Stella thinks it is poetic. She sees it as part of the Spanish death thing, giving people a decent opportunity to get killed.

The wet sand is silvery. At the back of the bay, beyond the reach of the sea, it becomes yellow and rises to a stretch of low dunes. Nothing has taken root here, no grasses, none of the glaucous plants that hold down the soil further inland. Hippies have built windbreaks with small rocks, semicircular half-huts where they play house, huddle up over a joint, build a little fire and leave scorched hearthstones. The ash is soon blown away.

The eastern cliff is the edge of the Picos d'Oro mountains, which rise to three thousand feet. The cliff curves round to make a colossal basin which the surf fills entirely with spray. When the tide is in and the sun shines you can watch the rainbows in the bowl of the cliff all day, little arcs forming and fading and forming again and again until the light is gone. The waves roar; you have to shout into the noise.

The beach is the other way and Placido doesn't want passing trade. He wants the people who trust their dreams. We are the ones who will follow the faded sign pointing in the wrong direction down a street fit to die in, because we have faith that what we seek will be there at the end. I am one of those, I found this place. So far in my life, I have absolutely believed that what I wanted would be there at the end. Now it seems possible that I was wrong.

The street ends at the bar. Most of the old streets on the island are like this, pointless strips of sandy earth scattered with small black pebbles. Placido's street is atypical because it goes somewhere. The old houses here express a trust in their function. They say that the lives lived inside them have a purpose, although until recently, there was no reason to live here and so no reason to build anything.

There are no footprints, no tyre-tracks, no paw marks, no dog turds, no litter, no flies. The wind erases everything, sweeping whatever is unwanted out into the ocean. There is no need for paving because there is never mud, because there is never rain, except when there is. But when all the rain collected in the idiotically primitive device which I sometimes tend at the Instituto de Geografia is added up, the annual fall in Los Alcazares isn't usually more than an inch.

With the wind and the sun and the dust, people stay indoors when they can and keep their shutters closed, so the streets are deserted. Not that Quemada would have much street life. When I first saw it the whole place was maybe six houses, plus the boat house and the bar.

I first came here with Stella. I wanted to follow the sign and she, who always knew how to set me free, followed me. She had taught me how to find water holes of pleasure in the desert of my life. Placido's was the best of them. Now I come here and she doesn't. I brought Matthew here.

This should be a place for lovers but not many come. Perhaps lovers are too anxious for their perfect moments, too unsure of each other to take the chance and follow the sign, and so they miss the peak experience for which they're searching. Instead they find something pleasant but mediocre. They turn the other way, to the new restaurant on the hill, a smart place with white sun umbrellas over the tables, but nothing compared to Placido's.

Stella doesn't come to Quemada at all now. The island has no more pleasures to offer her, she is bored with them all, especially since I introduced Matthew into our environment. I've come because I'm sure she wouldn't come here with him, but I don't like having my dream faded and blemished and compromised by these pathetic moves.

The door is usually open and the curtain of plastic strips in truly horrible colours – brown, orange, green, cream – hides the interior. There is a stone floor and a Formica-topped bar and a poster of the fish of the tropical Atlantic as an aid to ordering. Maybe there's a man, or two men, sitting at one of the cheap tables, smoking. From time to time – you learn never to expect normal sights at Placido's – a bowl of octopus salad or a platter of tortilla may sit on the counter. The door behind the bar is open sometimes: you get a glimpse of black rocks and sea. Today it's docile, wave after wave lapping at the rocks without argument.

You go through this room to the terrace, which is a small area of gravel fenced in to the height of the table tops by screens of split bamboo and shaded by a roof of the same flimsy stuff, although people mostly come here in the late afternoon, when the sun is no longer cruel. The tables are wooden, the legs painted green. 'This is very Zen,' was Matthew's comment. It is plain, it is essential. There's very little wind because the cliffs cut it out. You sit down.

It feels as if the beauty begins after that, although you know that the beauty had no beginning until you believed in it. The rocks run out to the sea, the waves break over the rocks and the sun sets. Stella says this island has the best sunsets in the world, and she has spent a lot of time in her life checking out the contenders, so I believe her.

On the south side of the island you see the sun fall out of sight behind the mountains, making them look harder and denser as the light fades. Here on the north side the sun passes through layers of vaporous sky, gathering colours as it sinks into the sea, slow-motion fireworks, violet, orange, pink, red. The last rays blaze up from below the horizon, tinting the underside of the dark clouds and gilding the waves.

The sunset takes about two hours from the time the first wisps of rose appear in the sky. This is an island full of wonders, but the sunset is the greatest of them and Placido's terrace is the best place to see it. Sometimes people applaud when the last slice of flame disappears into the ocean. Placido despises that, he slams the door behind the bar and starts yelling at his boys to fetch up more beers from the fridge and get more fish cleaned.

Beauty and pain, what a mix: they make each other worse. Pain makes beauty unbearable; beauty turns the knife in your wound. These last weeks I have chosen to drive around all the ugly roads on the island because I'm feeling enough pain already. I took the fast road from Torrenueva, and the road along the neon strip through Playa de los Angeles, and the airport road out to Ubrique and the road to Santesteban del Campo which runs by the water park and the derelict greenhouses flapping dirty plastic in the wind.

I took my seat, the best seat, the one at the corner table where you get the ultimate experience, where there would be nothing between us and the rocks and the water and the sunset, wondering why I wanted to torture myself, what kinky geophysical S & M session this was going to be. There was a mackerel sky and the sea was milky slate.

This was Matthew's idea, he chose this for us. 'Let's meet at Placido's,' he said, as if he were saying nothing important. 'We've got to talk. I'd like to get away.' He thinks if he chooses my favourite place to tell me I won't cry so much when he says he's leaving. He is thoughtful, even if he gets it wrong sometimes. I haven't seen him for five days. We have never been apart before.

I am no good with love. It's new to me, I don't know about it. What are the essential properties of love? Should it make me happy? Should it give me pain? What's happy, anyway? A deal you make with life, Stella said once. She used to straighten me out over this kind of thing, but I can't ask Stella now.

That was my line: 'We've got to talk.' Weasel phrase. I know what I meant when I used it, which was, 'Bad news, you're not going to like this.' I never actually wanted to talk to Conal, or hear what he had to say; I just wanted to act out civilised behaviour, to look as if I were doing the kind of thing that a thoughtful, responsible, intelligent wife would do with her husband. I wouldn't sink to his level. Being good was my only revenge.

That was my personal delusion because everyone else around me was too wrapped up in their own things to notice I was alive. I decided, when I was very young, around the time my son was born, that if I was going to be cheated over love, I would not retaliate. I would still act the way people should, the way good people acted, the way people who loved, who were loved, who went to restaurants together, who lived in pale-walled apartments with shelves full of books acted. Then I met Stella, someone who had pale walls and books; my life became a *folie à deux*.

My husband and my son had my body, but Stella had custody of my soul, until Matthew arrived. Matthew did decent behaviour big time; that was why I believed in him. But Matthew, I discovered, is a great faker. He has a gift for it and most of his life he has faked for a living. 'We've got to talk.' I do not like that. All the same, it's a fact.

I can't resist the sunset, so I got here early, when the only other people were two Swedish boys by the door, lingering with a couple of brandies, picking their teeth at long intervals, their conversation like drops falling in a pool, just audible over the grumbling surf.

Stella's husband was killed a week ago. They found his body in his car, which had run off the road that winds down from their villa through the vineyards, and crashed into a valley. This happened at night. It is pretty easy to run a car off many of the island's roads at night, because the Tarmac is black and the lava rocks are black and the district governments are not bothered about painting white lines along the roadsides, let alone putting up crash barriers. The Spanish death thing again. Somebody told me that the island has the worst road-accident rate in Spain; that would be quite an achievement, if it's true. People are also not bothered about verifying facts here.

It is true that Stella's husband is dead. I went with her to the hospital to make the formal identification, facts matter to me. It was a bad thing and I cared about her, but I also wanted to go because I was afraid that she would pick a man, most likely Matthew. 'Oh my God! You're not going by yourself! No, no, darling, you can't possibly. Don't even think about it. Listen, I'll drive you, we'll go together, take my car . . .' So I went with her, another spot on my dream, the pox of deceit rotting it away.

He was a mess, although I have seen worse. His face was split open like a cracked melon, the nose and mouth were mush, one of the eyes was not exactly in its socket. The gashed skin was white like raw pork rind. The nurses had washed him and tidied him a little. The dead must be buried within forty-eight hours here, one of those exotic hot-country customs Stella finds so exciting. That we both find exciting.

His hair was wet and someone had combed it to the side. Tom had hair like a lion's mane: it stood up from his forehead in dark brown tufts, beyond combing. Stella reached over and tried to make it lie right, a tender gesture, with her stiff suntanned hand. 'Poor dear, he must have been so unhappy.' She was yelping into a tissue; Stella was not made to weep. 'I should have been there for him.'

Later in the day, when we went back to their villa, her mood changed. 'Stupid, stupid, stupid,' she said and over again when she was in one of the bathrooms and thought I couldn't hear. 'Why are men so fucking, fucking stupid?'

Tom was in a little room at the back of the hospital and one of the doctors had signed a death certificate. Here on Los Alcazares we have only eighty thousand inhabitants, plus a hundred thousand tourists a week, which means that a morgue and a post-mortem are luxuries for which we do not qualify. If a full autopsy has to be done, the body can be sent on one of the police boats to the regional capital on Gran Canaria. Nobody bothers much about foreigners, even though most of the population weren't born here. And in this case the cause of death was pretty obvious.

I ordered a beer. Placido only keeps Cervesa Tres Reyes; the man has a lot of focus, he's a *conejero*, Canarian homeboy. He has travelled – once he went to Vallodolid to visit his wife's family. He serves Americans and Germans and Belgians but he sees no reason to keep their native beers. We all admired this, Stella, Tom and I, and later Matthew. We all liked to think of ourselves as such absolute folk, although Stella was the only one whose life produced evidence of it. Now my lover is coming to tell me that Stella has him, absolutely.

* * *

My life has been very corny. Fate saves all the worst cliches for me. The way I met Matthew was so corny, I should have refused to believe it. I would be ashamed of it if things had not turned out so gloriously. Plus I don't have the same shame threshold as most women.

The whole event is like a video stored in the archive of my memory which I can get out and run any time. While I waited for him I ran it over and over for myself. I can run it in slow motion and pause the best moments. Here I am at the bus stop in very heavy rain, stepping back as the bus pulls up and sends a wave of gutter water towards my feet. It's evening in winter and the lights of the bus glow out into the dark street. If I look carefully, I can see the blurred dark shape of Matthew's jacket just inside the window. I'm not feeling anything much: I didn't use my feelings then, they were hung up in a cupboard waiting for the right occasion. It's the end of the day, I have to go home and I feel sad and cramped.

The bus stops, the doors crash open, I fold my umbrella, get on, pay the fare and take the nearest seat, on the benches that run lengthways along the vehicle. I'm carrying a bag of work, twenty-seven essays by eight-year-olds on How Rivers Begin. I put the wet umbrella on my left and keep the work on the seat to my right; then I look up and my whole life goes off in my face like a bomb.

I always pause this moment. In real life when you pause a video it's not very satisfactory. There is a tendency for the picture to shake, and it's like that with my memory, I can't quite make out the details. All that's really clear are Matthew's eyes, with that laser look he gets when his feelings erupt, and the eyebrows drawn flat, each black hair etched against his skin, dragged from vertical to diagonal. I can also see the raindrops on his black leather jacket. And his lips. He had a day's growth of beard, which made them seem bare and ready to kiss. What's most clear is something invisible; the charge there was between us, the hissing lightning of affinity.

Next I see us thrown back in our seats by the explosion. That really happened, it's not my memory editing in comic strip effects. I recoil and he recoils, and his foot shoots out and knocks my umbrella over, and he snaps forward and picks it up, and then we get the first line of dialogue: 'I'm sorry.' A Cary Grant moment. Corny or what.

Then comes the funny part. Matthew has to think of a way to start a conversation. He looks at the umbrella, which is the most boring piece of haberdashery ever made and no help at all. He looks at the bag, which is a black nylon thing and closed, so no clues there. He dare not look at me in case the lightning strikes again and knocks him over – he told me afterwards he actually felt the force was that strong, that he would be thrown right across the bus if our eyes connected again. I'm looking at the floor myself, knowing that he's struggling with all this, understanding it all absolutely with that instant transference that's part of our thing. I am also feeling as powerful as Cleopatra, another new sensation.

In the end he just laughs, and shrugs because there is no natural entry to our love affair, and manages to look at me with half-closed eyes, and says, 'Are you getting off at Custom House Walk?'

'No,' I say, 'my stop is out at Green Lanes.'

'Why don't you get off at Custom House Walk,' he says, 'then we can have a drink together.'

I had to say yes. Saying no would have been like trying to make the world turn backwards. I put my right hand over my left to hide my wedding ring and found he was watching me. 'Too late,' he said.

Maybe because I became an adult too soon and with so much disgrace, I tried to compensate ever after. All my life was maintained at high standards, everything I did was policed by my conscience. I never wanted to be bad in any way, but I was out of practice with surprises. I was not expecting lightning to strike twice in the same place. So saying yes did not feel sinful at all but completely correct. Only the very feeble voice of reason said that no good could come of what we did.

So there is Matthew handing me down from the bus. He has a special manner for these somewhat wussy acts of chivalry, a habit of quarter-turning away from the woman so that he can be polite and macho at the same time. Matthew has a natural aptitude for inspiring romance and when I remember him doing this it makes me think of a highwayman gallantly handing down his victim from her coach.

We went into the cheesy little bar in Custom House Walk, the kind of place that has wooden wine box lids and hundreds of yellowing business cards pinned to the walls. We had two glasses of their Rioja – already, please note, the Spanish motif. It was half an hour before we admitted that it tasted like turpentine. We didn't say much but we laughed excessively. And at the end of it, Matthew took someone else's card off the wall and wrote his number on it with the waitress's pen, and said, 'I would like you to call me. Please.'

I found I wanted to cry because at the base of his neck where his collar is open his skin is very fine and smooth, the texture of cream. This is still the dearest part of his body to me. I took the card from him.

I can't remember exactly how I was getting through life then. I wasn't dreaming of meeting a handsome stranger; I have the impression of a state of existential patience. I know I didn't dream actively; that was something I'd let go of when my marriage began. When I say I followed a dream in coming here, I mean the sort of vision that burns dimly in your mind, the little votive light to the person you know you are at heart which gutters feebly in the huge dark cathedral of who you have to be to get by.

I cherished that flame but I did not pursue it, and if Matthew had not been on the bus I would have kept the flame for nothing; it would have died when I died and nobody would have known it existed. That is now a frightening thought; it makes me feel I was standing next to death, as if a truck came along instead of the bus, and hit the person standing next to me at the bus stop, and killed them. It could have been me.

* * *

Los Alcazares gets television from a satellite in seven languages. Telephone calls go by satellite too; you can get a lot of echo or you can get a completely clean line to the mainland, as if you were calling the house next door. The newspapers come from Stockholm, Geneva, Washington, Paris, Frankfurt and London at least a day late. People are on the Net, but the wonders of the World Wide Web seem puny next to the miracles you can see out of the window and besides, there's really only one way to find out what you need to know here. Los Alcazares lives by word of mouth – it's one of the many medieval aspects of island life. To get information, you go to a bar and ask. What you are told may or may not be true, but after a few weeks here the truth starts to become unimportant.

I had been here two weeks when someone told Professor Emilio Izquierdo Menendez, director of the Instituto and of a joint project with the Canarian Oceanography Foundation, that there was a woman geography teacher on the island who had good Spanish. It was to be presumed that I needed a job, because most foreigners who come here need work pretty urgently. Milo did the proper thing, and sent

Eva, his assistant, to find Stella and ask for an introduction. On the island, people do not make calls or send letters; they know each other, by reputation at least, and they talk. Stella brought Eva to the bar by her office where we met in the evening, and very shortly I had a desk at the Instituto.

Now when I am not scrambling out to the sea-level monitors along the north coast, I'm making a new translation of the journals of the Cura Don Agustin Perez Rosario, the parish priest of Yesto, one of the few literate people who were able to witness the creation of Los Alcazares as it is today. When Milo's survey is completed, I will also translate the whole report, thereby, he hopes, helping to get it published in *Nature* magazine and discussed across all America, so that the United Nations will honour the spirit of the International Decade for Natural Disaster Reduction and give him money for a vulcanological station here.

Yesto now is hardly even a village. It is just a junction on the highway to Puerto de la Frontera where the road to the national park joins the main drag. There is a bar like an aircraft hangar for the coach parties, the old church standing between two dying palms and a stupendous stretch of dual carriageway built with EU investment and landscaped with hundreds of scarlet canna lilies.

Now there is naked rock as far as you can see in every direction around Yesto, but when my Cura said his first mass in the church in 1790-something it was a market town nestling in wheat fields and vineyards, the centre of the most fertile region on the whole island.

This is how the Cura Rosario recorded the first signs of trouble.

20 September 1793: To Almonte yesterday to give thanks for the vintage. There has been rain this year, the harvest is good and there was much celebration. One would imagine that in this cruel climate the grapes would wither on the vines, but God has given these people such ingenuity that the farmers first dig for each vine a hollow in the earth to catch the dew and shelter the young plant from the wind. For further shelter a wall of stones is built around the edge. A cactus is rooted first at the bottom of the hole and the vine grafted on to its stem, so that the succulent plant can nourish the vine with its moisture. The wine has a smoky taste; they would not think much of it in Castile, but here one can get used to it. Matured with sugar and brandy it becomes more appealing.

As I rode home at midday a white rain, like a fall of snow, came down so thickly that my mule became Balaam's ass. He could not see his path and refused to walk on, though I beat him with a thorn branch until it split in pieces.

* * *

Here is a story that tells you about Stella. Her villa, like all the old houses on the island, has an underground water cistern called an aljibe. The house was built as a hollow square, three identical single-storey wings around a courtyard with the external wall making the fourth. All the roofs slope to a system of gutters which funnel the dew and rain into the aljibe, where it can be stored with the minimum loss from evaporation. It's an excellent system, invented by the Arabs, and even now that the island's water comes from the desalination plants, the water truck will pipe its costly load directly into the aljibe, where one exists.

Stella is good to her houses. She never rests in her home but runs about looking after it, patting, stroking, arranging, offering it flowers or new pictures like little gifts. In the courtyard she wanted to tie in a new branch of the great pink bougainvillaea which grows in the corner and she had to stand on the shallow dome of the cistern to catch it. The cistern has a wooden hatch at ground level to allow for cleaning, and she saw that it was broken.

'Tom!' she called, tottering into the living room on her ridiculous sandals, 'Tom! We must get this fixed at once. We can't have a hole in the aljibe. Some child will fall in and drown and poison our water. You must call the builders, Tom. Tom!'

Tom came in from out back where he had established his office, smiling because she is funny and he loved to serve her, and said, 'Some child will fall in and poison our water? What child is this, Stella?'

'Any child,' she insisted, sagging against the door frame with her cheek to the wood. In the presence of a significant male, Stella went into Marilyn mode. 'It'll be a nuisance, Tom. Can't you make them fix it?'

'Sure,' he said. 'Does it have to be today?'

'To-om! It's a hole in our aljibe.'

'Of course.' He looked at his watch, because although he had been two years on the island at that time, he still needed to remind himself of Spanish working hours. Tom adapted slowly, which was one of the things Stella had against him.

So she sighed, 'Aren't you going to call them, Tom?'

'Sure, sure.' You could almost hear the wheels going round in his head while he worked out how to make the request in Spanish. Tom was not a linguist either, which also counted against him with Stella. There are women who bring out the worst in men who work with their hands, and she is one of them.

Tom sloped across the room to the telephone, rummaged for the number in their book with his big square-ended fingers and made the call.

While he was speaking, Stella, who by this time would have told anyone who would still listen that she despaired of Tom, that island life had ruined him, that he was hardly a shadow of the wonderful man she had married, tripped across the marble floor and hugged his free arm. She applied the length of her body to his arm, rising on tiptoe so that his hand fetched up in the region of her crotch. She disengaged herself exactly at the moment he finished the call, and tripped out into the courtyard again, throwing an idle, 'Well done, darling,' over her shoulder.

This episode is typical of Stella in four ways. First, she plays any exchange with a man as an erotic encounter in miniature. When I met her she wasn't like this. She didn't need to be, she had pure, natural glamour. It was during her single years, when her star faded, that she became compulsively seductive.

Second, she believes that men are here to serve her; she believes this so completely that it's true, her men all adore making themselves her slaves. Of these two features of Stella's personality I was in awe for at least the first ten years of our friendship, without understanding that Stella's concept of service is not gender-specific, and that I was also serving, but I enjoyed it so much that I never noticed.

Third, she can't tell the difference between tragedy and nuisance. This is quite heroic, when what others experience as tragedy will impinge on Stella as a nuisance. On the other hand, to Stella a nuisance is actually a tragedy, because it derails her primary life activity, which is having fun.

Fourth, note the lack of proper concern for the notional child whose drowning would create such a nuisance. Stella actually proposed this scenario with a relish. Her eyes flashed when she said, 'Some child will fall in and drown.'

She looked at me when she said it, because although she spoke as if she were joking, she wasn't, and I knew she wasn't. We are friends, we can talk about anything, we keep for each other those parts of our hearts that can't be shared with anyone else. We confess, we accept, we absolve each other. She was trying to say that we could even talk about the death of children. Maybe she can, but I can't.

Stella regards children as a supreme nuisance, or indeed a supreme tragedy. Tom, unlucky fellow, had married her with the gut feeling that there was some connection between marriage and children. It was one of those Maupassant-dark misunderstandings between the two of them; he had imagined that she wanted to get married in order at last to have a child, while she had just wanted a husband.

This mismatch of life goals was beyond Tom's understanding. He was flummoxed; he came from a world where girls entrapped men to get children. For two years, since he got off the plane with a few grains of the wedding rice still in his hair, he had lurched uncomprehendingly after his brilliant wife expecting her at any minute to stop flitting from bar to bar all night and stay home to decorate a nursery.

My story, of course, had pushed the child button with Stella. 'That is one bum rap,' she pronounced. 'A life sentence. Oh, I just can't believe something so cruel could have happened to you. I want to make it all up to you right now, I want to give you some real good times.'

She saw me as disadvantaged when I had a child, and I saw her as disadvantaged because she had no child. I no longer have a child and the equilibrium is out.

CHAPTER 2

With Us, in Spirit

Tom was to be buried in the island's central cemetery which lies on that ugly road between Villanueva
and Santesteban del Campo. Officially Los Alcazares
is Catholic. Every village has its church. You can
tell which shops and restaurants are Spanish because
they shut for the big holy days. Two nuns keep the
cemetery immaculate and switch on the electric
bulbs over every burial site at dusk. Up on the bare
crown of the highest mountain, a fit venue for
Walpurgis night, there is a monastery, a white
matchbox containing one Benedictine anchorite.

Los Alcazares is a very spiritual place. We have a
lot of faiths here. The New Agers say that three of
the world's major ley lines cross here, that we are a
node on the energy circuit running through
Glastonbury, Jerusalem and Marrakesh. Anyway, we
have a lot of faiths here. Down in the fleshpots of

Angeles, we have an Anglican church and two Lutheran churches; there is a Tibetan Buddhist *gompa* in Aranda and a Zen buddhist *zen-do* at Tamiza; a Methodist chapel and a Christian Science reading group in Villanueva, a synagogue at Aranda and an old mosque for the Moroccans in Ubrique. Carole, Tom's masseuse and Stella's hairdresser, has fallen in with some Reiki healers at Puerto de la Frontera who have meditation evenings twice a week. There are some druids in the south who hold a full-moon festival every month, and a bunch of weirdos, mostly Swiss, who live in caves somewhere inland and call themselves the Children of Hildegarde; they are training themselves to levitate *en masse* so they can fly to the moon when the end of the world happens.

Tom was buried by the Anglican priest, Martin Donald. We call him Father Martin, another of the many things we do here which we would not do at home. Stella wore a mantilla and black stilettos, I broke out my tuxedo suit with satin lapels and Matthew stood between us wearing his black leather jacket for the first time since we'd left England. In this carnival gear we joined the crowd at the cemetery. Stella started dabbing her eyes under her veil as people muttered how sorry they were.

All Tom's island life was represented: the first condolences came from Tom's doctor and closest friend, Isleywn Pritchard, who dispensed a hug and said, 'Indeed a tragedy for us all.' Next, Maryse, whose voice is reputedly on Elton John's last three albums, although nobody can believe anything like that here because people arrive with all sorts of histories. Stella toyed with the idea that Tom had been having an affair with Maryse. She fluttered over in midnight blue chiffon and a cloud of scent which even the wind could not disperse, and exhaled her sympathy: 'Bless, Stella darling. This is bad, isn't it? Life can be so hard. I don't know what to say.'

Carole wore her pinstriped suit with shoulder pads, the skirt tight around her conical thighs. Leif, Tom's chiropractor, wore a yellow silk shirt because he said Tom made him think of the sun. Sam had put in all his earrings for the event. Sam's business is Radio Angeles; for Tom he had pre-recorded his morning show and left the computer in charge of transmission in his apartment on the marina.

Fred Dagenham, who runs The Crown and Anchor down on the harbour in Angeles with his wife Bunny, had put on his British Legion tie. Terry Race came last, slinking nervously to the back of the group. Terry lives on his yacht at the marina and takes tourists sport fishing off Punto Grande. He had found a brass-buttoned blazer to go over his Levi's but he didn't look comfortable in it. It was a Tuesday, which made the events that followed more surprising.

Father Martin gave a eulogy, which Stella had composed but said she was too distressed to deliver. 'Tom Banks was a very special man,' he told us. 'Not just because of what he was in the wider world but in the qualities for which we here on Los Alcazares came to cherish him, for his good nature, his kindness to those in trouble, his generosity as a host, the warmth of his personality.' Stella sobbed at this point, a twisted little noise under the shaking veil, and leaned towards Matthew, who put his arms around both of us. Jealousy wrung my stomach. The sky was cloudless, the sun was scorching but the wind blew steadily so most of us kept our dark glasses on. We looked pretty surreal.

To hear what our spiritual leader was saying we had to stand close around him. Father Martin is probably about fifty, a patriarchally huge man, maybe 6 foot 5, who has a big nose and grey hair shaved very short to ear-level and then allowed to be floppy, so he looks like a Norman warlord. The sun has burned his nose red. His church, like The Crown and Anchor, the Beaver troop and the animal hospital, has become one of the cornerstone institutions of the British community here even though most of its supporters are probably unbelievers; it's just a part of our national identity, now we are thousands of miles from home and have to speak at least three different languages a day.

'When Tom entertained us, as he so often did,

with the stories of his newspaper days, I felt privi-
leged to be in his company,' Father Martin
continued, evidently on his own initiative, 'knowing
that he had been one of our leading journalists.' Not
to speak ill of the dead, but this was an exaggera-
tion. When he married Stella, Tom had been made
redundant from the job of sports reporter on a
provincial evening paper to which he had clung by
his fingernails for too long. With her to bully him,
he was supposed to set up a foreign property magazine designed to stoke people's dreams with
hundreds of pictures of villas, pools, palms, golf
courses and beaches.

'Tom was a man to whom honesty was not an old-
fashioned concept. I'm sure his colleagues in the
media would join with us now in honouring him as
a man who may have been, at times, perhaps, too
much of a good deed for this naughty world.' Father
Martin was proud of that observation, a good gloss
put on the fact that in business Tom had been an
idiot. Island life exposes such weaknesses immediately. I saw Stella lift her nose and nod, accepting
this camouflage for her late husband's only real
shortcoming.

Father Martin invited us to join in prayer and
steamed through his Sunday specials: Queen
Elizabeth and the British Royal Family, King Juan
Carlos and the Spanish Royal Family, archbishops
and cardinals on both sides, the President in case he

had any Americans in, the European government because their designation of Los Alcazares as an Objective One Area has meant the second desalination plant, the new roads, the electricity grid and the satellite phone connection; the United Nations because their appointment of the island as a reserve of the biosphere has added the wind-farms, the Instituto and a portion of Milo's time. He finished up with the people we knew, the sick, the sad and we the bereaved.

'Stella, his wife, his friends here on Los Alcazares and of course Tom's relatives in England . . .' Matthew and I were probably the only people there who noticed that we were not specifically invited to pray for Tom's first wife and their three children, nor was any mention made of his family in the eulogy. The very word 'relatives' was mumbled, but even so Stella stiffened when Father Martin said it.

Our vicar went straight on into the committal, running through 'ashes to ashes, dust to dust' quickly and quietly because it was not at all appropriate for the actual method of interment. Next came his big number, the processional hymn. Father Martin reached for his cross and led us off down the central aisle of the enclosure, away from the coffin. He does this to stop people seeing what happens next.

The cemetery contains a semicircular white wall

about fifteen feet high, built of typical island materials – grey breeze blocks faced with whitened plaster – enclosed within an area marked by a lower white wall. The concave façade is divided into slot-shaped rectangular sections, and when the time comes a burial chamber is built with more blocks behind a slot in the façade, which will then be sealed with a memorial stone.

During the burial service the coffin stands on a wheeled trolley. To hide the trolley, it is draped with a white cloth which the wind flaps around irreverently. At the right moment, four or five guys who look as if they've been press-ganged from road-mending wheel the trolley to the wall and shove the coffin through its slot into the vault knocked up a few hours earlier. Then they start up the cement mixer and shovel wet concrete on top of the casket.

So the wall of the dead rises with an ugly lack of ceremony.

Los Alcazares is composed mostly of solid rock. Trees are rare. The prehistoric inhabitants embalmed their dead with a mixture of goat fat, herbs and pulverised minerals, then buried them in mausoleum caves or left the body on a plot of sacred ground and built a memorial cairn of stones over it.

Spadefuls of concrete thud on the casket, which people find distressing, especially since the work gang are not dignified professional grave-builders.

That's why Father Martin instituted the processional hymn to distract the congregation while the actual burial is in progress. So there we were, hobbling over the stony ground, gasping 'For All The Saints' into the wind.

The British at worship sing in a strange way, side-by-side with eyes to the front, half-chanting between our back teeth, nobody wanting to raise their voice to a volume that would embarrass the rest. The congregation was made up of fourteen Brits and ten Spanish, plus Leif and Gabrielle, his French wife, who keeps immaculately a little garden centre outside Angeles supplying geraniums and cacti to new villa owners.

The boundary wall is low. As we approached the entrance gate we got a clear view of the two police vehicles roaring up the road. They squealed brakes and pulled over to double-park by our cars. A squad of guardia jumped out with rifles and ran through the gates. Father Martin raised a hand to bring our procession to a halt.

The police captain approached him with a piece of paper while the officers ran up to the grave and ordered the cement gang to stop work. They dropped their shovels immediately and stood back, putting on those expressionless faces which the Spanish keep for trouble.

'*Buenos dias.*' Solemn in face and voice, gratingly English in accent, Father Martin greeted the captain, who responded by snapping out a few sentences and handing over his paper. Father Martin looked it over. Then he turned to us, drawing Stella, Matthew and I a few steps away from the rest for privacy.

'He has an order to take the – to take Tom to Tenerife for an autopsy.' Father Martin turned the paper over. He reads Spanish much better than he speaks it. 'Signed by the mayor and the regional governor and our consul.'

'Why?' Stella demanded from the sanctuary of Matthew's supporting arm. 'I want him here, with me. That's what we planned, that's what's in his will. Why has he got to be disturbed? Why can't he rest in peace?'

Father Martin took this question back to the captain. The answer was short but the body language was explicit. 'He doesn't know. He has to enforce the order, that's all.'

Stella's veil shook. I could see that her eyelashes trembled. 'This is just disgusting,' she announced, her voice ragged. 'I can't bear it, I can't bear having him moved and cut up and God knows what. Why, for God's sake? What's the reason for . . . ah!'

An official Mercedes had glided to the roadside and its passengers were getting out. From the front came Margaret Amoore, the British vice-consul on Gran Canaria with responsibility for the smaller islands, shaking out the skirt of her printed dress. A dark-haired young man ejected himself from the back. He wore a smart wool suit, not a good idea in this hot and dusty climate. Another man followed, tall, maybe twenty-five, his clothes crumpled, with prematurely thinning fair hair but otherwise a ringer for Tom; he helped out the last passenger, the youngest, a spectacularly glamorous woman with a mass of glistening blonde curls.

'Well,' Stella muttered to us, now suddenly calm. 'The family's all here. Almost. That's the son and the youngest daughter.'

'My God,' I whispered back, 'how did they get here so fast?'

We have one airport, outside Villanueva, and it is run on very egalitarian international principles; one day per country. All the scheduled flights come in or out on Monday, then charters from Germany come in on Tuesday, from Sweden, Norway and Denmark on Wednesday, from Britain on Thursday, and from the Spanish mainland, where Los Alcazares is popular for weekends in the sun, on Friday, Saturday and Sunday. Every morning at 11 A.M. there is an inter-island flight, either from Gran Canaria or Tenerife, which returns the same evening. So if anyone from England, like Tom's family, wants to come out on any day other than Thursday, they have to use a bit of ingenuity.

'Scheduled flight to Las Palmas, I suppose. The only way, isn't it?' Her tone was defeated.

'Did they tell you they were coming?'

'Of course not; please, Kim, don't be stupid. This is a set-up, can't you see? They just want to hurt me. They never accepted that he loved me, any of them. I told him the funeral would be today, the son, I mean. They're doing this to get back at me.'

At the wall, two of the guardia, with some reluctance, put down their rifles and took up shovels to begin digging out the coffin. The group by the Mercedes formed and made their way towards us. The man in the suit took the lead and spoke to Father Martin. He was English; now I could see him properly he looked exactly what he turned out to be, a fat-cat lawyer.

'You must forgive us for interrupting your service,' he said. 'I am here as the solicitor acting for Mr Banks . . .' He nodded at the fair-haired man, who now took up a position with the two women at a safe distance from us, as if Stella were an infection he didn't want to catch. 'And we have obtained a coroner's court order that requires, in view of the circumstances, an autopsy to be performed by a surgeon appointed by the court before any burial can take place.' I felt Stella's hot anger despite the mass of Matthew's body between us. 'What that means, as I understand there are no facilities here on Los Alcazares, is that the procedure must be done in Gran Canaria. My clients have chartered an aircraft to enable things to go forward as quickly as possible.' He was making a good impression on the rest of the

Brits, going to great lengths of circumlocution to avoid using words like 'body' and 'coffin'.

'I refuse,' said Stella suddenly. 'I refuse absolutely; this is outrageous. He was my husband and he wanted to be buried here. There's no reason for any of this, you have no right . . .'

'My client does not intend to dispute Mr Banks's wishes for his final resting place. However, he has the right to know how his father died. After all, it was not an expected event.'

'It was a car crash, we've already spoken, I've told him . . .'

'And I'm sure the autopsy will confirm that, Mrs Banks.' And he looked her straight in the eye through the mantilla, clearly implying that if she protested any more it would be noted. Then I felt Stella subside.

'Oh, do whatever you want,' she whispered. 'I'm sure you've got all the right bits of paper. He always said his first wife just wanted to bleed him dry. I suppose she didn't want to miss their last chance.' Those who heard this gasped, even Carole, who had collaborated with Stella for hours in passionately bad-mouthing Tom's family. Tom's daughter, out of hearing but sensing outrage, gave a small scream.

The son shook his head. 'That wasn't necessary, Stella.'

'This isn't necessary either. Tom always wanted to

be buried here. It's just cruel, you're trying to make me suffer, you're always trying to do that, all of you. For God's sake, you're adults, your mother is an adult, your father was an adult, you have to accept his choices . . .'

Stella was on the edge of tears, stabbing a finger at the son so violently that her whole body shook. With her stilettos and the stony ground, it seemed likely she would fall. Fred Dagenham rolled forward and took her arm. 'Steady,' he said. 'Take it easy.'

That kind of advice is usually enough to make Stella blow her stack so Matthew, the peacemaker, took control. His voice is powerful but he speaks quietly, as if its range embarrasses him. I can't remember ever hearing him shout, except once at Quemada in a storm, when he got joyously drunk and waded out into the sea to tell the waves he loved me. 'Have you met this kind of thing before?' he said to Father Martin.

'Not exactly. Not out here. I don't know what the Spanish law is in this situation.'

'We all know what the Spanish law is in any situation,' sneered Carole. 'In the event of guardia turning up with guns, you do what they say. Even if they want to kidnap your husband's dead body.'

There was another little mew of distress from Tom's daughter, and a lot of uneasy shifting among the mourners behind us. Stella was definitely weeping. I put my arm around her; I had to. We could all hear the scrapes of the shovels freeing the coffin from the concrete.

Matthew asked Father Martin for the official paper. A cluster of seals had been stamped along the bottom of the page.

'It is the proper thing,' Margaret Amoore assured us. 'I got instructions from London yesterday and made the application to the court the minute they opened this morning. I'm afraid we have to comply now.' She was anxious. Margaret comes from that generation of women which rarely attained authority without a struggle, so she can't be a stranger to conflict, but still she hates any kind of fight. In disputes she will always try to be brisk and bully you into the course of least resistance.

The guardia threw their shovels down and began to drag the coffin out of its slot in the wall; the cemetery work gang, sitting on the pile of blocks waiting to top off the immuration, shared around a pack of cigarettes.

'He can come back, can't he?' This was from Maryse, clearing her husky throat as she went on. 'I mean, when it's over, he can come back.'

'Oh yes,' Margaret Amoore assured us generally. 'When it's been done, he can be returned and buried exactly in accordance with his wishes.'

'This is all in line with what I would expect in England,' Islewyn announced.

'Mr Banks and his sister have no objection to the burial here,' the lawyer said.

'That's right.' The son had an air of condescending righteousness.

Maryse came fluttering over and took Stella's arm. 'Darling, look,' she murmured. 'Darling, you're in shock, you can't get your head round this. I know it's horrible but you've got to go along with it. You don't want the guardia running you in and getting nasty, maybe starting some inquiry and turning over your whole life and finding what you don't want them to find and busting you maybe for something trivial like some permit you haven't got . . .'

Maryse hit the right button. Spanish law is so complex, and its enforcement out here so random, no one can ever be confident that their affairs are in order. Stella certainly had secrets: she said calculating tax made her brain hurt and she always had a few knobs of hash at home.

Still, Stella said nothing, but stood on stiff legs, shaking her head. Fred Dagenham gently pulled at her arm. 'Tell them to get on with it, love,' he urged her. 'It's only a day, that's all the time it takes. We'll all be back here on Friday.'

Now Stella started crying for real, her ragged tissue coming away from her eyes black with running mascara. 'This is such a mess,' she said, 'I wanted it to be done properly.'

'Bastards,' Carole muttered this loud enough for us all to hear. Distaste showed in Father Martin's fleshy face.

'It will be done properly,' he assured Stella. 'I'll see to it. Like Fred says, Friday I should imagine. That's reasonable, isn't it, Margaret?'

Our vice-consul spoke to the police captain and agreement was obtained. 'Friday, he's promised me,' she said brightly.

Matthew looked at Stella and raised an eyebrow, but it was more of a command than a question. In response she let the sobs go and collapsed against him. 'She's upset, of course,' Matthew told Margaret. 'She'll be OK. They can do what they have to do.' I was proud of him. I always am when he wades in and sorts things, but I was angry too; I saw that this tragedy had crashed into our life and pushed him closer to Stella. I have only these two people left to love. Tom, with the family he had thrown away for Stella, had been a much bigger obstacle between them than I was.

By this time the coffin was on the trolley, and the guardia wheeled it over the rocky ground to their vehicle where they heaved it through the rear doors and climbed in after it. The strangers got into their Mercedes and left; Margaret looked pained but no one actually apologised. Sam and Terry voted for taking Stella down to the Lumumba bar on the marina for a drink. Not that any of the hardcore ever needs an excuse for a drink.

* * *

The next day, life kept rolling. This is always strange. Death changes so much but that's still much less than everything.

'Kim,' called Eva optimistically, swivelling her chair around to talk to me. 'Kim, are you my friend?'

'Depends.' I kept my head down over my keyboard; I was wary. Eva is a natural-born gypsy princess. She sits behind her terminal as if she were waiting for Goya to paint her. At least fifty per cent of her energy goes into devising errands for the men at the Instituto to perform. As I'm effectively the only other woman in the place, she normally insists that I also exact these tributes. I'm never sure I can get into the right mode of political inertia.

There is a subtle difference between Eva's style and the way Stella puts her man to work. Eva is a dominatrix for the hell of it, and although they moan, the guys love playing slave. Stella needs people to do things for her. She misjudged Tom; she needed more than he had to give. I could say that she destroyed Tom. Respect exists between Eva and Stella, but they are not friends.

'Milo wants someone to go out to the sea-level monitors with him this afternoon,' Eva informed me.

'I didn't know Milo was here.' Our professor is based at the parent Instituto Canarien de Geologia y Geografia in Tenerife.

'Yes, he's coming this morning. Bringing us one of his new toys. Sea-level monitor. Full moon, spring tide, it has to be today.'

'I thought you and he . . .' Matthew labelled Eva 'one of those Madrilena babes who's catting around all she can to make up for two thousand years of machismo and Catholicism'. I wouldn't know a Madrilena babe from any other species, but it seems that my lover would. He made three car commercials in Spain and he said he knew Eva's type.

Eva flirts operatically with Milo, who's short and chunky with a Julius Caesar haircut. He swaggers around her like a dictator whenever he visits. You could cut the chemistry between them with a knife.

As soon as Milo leaves other men jam our phone lines all morning trying to fix their dates with Eva. I don't answer Eva's phone any more – it makes me feel as if I've never lived at all.

'So? We're getting a new monitor and someone's got to learn how it works and I've had it with breaking my fingernails getting into that stinking wet-suit. It makes me sick just thinking about who's pissed in it before.'

'Thanks,' I told her. 'Why me? What did I do to deserve the honour of getting into the stinking wet-suit instead of you?'

'Nothing. You're new, you have to learn.'

'That's right,' agreed Dima, one of the Russians supposed to be working on a geothermal project in the next room.

'Shut up, *cuno*,' Eva advised amiably. 'And what's that in your arms? The body of the last woman crushed to death in your bed? You disgusting slab of blubber.' What with the moustache, the drooping, red-rimmed eyelids, his rasping, mouldy breath and the way the seat of his trousers bags out while his gut hangs over the belt, Dima makes everyone think of a walrus.

'How could I sleep with another woman when I am in love with you?' he demanded.

'Easily. You are a man, aren't you?'

While Dima was wheezing and trying to come up with an answer she leaned over the desk and took a peek inside the bag which he was clutching to his chest.

'What have you got in here? Clothes! Yeuch! Dirty clothes. Dima, why are you bringing me your stinking laundry? I'm not your mother . . .'

'They're not dirty,' he protested. 'I look them to lavanderia this morning. Cost me fortune but I promise they're absolutely clean.'

'So why are they here dripping all over our office?'

The bundle was not dripping, but she tricked him into checking the floor.

'I dry them here,' he explained. 'Save money.' Water being precious, washing machines aren't standard kitchen fittings on the island and the lavanderia is spectacularly expensive.

'No way! Dima! This is a temple of science, you can't hang washing lines outside it. Forbidden. Milo would go crazy.'

'Not outside.' Dima was rolling his eyes at her pleadingly. 'Inside.' He pointed down at the floor. 'Nice and warm down there.'

He was talking about the excavations below the building, where the newest instruments sit silently at the end of a downhill tunnel, registering the invisible life of the earth, the force of its shivers and shudders, the swings of its magnetic fields, the gases in its farts and belches. All this information feeds directly into our computer system. Any time we want to know how mother earth is feeling, we can get her vital signs on our screens in a few keystrokes.

It's hot down there, hotter than a sauna. To visit the lowest instrument chamber you have to put on a silver heat-suit, gloves, a thermal helmet, a breathing mask and thick-soled mountain boots, and it's still like being in an oven.

Los Alcazares was born from a wrinkle in the ocean floor, the wrinkle that is now the La Mora mountains. The earth's crust is thin here, only about five kilometres deep, whereas on the mainland of Europe or Africa it is ten times as thick. There's not much here between us on the surface and the heat of the centre of the earth.

'I'm not hearing this,' Eva declaimed. 'You are drying your washing with our seismograph? Our new digital seismograph which cost Milo at least one and a half billion pesetas?'

'It wasn't your money,' Dima reasoned. 'I don't put clothes on seismograph. There's a nice rail down there. They dry in couple of hours, even my jeans. What's wrong with that? You should be pleased I like to be clean and smell nice for you.'

There is a guard-rail running around the instrument area with no obvious purpose except to make inspecting the gear more difficult. One of us checks on the installation every day in case of a rock fall. Dima must have been stealthy; we'd never noticed his washing disfiguring the rails.

Eva decided she wasn't really annoyed. She tossed her long black hair, stuck her nose in the air and pronounced, 'Well, OK. But not today. Milo's coming this afternoon. Suppose he went down there and found your underwear all over the place?'

'What underwear do you mean?' Dima enquired craftily.

'Assuming you have any. You're such a peasant, I'm surprised you know what it is. Go away please, we're working here.'

He shambled off to his desk. Only eight people work full-time at the Instituto: the men are four geologists, two from Madrid, two from Moscow, working on the geothermal energy project, and Mark, a geophysics student from Perth, who is finishing a thesis on the erosion of the islands over the last four million years. The other woman is Suzanne, a very pale, very shy palaeontologist from Copenhagen, studying the blind white crabs that live in the caves. According to Eva, Suzanne is so silent, white-skinned and tentative that she probably emerged from a lost subterranean genepool herself.

We speak English and Spanish together, hardly thinking about which language we're using. Eva rules this province by fascination. She is the most exciting phenomenon this international convocation of anoraks has ever observed.

* * *

A few weeks ago I began to dream about falling from the Mirador, the highest cliff on the coast. Up there is a narrow balcony carved into the cliff face. The dream begins with me climbing up a spiral staircase built in a tunnel through the rock. The staircase has white treads and white walls. As I step outside on the balcony the rock parts like sliced flesh under my feet, the iron railing collapses and I start falling thousands of metres through the air. The eagles wheel around me as I fall. The dream changes before I hit the sea.

Maybe it's true about the ley lines. It is true that we all dream wonderfully here, even I, who haven't dreamed since childhood. My night visions are as clear and well framed as if they have been shot by a master cinematographer.

After the falling part of the dream I am in a narrow space trying to open a door. I have been waking every morning at dawn, knowing that I've been dreaming of pushing open a door. The door wouldn't open, there was something behind it, pushing against me. The harder I pushed, the more it resisted. It was something terrible which I had to see no matter how bad it was, because something else was threatening me, something behind me, tracking me. I knew I would be safe as soon as I got the door open and saw the terrible thing that was behind it.

I was in panic because I couldn't open the door. I put my shoulder against it and braced my feet on the floor and pushed with all my strength. Then I turned and put my back against the door and pushed again. The door started to splinter; it was going to break up. I pushed one last time and it opened. Then I woke up.

This dream frightened me as much as if I were still three years old. A few weeks ago I woke from it with my heart leaping in my chest and my eyes aching because I had been crying. The sheet was wet where my tears had run down. The T-shirt I sleep in was damp. I had kicked away our quilt and my pillow was out of reach. I sleep curled up, and this dream makes me roll around our bed like a mad hedgehog.

Matthew is a starfish sleeper. His arms and legs lie in the bed like logs and he sleeps so deeply that I can steal a hug from him by creeping up under his outflung arm and resting my head on his chest. I like doing it; if I woke him up and asked he would hold me close as long as I wanted, but the theft of his protection feels more luxurious.

That morning I was afraid to go back to sleep in case the dream started again, and I was afraid that if I lay down and took comfort from Matthew I would fall asleep. Furtively, I got off the bed, rolled back the glass door to the terrace and went outside.

We sleep with the doors unshuttered so we can wake up to our beautiful view. Our apartment is part of an old farmhouse on the edge of another of those unexplained rows of houses which only just add up to a village. Our bedroom looks out over black fields with black stone walls stretching away to a small brown mountain, a minor crater from the first eruptions. The mountain brings our horizon very close; the effect is surreal because all the distances in the view look wrong. If you drew the scene it would look like a drawing by someone who can't understand perspective.

Dawn was a while away; the edge of the mountain was solid against the sky but the stars were still bright. My heart slowed down. As I moved through the cool air I realised that my skin was wet with sweat as well as tears. At the edge of the terrace I sat down on the tiles and tried a seeing meditation which Carole had just taught us, focusing on the leaning palm on the skyline at the base of the mountain.

My thoughts looped around a while, then flew away. I was surprised at how easy it was to clear my mind. My breath came and went. Cold settled on me like a brittle coat which would crack if I moved. The light grew stronger, the tree became green, shadows thickened behind the boulders on the mountainside. The chill of the air and the clarity of the light were echoing in the space inside my mind.

Matthew woke up. I felt his consciousness appear in the room behind me like a heat spot. Immediately my head was full of questions. Should I go in to him, or would he come out to me, or would he see what I was doing and leave me alone because he liked me to meditate? Was he angry that I had left our bed, was he worried about me, was he annoyed that he was worried about me or was he thinking of what it would be like to sleep with Stella? Had he already slept with Stella?

From peace to pain in three moves. Something slipped away from me in those moments, something celestial which had been at my fingertips. The golden carp of wisdom flipped its tail and vanished. I got up, slipped on the tiles, felt a twinge in my knee, felt cold and stiff, felt angry. A slink in the corner of the terrace told me that some animal had been watching me.

Matthew was sitting on the end of the bed pulling on his shorts and when he looked at me his eyes were still blurred with sleep. He said, 'Hello.'

This was one of our scripts. I was supposed to say, 'Hello back,' but I didn't because I didn't want to be cute. So he said, 'Are you OK?'

'Yes,' I answered. 'I woke up and I couldn't go back to sleep.'

'Aren't you cold?' This was not all that he wanted to say, but he was choosing to be concerned about something neutral. I accepted that.

'Yes,' I agreed. 'I'm freezing.'

'Your face is white.'

'I was meditating. I didn't realise how cold it was.'

I expected him to come to me, or to bring me the quilt. Instead he rubbed his face with both hands, washing off the sleep. 'Did something wake you up?'

'I don't know. I just woke up, that's all.'

Our clock told us that it was just after six A.M. I had been outside nearly an hour. Matthew stood up and went into the bathroom. All the small apartments on the island are the same, with the bedroom at the back, a short corridor with the bathroom off it, and a galley kitchen that gives on to the living area at the front. He shut the door. I heard him use the toilet, run the shower, clean his teeth.

He came out with a towel around his waist and drops of water standing on his skin. He has no idea how beautiful he is to me. Most beautiful at the times when he is doing something so habitual that he is not aware of his body. It's like a shock, it makes me breathless. One time when I tried to explain this he was embarrassed and didn't want to hear me.

'Put something on,' he said, 'I'll make us some coffee.'

I couldn't think what clothes to put on, so I pulled the quilt off the bed and went to sit outside again, this time in one of the chairs. He came out with the coffee jug and two mugs. We both drink strong black coffee, which proves that our love was meant to be.

The sky in the east was very bright; the edge of the sun might have been showing already. Little birds were cheeping in the aloes that grow beside our building. I don't understand why the dawns are so colourless here. Something must happen to the water vapour in the atmosphere during the night.

He poured the coffee and we held the warm mugs. 'It's a city smell, isn't it, coffee?' I skimmed the idea off the top of my mind. 'It's all about espresso or latte, going out, ordering in, not having time for more than one cup . . .'

Matthew didn't answer. He let me run out of words, then he waited, looking into his drink. At last he came back to our business and said, 'There is something, isn't there? Kim?'

Away across the fields somewhere a cockerel crowed. 'Look . . .' I began, trying to see ahead. I was afraid of so many things I couldn't recognise any of them. 'It's . . . I don't know. Tom dying, I suppose.'

'You don't have to tell me,' he offered. 'But there is something, I know there is. Something about us. It's eating up half your mind. You're not with me any more. I've been feeling it from before what happened to Tom.'

'I don't know.' I was desperate for camouflage now. 'I think it's just . . . another death.'

The far-off cockerel crowed again. Matthew tried to look at me and couldn't do it. 'Don't guilt-trip me,' he said finally. 'I'm not Jesus, I'm not going to give you the best of three cockcrows before you betray me. It's not me you're doing it to, anyway. It's us. We deserve the truth, even if I don't.'

'I can't talk about it,' I pleaded. 'Whatever it is. I don't know what's going on with me. I can't tell you what I'm thinking, my head's just a mess.'

He stood up and put his hands behind his head and stretched, as if he could loosen up the tense

atmosphere by the action. 'Now I feel like I'm putting pressure on you. Maybe you need some space.'

Before I understood what he was doing he went
inside, got dressed and left. He didn't kiss me goodbye then. I don't think Matthew would ever give me
a kiss he didn't mean. I was still sitting wrapped in
the quilt and holding my coffee when his car started
and he drove away, leaving the birds in the aloe
hedge to flutter and twitter after the disturbance.

Stella used to be my rock. I always called her
when I didn't know what to do. Was Matthew going
to Stella? Should I call her and find out the worst? I
got as far as picking up the phone, but the line
hissed at me. I assumed it was a fault; they work on
system faults at night. I decided to go to work early
and went to find clothes and make-up, the equipment for putting myself together.

There was a cat on our terrace. It was bony but
big for a stray. I went to lock the doors, expecting it
to run away, but it stayed sitting neat and upright
with its tail wrapped around its feet. It looked quite
Egyptian, except it was black and white with a silly
face.

Heading to the door through the living area I saw
that a fax had come in. So there had been no fault on
the telephone line; the fax had been receiving when
I tried to call. It was from Matthew's agent and all it
said was, 'Call me today if you can.' I took it with
me. It sat on the passenger seat in my car.

This was the day Matthew usually gave to Sam at Radio Angeles. As I turned on to the main road I thought of three ways to go. I could turn right soon and drive up to Stella's to see what I might see; I could turn left later on and drive down to Sam's place on the Marina with the excuse of giving Matthew the fax. Or I could keep on down to the Instituto.

It was still very early. Matthew could have gone anywhere. I didn't know if I wanted to see him anyway. The turning up to Stella's came before I had made a decision so I passed it. Then I took the road down to Sam's.

They were on the quayside, sitting at one of the tables outside the Lumumba. Matthew saw me as soon as I saw him. He came forward and caught me in his arms. I started crying. Sam rolled his eyes, threw down his newspaper and ambled off home to give us some privacy. We had a chaotic conversation of which I can't remember much except that we both said sorry many times. We remembered the argument which, until that night, had held the title of Our Worst Row. The issue had been whether Alanis Morissette was a cultural disaster or just bad. He had said disaster, I had said bad. I can't remember how that one finished.

We were pretending that we hadn't seen what the morning had shown us: there were issues between us now. Something was wrong and from that night we both knew it.

CHAPTER 3

Viral Load

Many things get in the way of growing up; my first road-block was glandular fever. Most of what I remember about my adolescence is a hallucination of sweaty sheets and days blurred together by weakness and boredom. There were months, in my fifteenth year, when I was too feeble even to watch TV.

When he got home from work, my father would come up and read to me until my mother called him for their dinner. He was self-conscious and he read badly, but I loved to have his whole attention. Dialogue embarrassed him so he picked books without much talking. His favourites were spy stories. He sat on the plain chair beside my bed, the chair that was there for my father and the doctors.

My bed fitted into the corner of the room. My mother brought me meals on a tray which I could balance on the quilt over my knees; she liked baked potatoes because they were no trouble and had more vitamins. One day when my arm lost its strength halfway to my mouth a forkful of buttery mash hit the wall and made a greasy mark on the wallpaper. I would lie for hours entertaining myself by trying to work out what the mark looked like: a butterfly taunting a cat? The head of a Nero on a Roman coin? The man in the moon eating an asteroid?

'Of course, you were just trying to get your mother's attention,' Stella diagnosed. 'I'm not saying you weren't really ill, or anything. But it's a natural thing for a child to do, isn't it? To be ill, to cry for help?'

'But it didn't work.' I thought about my parents. They are the happiest couple most people know. I am 37 now and finally I have fallen in love. Maybe I still am in love. I can't connect what I feel for Matthew with whatever holds my mother and father together. It is like an electromagnetic bond, linking them, repelling others. My mother and father live in their own dimension, a pocket in the space-time continuum exactly big enough for the two of them. Which meant no room for their children, for my brother and myself.

'But your mother had to run around looking after you. I mean, what about *her* life?'

'Her whole life is my father. It's . . .' I was going to say, 'like you and Tom,' because at the time we had this conversation Stella was convinced that Tom was the centre of her universe and all she wanted in the world. Maybe I had a feeling about that, because I changed what I was saying and finished, 'it's a perfect marriage. They love each other so totally they've nothing left over. They've always been like that.'

'But she had a job, didn't she? Didn't you say she was a teacher? Didn't she have to give that up, if you were so ill?'

I began to feel breathless. These conversations were too much for me, I hadn't the strength any more.

'She should have stayed home to look after you. Your father had a good job, didn't he? You needed her, you poor little thing. We all need mothering when we're ill. Didn't you miss her?'

'I don't remember. You don't question what your parents do, do you? I was quite happy. Given how ill I was.'

Only as my life had unrolled and I myself became a mother, and put distance between myself and my family and struggled into a career, had I sometimes asked myself what my mother might or might not have given up for the sake of her children.

'She went to work every day just the same. I was by myself most of the time. It was OK, really it was.'

'Horrible,' said Stella. Solitude is torture to her.

'I enjoyed it sometimes.'

'You can't have.'

But there had been luxury in being alone. It was then, I suppose, that I cleared the space in my mind for my inner life, laid the foundations of the chapel where I would sit meditating with my flame.

'That was an unforgivable thing to do,' said Stella. 'That's neglect. They could have been prosecuted. And there was your brother, taking up all their attention. Don't you see that's how it must have been?'

'It doesn't seem to me that they took any more notice of him.' My brother was a swimmer. He was an outstanding athlete; for a few years he was an Olympic champion.

'Oh, come on . . .'

'Rob was never in the house. I don't remember him being there at all when I was in senior school.' And that was a relief, not to be constantly alert for the thumps, cheats and insults which boys think are just play. 'Once he made county junior champion he just belonged to his coach. He was never in the house after that. He complains that Mum and Dad would never take him to any competitions or anything. Or go and see him at events. Even when he was a champion. They just said they could see him on the TV.'

Stella made a colossal fuss of Rob when he came out here last year. His visit made a big swirl in our little pond, even though he retired from competition ten years ago. He has joined a sports promotion company and occasionally turns up in ads endorsing goggles or swimming trunks. Insanely, Los Alcazares stages a world-class sporting event every spring, a biathlon contest hosted by the developers of a big German spa hotel up in the north. Rob came out for that, really to have a reason to come to see me. We're good friends now.

He finished 112th out of 139. My brother is three years older than I am and always was a lot less impressive on land. Stella gave a biathlon barbecue and Matthew had to step aside for a while and was jealous. He got drunk with Tom. I assumed he was jealous over me, but perhaps I was wrong. Now I scan my memories all the time, looking for evidence.

'What kind of people can have a son who's an Olympic champion and not go to see him win?' It was Stella's mission to compensate the victims of parental crime.

'That's Mum and Dad. All they need is each other.'

'I think that's sick.' She drank a full glass of wine in one gulp to indicate her disgust.

'I think it's rather beautiful.'

So it is, the love of my mother and father. Every photograph I have of them shows them as close as siamese twins, my mother barely reaching my father's shoulder, the mass of my father rising protectively next to her. 'Your father will be home soon,' she used to say as if announcing the second coming of Jesus. 'I'm not sure your mother would like that,' was the worst he could do in the way of disapproval. They share no other passions. When they are together they seldom talk; they are happy like grass growing. This great silent love is a mystery to me.

'It's selfishness,' Stella declared, reaching for the bottle to refill her glass. 'Where's the beauty in that? You must have been miserable, ill and all alone.'

'I had a dream once, that our house burned down while I was helping my father wash the car. We just stood and watched, the two of us, while Rob and my mother burned to death. It was a very clear dream. I remember Dad holding the hose and the water running into the gutter. Then we finished the car, just the two of us, not speaking, just being together the way he could be with my mother.'

'Damn. That is so fucking obvious. I hate that. I hate it when your subconscious just comes out with stuff.' We laughed and refilled our glasses.

'Rob gets angry about them now.'

'I remember. I remember that, he told me he was pissed off they never took him to competitions like the other kids' parents.'

'I thought whoever I loved, we would never be able to be like them.' My fears are like vampires; they die in the daylight. Stella tempts them out, she frees me from my terrors. Most of them, anyway. 'When I started going out with boys and thinking about getting married – you only have your parents to follow, don't you? And they've got this perfection nobody can explain.'

We were in Stella's office when we had this conversation, waiting out siesta time under the photographs of villas for sale which she kept on the walls. While all of Spain was dozing in the heat and letting its lunch settle, people in Northern Europe carried on calling, faxing and e-mailing, only shutting down at about the time when the Spanish got back to work. Failure to amortise the two schedules might delay a sale by twenty-four hours so people like Stella, with multinational businesses, were trapped in their offices at siesta-time.

'I'm a prisoner!' she used to protest. 'I'm chained to the phone, I'm stuck here eighteen hours a day and it's like an oven in this place, I'm going mad in here, it's like Japanese torture . . .' Everyone who knew her and who passed through Playa de los Angeles between one and five would call in at the Residencias to help her through the afternoon. She could make anyone's arrival into a party. People brought bottles of wine, they filled the fridge full of beer. The Bar Macarena over the road would send up tapas. Siesta-time at the Residencias office became an island institution.

So, my illness. Picture that virus – well, you can't picture it. The thief of my youth, the rapist of my destiny, is so small your eye can't see it. Even if you catch it, kill it, stain it and put it under a micro-scope, it won't be more than a speck. Tiny but deadly, smaller than a single spermatozoon; a few molecules to start or stop a life.

I came to think of the virus cruising in my blood-stream like a shark. It played sadistic games with me, lying dormant for months until I bloomed a little, then coming back to strike me down all over again. It seemed the beast was never going to finish shaking my carcase.

I forgot what it was like to be able to run. Before the illness, running was my natural pace. Every cor-ridor in the school building had been an invitation to sprint. On any sports team I had always been the fastest attacker. Certainly, I had been able to outrun my brother.

My life was laid waste. Friends got bored with coming round to see me. A lot of classes were missed, a lot of homework was never done. The teachers kept me back a year. I was resitting exams when my original classmates were undergraduates. Some papers had to be written from my bed, with an elderly teacher invigilating in my bedroom to ensure that I had not smuggled any books under the quilt.

This is why I became a geographer. The earth was so easy to explain. Why was the sky blue? Well, because when light waves from the sun hit the zil-lion molecules of the earth's atmosphere they are scattered and refracted into frequencies; blue light, which has the highest frequency, is scattered most and gets to our eyes first. Quite logical, captain. All I had to remember was two words, the name of the process: Rayleigh Scattering. I could work out the rest. In geography I could make up exam answers and get them right. In French and chemistry I didn't even know where to start guessing. So I passed exams, but my scholarship, such as it was, always felt unstable.

When I was finally packing for university, my mother brought me an armload of freshly washed clothes – she only ironed for my father. 'Well,' she said, putting them down slowly as if suddenly realising that the job of nurturing me, which she had done grudgingly, was now to end, 'you'll be the first woman in our family to go to university. Think of that.'

'It was different for you.' I wanted to excuse her. It always seemed too unkind to criticise my mother, or even let her reproach herself.

'Yes,' she agreed. 'It was different for me. Things were different. It was a different world.' This was the deepest conversation we ever had. I could see that what was boiling up in her mind had brought her to the point of panic. She spoke as if what I was doing was inevitable but in some way wrong, even an offence against nature. My mother, in her cocoon of perfect marital love, had felt something from the world outside. She was jealous of my freedom.

I ended up at a university full of people like me, all educationally challenged. It was a combustible campus inhabited by virgins and party animals. The virus backed off for a full year. I first met Stella: Estelle Mahoney. I can see the name now on the door of her room at our hall of residence.

* * *

When Milo arrived I drove them both out to the coast. At two hundred metres away the Instituto becomes almost invisible. It's a one-storey, flat-roofed construction in the same style as the tourist complex in the National Park, built from the bubbly lava rock and nestled into the bare skin of the earth. The architect was a genius. The shape of the Instituto is so organic that you can drive right up to the door before you believe that this really is a building, not just another extrusion of basalt. Only the sun glinting on the windows gives it away.

'Are you happy in your work, Kim?' Milo asked me.

'Of course,' I assured him. I'm not used to answering questions about happiness. I know what I'm supposed to say, but it's only since Matthew that I've been able to ask myself the question.

'Eva isn't bullying you?'

'I don't bully anyone,' she protested from the back seat of the car.

'Nothing I can't handle,' I said.

'The translation isn't too difficult?'

'It's hard going sometimes but I can cope.' The work is extraordinarily tiring, which is why I can only finish a couple of pages a day and I'm glad there are other things in the job specification. When it's time to go home I sometimes think I'm too tired to drive.

'And you're not bored? I'll be able to give you more interesting work soon, I hope.'

'I'm not bored. I like working on a real project. Doing hands-on work, after teaching.'

'You're not lonely out here?'

I had to think about this one. The Instituto is in the far northern corner of the National Park of Tarfaya. Although there are eight of us in the building, and others come and go, and we have homes and loved ones and people to call all day, we each feel alone. We can look up at the night sky and tell ourselves the guys on the space station are light years lonelier than we are but it doesn't make any difference. We are living with the truth about the planet and our lives seem so tiny that we might as well not exist at all.

'Dima has a joke for the new people,' I told Milo. 'He said to me, "After a couple of weeks out here, you'll be so lonely you'll start talking to the rocks." Then he says, "But don't worry, that's quite normal. The rocks are shy, it takes them time to get up the nerve to start talking. After a while the rocks start answering you back. Then you think you're going mad. But don't worry." Then he says, "The time to worry is when they start telling you no woman on the island has more beautiful eyes. When they start with that stuff, just let me know and I'll sort them out for you.'"

Milo laughed and looked at Eva in the rear-view mirror. Eva's posture indicated that compliments were boring and anyway she had the most beautiful eyes on the island. So Milo returned to me. 'You are feeling lonely?'

'Just a little bit. Maybe.'

Eva said, 'We feel a little small, that's all. Next to all this . . .' She flicked a languid finger at the landscape. We were driving across one of the most beautiful areas in the park, El Mar Negro.

Tarfaya, in its awesome rocky way, is a riot of colour. Every one of the twenty-four craters is an individual, from the biggest black mountain where the tourists queue for camel rides to the twenty-foot frozen rock fountain outside the Instituto.

The rocks are purple, red, orange, ochre, yellow, white, grey and green. They sparkle rainbows with mica and glisten with olivine. They are as smooth as melted chocolate or rough like coral, harder than iron or crumbly like bread. A lot of them are petrified in mid-action; eternally, bubbles of rock are bursting, smears of rock are drying, waves of rock are swelling, drips of rock are falling. There are smooth ponds of golden pumice gravel and high walls of lava crust the colour of dried blood.

Artists will tell you that there are a thousand different shades of white, but you've never seen black until you've got out of the car at night in El Mar Negro. Then you see blue-black, yellow-black and red-black, even a sort of ash-black that definitely isn't grey.

Unlike the cruddy stuff where Tom died, in our black sea the lava must have been very hot and liquid because it set fast into black waves. At Jimena, where this sea of lava meets the ocean, you see waves of water crashing into the waves of rock.

The surface of every wave is covered with wavelets whipped by the wind, razor-sharp. We have no water, therefore no erosion. If a car goes off the track here its tyres are instantly ripped to shreds. The tourist board pays for the removal truck the same day.

It was afternoon, and the sinking sun was adding shadows to the still black swell. Lichen has attached itself to the leeward side of every wavelet. The lichen is greeny-white and looks like foam on the waves. Apart from us, the tourists and the camels, the lichen is the only living thing in the whole area.

We passed the northern border of the park near Yesto, where one of the surface seismographs lives in something like a concrete trunk. Every day, either Eva or I check the surface equipment. The surface seismographs are beautiful little brass instruments, relics of the childhood of geology. Each has a nib on a long arm tracing a line on a sheet of graph paper stretched around a rotating drum. The needle registers the movement of a tiny metal cube mounted on a fine spring attached to a rod which has been driven into the ground.

Next to the seismograph is a magnetometer and some small bore holes fitted with permanent pipes and valves for gas sampling. On the hillside above are tilt meters and crack detectors. These are pathetically crude, not much more than a spirit level and a wire stretched between two measuring scales. They have been fitted over fissures in the lava to measure the movement in the rocks.

One of Milo's propositions is that very slowly, slower than the creep of a glacier, Los Alcazares is breaking up. He installed this stuff to prove it. The gas samples are crazy, but not in a way that means anything. Nothing has happened in my time here, but most of our outside instruments are as old-fashioned as a steam engine.

'Flatlines,' Milo said wistfully as we passed the monitoring station. 'Always flatlines. Nothing going on down there, nothing to worry about, everybody can be happy.'

'You'd have liked to be here in 1790,' I suggested.

'He'd like to be in Hawaii now,' Eva said from the back of the car.

'Hawaii,' said Milo with contempt. 'The Pacific isn't important. They make me sick, going on about their ring of fire. It took them twenty years to figure it out. This is bigger than the Pacific. In human terms, much bigger. But they get the money. They can't do anything in Hawaii that I couldn't do here, if I had the money.'

'In Hawaii they're live, right? Isn't this region dormant?' I wondered if I was asking a stupid question.

'What does dormant mean?' Milo asked scornfully. 'It's not a scientific term.' Then he fell silent, as if he thought he was giving too much away.

'It's this place. It gets you. When I first came here,' Eva pulled a face of disgust, 'I thought he was mad, bringing me to somewhere that's as ugly as a motorway shoulder. Dead like a desert. More dead than a desert – at least there are beetles in a desert. Two days later, I was thinking, hey – that's a pretty pebble. Three days, you think, wow! That's a beautiful stone. One week, you think this is the most beautiful place in the world. Then you never want to leave. That was your plan, wasn't it Milo?' She tickled the back of his neck.

He swatted the spot as if a fly had landed on it. 'Earth, water, air – that's it. Just the elements. But that's all you need to make life.'

'And fire,' Eva pointed out. I pretended to watch the road but I saw him try to catch her fingers with his.

Our boat, an old navy-surplus inflatable, is kept in a hut which is hidden on the seaward side of the workers' cabin at the salt pans. We got there half an hour before low tide, and a couple of technicians met us, lugging the scuba gear. Eva sat in the car and started painting her fingernails while we hauled on the wet-suits.

The boat scudded around the coast to the spot on the shore where the sea-level monitor is fixed. There's a little red buoy for hitching it at a safe distance from the cliffs.

The old monitor was a glass-tube affair held by brackets to a ten-foot iron girder. Beside the girder is a rusting iron ladder and a concrete platform, only big enough for one person to stand on at a time. Milo had decided there was no need to dismantle the old monitor. The techies kitted up and tipped overboard with their underwater welding gear while Milo rehearsed me in reading and resetting the new instrument, a small cylinder of grey heavy-duty plastic containing the keypad and display, with sensor cables held in place on a titanium arm. Then he got anxious and put on a mask and snorkel to go down for a look underwater. He splashed a lot and came up three or four times before he was satisfied. The techies helped heave him back into the boat.

An hour later the new instrument was in position. Back on shore Eva passed round a bottle of brandy to warm us.

'He's really anxious about this,' I said to her, while the men were discreetly stripping off their wet-suits around the corner of the boathouse. 'He went down to see what they were doing.'

'Milo? He went in the sea?'

'Not a pretty sight.'

'He hates the water. You know he paid for that thing with his own money? We tried everywhere for a grant but the EU decided to fund a sea-level project in the Mediterranean, not here. He was so pissed off.'

'But there's a whole new crater coming out of the sea near Crete. Two million people living around Vesuvius and a new magma chamber ten miles north of Rome – you can see the logic,' I argued cautiously.

'Milo thinks he'll get better data here because we're out in the ocean. So he sold his apartment. To buy that thing.'

'Do we need a new monitor? OK, the old one's primitive but it still works fine.'

'He says we need it.'

'But why's the sea-level so important? I'd have thought the old stuff on land needed to be replaced first.'

'He read some study of prehistoric volcanic activity and decided to do it this way.'

'He's obsessed,' I suggested.

'Not necessarily.' Eva admired her manicure. 'Espresso Ecstasy – nice colour, eh?'

Milo came back, rubbing his wet hair with a towel and carrying the half-empty brandy bottle which he offered to me. 'Good thinking,' he said to Eva. 'Warms you up.'

She blanked on his innuendo and said, 'Tell Kim why we need the new monitor. She thinks the old one works fine.'

'Sure it does, but we need respect for our data. The more modern the equipment, the more people believe it. Our research gets respect, we get money, we can carry on, do more.'

'But why the sea-level? I don't understand.' Maybe it was the brandy, but I was feeling argumentative.

'To predict the way a volcano will behave in the future you can look at typical volcanic activity in the past – that's why your Cura is so useful to us, yeah?'

'Sure,' I agreed. We climbed back into the car, grateful for the cosy interior after the wind outside. This time Eva drove.

'A study last year suggested that volcanoes get very active when the sea-level rises. Twelve thousand years ago the sea rose thirteen metres over two hundred years and immediately there was a big increase in volcanic eruptions.'

'Global warming. Got it.'

Eva winked at me, steering with one hand while she took a last swig, capped the brandy bottle and stowed it in her bag.

Milo leaned out of the window to look in the wing mirror and slick down his hair. 'Ninety per cent of volcanoes are in coastal regions. If the sea rises and erodes the old craters – big risk of an eruptive crisis. Really big. Global climate change, second ice age . . . I'll give you the paper to read.'

Recrossing El Mar Negro, Eva said, 'It's not really lonely here. You just feel like it's nothing to be human, nothing at all. But then you realise you have a purpose in being here.'

'Philosophy,' Milo was disdainful.

'Look at you,' she challenged him, 'or Kim. Any of us. When you first come, it's only another place. Then you start to feel there is a reason you got here and you stay to find out what it is.'

'Oh God, my assistant's turning into a hippy.' Milo put a hand over his eyes.

'He doesn't like me to think,' Eva confided over her shoulder to me. 'It makes him nervous.'

'I'd like you to watch the road,' Milo said. 'Your driving makes me nervous.'

A wise person does not say things like that to Eva. She did a handbrake turn where the Instituto road loops back from the main drag to the Visitor Centre at Tarfaya. The squeal of the tyres and the hiss of the gravel echoed off the crater walls.

The Visitor Centre is a much bigger building than the Instituto. The architect fitted the essential facilities into a chain of shallow craters. The huge Panorama Bar gives its customers a view over the lunar park to the west. In front of the Centre is an arena walled with iron-brown rocks and floored in red pumice where the tourist guides do their circus act. At the base of the rock walls are bore holes down into the hot substratum. The guides tell the crowds to stand clear and pour water into the holes with long-handled metal ladles. In thirty seconds the water returns as huge spouts of superheated steam. While people are applauding, the guides get hold of their pitchforks and stuff some dead thorn scrub into the bigger holes, where it bursts into flames.

After this Biblical effect, the impressed visitors can march into the bar and order pollo el diablo, chicken barbecued on a massive iron grill in a separate cook-house which is built right over a small fuming crater. The chicken cooks on the heat from the centre of the earth.

There are pictures of the building works at the Instituto, showing the masons walling the interior of this devil's barbecue in their silver Nomex spacesuits and primitive thermal helmets. To me, all this is frighteningly cheeky. Tarfaya went up over two hundred years ago. Two hundred years is a lot of time to people but nothing in the life of the earth, let alone the life of the universe.

To the international leisure industry, the volcanoes are an exploitable resource which they can use to sell good times to a million suckers a year. I don't know how the earth feels about this. I'm a scientist, I can't anthropomorphise. All I can say for sure is that when I see the cooks at Tarfaya barbecuing chicken wings over the mouth of a so-called dormant volcano, the thrill I get is a guilty one.

CHAPTER 4

A Vessel in Distress

I finished my beer. I was thirsty. If I wanted another, I could go back into the bar and get it. The sea was turning inky and above the horizon there was a clear band of sky which was very bright but fading in colour from blue to turquoise. I looked for the purple; Matthew talked once about a painter who said there was always purple in the horizon. Some thick, feathery layers of cloud were settling. The sun was losing power; it was quite comfortable to look at it, a bright yolk cruising quietly along its orbit through the dappled cirrus.

At the height of the heavens the little dabs of cloud drifted in orderly ranks, lined up north-west to south-east, crossed by the white line of a jet's vapour trail. I can never see a plane without feeling my hopes fly up to it. The aircraft was so high it was just a spark in the firmament, silent, almost invisible except for the lengthening slash of white in the blue. At that height it had to be a long-haul flight from Africa, maybe Iberia's daily run from Madrid via Casablanca to Mexico City.

Los Alcazares, as I have said, is a very spiritual place. Whatever formal religion each member of our community chooses to profess on occasions like Tom's funeral, we all share the creed of travel. We all believe in moving on, leaving your troubles behind you, cutting ties, making a fresh start; that's why we're here.

Never let it be said that we have run away. People sit with their drinks and agree that the lives they have left were mad, unenlightened purgatory. They lambast the boss classes, they run down their families, they congratulate themselves on their courage in making the break. These are our articles of faith. We never talk of going back.

Little by little, the hints drop. The Dagenhams have three sons and at least one of them is in jail, learning to be a plumber, doing very well; there are four musicians due money from Maryse; Terry's left behind a wife who has multiple sclerosis, and their two daughters who'll never speak to him again. Sam has an ex-wife who left him and took their baby with her. Carole only works for cash. Islewyn and Leif were not actually struck off their professional registers but they put their mission to make the medical establishment accept complementary therapies above the basic demands of career-building. Tom had the wreck of his career, Stella had her relationship history. I, of course, can trump all of these. But all of this is in the past, the province of long ago and in another country. We all survive by putting a lot of water between ourselves and trouble.

* * *

'This place. This *fucking* place,' Stella raged the day after the funeral. 'I've got to get away. I'm going mad here. I'll go back to England for a week.' She began to call around for tickets, e-mailing the charter carriers in England to find herself a flight. She got one, but Thursday came and went, and she stayed.

'I just keep thinking of him,' Stella would say, many times a day. 'I keep thinking he's just about to come into the bar and, if I stay, he'll walk in. I know it's crazy. Why don't we go to Marrakesh for a few days?' This would be to Terry.

'If I could get a crew together, we could go to Barbados,' was how he replied. Terry mistrusted any place that could not be reached by water.

'Sosiego. I'll go over to Sosiego for the weekend. I love it, it's so peaceful over there.'

Sosiego is our retreat, the runaways' escape. It is a true desert island, a little heap of rocks extruded four million years ago into the vastness of the ocean.

You can walk round it on the wide white beach in an hour. The climb to the summit of the central rock pile takes twenty minutes. You can see it from the Mirador, the swathe of white sand looming out of the distance with the hazy outline of rocks behind.

Sosiego is a place for travellers, not for tourists. It's a microcosm of what Alcazares was when Stella and I first came here and its simplicity means that it stays true to the spirit of the backpack while Alcazares has been lost to the heresy of the Aloha Hawaii Cocktail Lounge. There is one bar on Sosiego, two palm trees and a few houses for fishermen, much like La Quemada when I first saw it.

There are also some caves on the far side where a low brown cliff rises above the beach. Sosiego's rock is ochre and brown-black, and tumbled in colossal chunks like a giant's building blocks. On the north side there are gaps and crevices at beach level into which the wind has blown floors of dry sand. People have finished them off by walling up any holes with small stones. The most comfortable caves are furnished, which means that their last visitors have left whatever they expect the next visitor to need. Usually it's a blanket, a candle and a box of matches. Sometimes there might be a bag of grass or a paperback.

People visiting for the first time often think they will get back on the evening boat but when they get there, time fades out. Then they find a cave, with its little hospitality pack, and they stay to sleep with the stars and wash in the ocean at dawn.

The ferry to Sosiego leaves Puerto del Norte at eleven every day; to reach it from our house – it was accepted, especially by Stella, that Matthew and I would now have custody of her until the next man appeared – it would have been necessary to leave at about nine in the morning. She announced that she would go alone, although Terry half-heartedly suggested he might cruise over after disembarking his fishing party. I went to the Instituto, Matthew went to find Sam at the marina.

'You didn't wake me,' Stella complained when she called me at about ten.

'I'm sorry. We thought you were up. I'm sure I heard the shower.'

'Oh, well.' She was pretty unmoved. As I had guessed, her intention to go to Sosiego had been weak. 'I've called Las Palmas,' she went on. 'They've done it. They're going to bring him back by helicopter on Monday. They were trying not to mention that we haven't got a fridge big enough for a dead body over here. I thought they might stick him in one of the cold stores at a hotel or something.'

'You didn't say that?'

'Of course I did.' Even in this tragedy, her laugh was rich.

'Who to?'

'Only Margaret. "There must be hundreds of

walk-in cold stores here," I said, "I don't see what the problem is."'

'Wasn't she freaked?'

'Totally. But she owes me a freak-out, so we're even. And I really didn't want her trying to stick me with the bill. Or Tom's estate with the bill. Anyway, I made sure the consulate are paying. So they did that for him.'

'That's good. What about . . .'

'Father Martin, he'll be OK. I'll call him next. He'll do something, make it as nice as it can be, I suppose.' I heard her suck on a cigarette. 'What's this cat doing here?' she asked suddenly. 'I didn't know you had a cat.'

'We haven't.'

'A black and white one with a stupid face.'

'No.'

'Must be a stray or wild or something.' There are many vagabond pets on the island. If enough people complain, the police round up the dogs and shoot them. Maryse took on the cause of the animal hospital when she came out and is going to play a benefit to raise money for a full-time vet. 'Do you think I ought to feed it?'

'No, we'll never get rid of it if you do. You don't like cats, anyway.'

'No I don't. I just thought it was yours . . . you know. You and Matthew might be playing very nice house with two cats in the yard.'

'No.'

'So I don't have to worry about it.' Stella is active; when she is unhappy she needs to be doing things, or at least thinking of things to do. 'My clothes are all at the villa,' her voice dropped to hardly more than a breath, 'but I can't face going over there to get them.'

'I'll be through here by lunchtime, I'll come back and we can go together,' I offered.

'Would you? I'll be OK if you're with me. This is all a nightmare, isn't it?'

There is no quick way to do anything here unless it's done before one o'clock. There is no quick way to do anything with Stella when she is distressed. We called by the Residencias office to check the mail and messages, we stopped at the Bar Macarena because she had to eat and her favourite spinach with chickpeas was freshly made. It was four by the time we were grinding up the track to their villa.

Tom went off the road at the fourth bend from the top. The police had dragged the car off the rocks with the magnificent new tow truck from the accident repair place in Villanueva. It was now in the parking lot behind the police station in Angeles.

She stopped the car at the crash site and looked at it for a few minutes before driving on. The ground there is crusted black lava. Tom's car had made no impression on it. All that marked the place was a disturbance of the gravel at the road side, a few scrapes of paint on the rock and some snapped-off cactus branches.

Their villa is called La Pasmada, which was the nearest word to 'wow!' the postal service would accept. It has a great location on the saddle between two hilltops, with a view all the way down the spine of the western La Mora mountains and out to Fuerteventura. The villa and its add-ons – the garage, the pool house, the utility room – spills down the slope on the southern side and the terrace runs round the main building, making the most of the vistas. They are almost a thousand feet up here and it gets cold at night; in fact, it was already chilly when we got out of the car.

An empty villa is tragic, a forsaken place of pleasure where there is no laughter, no patter of happy feet on the marble floors, no noise at all except the humming of the pool filter and the cheeping of the finches in the hibiscus bushes.

'Remember when we first came here?' Stella asked me as she closed the door behind us. 'There weren't any birds at all, except the seagulls and the eagles at the Mirador.'

All the apparatus of enjoyment lay idle. The jacuzzi was still, there were no towels on the sun loungers, the ice-maker in the refrigerator chinked away, building a glacier because nobody had mixed drinks.

The shutters were closed. The maid had been in and the bed was made. Maybe more than one bed had been made. 'I can't bear to sleep with him any more, I can't bear sharing a bed with a man when the love has gone.' Stella said this several weeks before the accident. In silence, I had thought of my years with Conal. Matthew had said, 'I think you heard too much Barry White in the seventies.' I kicked him under the table at the Macarena. Now I noticed that she chose to tell both of us.

Stella trailed through the empty rooms to the main bedroom where she dragged out a suitcase and put a few garments in it. 'I can't think what I need to wear,' she said, sitting on the bed. I was feeling her wounds then; she seemed half her real size, a floppy little doll propped against someone's pillow, her eyes round and always open but seeing nothing.

I suggested she get rid of her stash. 'Done it, done it. First thing I did, Babes. No worries.' In the mailbox, I found a handful of letters, most of them sympathy cards. She poured us a couple of vodkas and we sat down to open them. When the guardia arrived, they found the identikit grieving widow.

Again, they came in a platoon. The police always look mulish in their minibus, as if they feel their masculinity is compromised by being passive passengers. There were some plainclothes men with them.

The captain spoke in well-rehearsed English. 'Señora Banks,' he addressed Stella. 'I regret very much informing you that we have to make some more inquiries about your husband's accident. We need you, please, to come with me and we need to make an examination of your house.'

'Why? What now? Have they brought him back already?' Stella had stood up to shake hands. Now she darted away from the table strewn with mail and stopped at the back of one of the sofas, which she leaned over as if thinking of sitting on it. One hand flew up to her eyes, shutting out the sight of the captain and two of his men standing behind him. She was holding her head up, which she does when she is frightened. Stella is a small, rounded woman but the line of her jaw is very fine, with a little cleft at the point of her chin, which makes her seem breakable.

'I have no information about that, I am sorry. Please come with us now.'

'But I don't understand – why?' Stella twisted obstinately on her heels. The rest of the police had dispersed all over the villa and could be heard opening doors and drawers.

'We need more information.' The two officers behind the captain were stiffening, as if preparing to drag her away.

'But what information? There isn't anything else to tell you. He drove off when he was drunk and had a crash. That's all I know. I wasn't there, I didn't see it.'

'Please get ready and come with us.' This was the right formula. The idea of getting ready somehow made it possible for Stella to do as he said. She asked if she could change her clothes, and had the officers searching her bedroom evicted while she did it. They wouldn't let me go in with her. What she wore was interesting, a prim little dress in dark blue with gilt buttons, as if she were already anticipating a courtroom.

'I need my bag,' she appealed to them when she reappeared. 'It's out in the car. We came in my friend's car.' Then she looked at me with the same wide-open face.

We went out to my vehicle, a rattling ex-rental Suzuki jeep. Stella rummaged behind the seats, then said, 'My mistake. I must have taken it in. I'm sorry, I can't think straight.' When she had her bag she appealed again, 'Will this take long? Can my friend come with me?'

They allowed this and I got into the jeep to follow them downhill. Something rustled in my seat and I assumed that Stella, whose own car is a mobile dust-bin, had managed to litter mine during our trip. When I had a chance I felt under my bottom, expecting cigarette cellophane or a chewing gum wrapper. Instead I pulled out one of the card envelopes with a message on it in smudgy black eye-pencil. 'Keep the faith, Babe. Love.'

I sat for an hour on a bench in the reception area

of the police station, feeling for Stella, wondering what this was about. Officially, drink driving is a serious matter, but here this is another law mostly honoured in the breach unless there's money in it for someone. Tom's insurers, maybe.

In the early evening there was very little activity, just a stocky Swiss couple reporting her bag stolen from their car. Perhaps because I was in sight for so long, the police captain decided to have me interviewed as well.

Another officer took me to a small, sweaty office. No building in Angeles is more than seven years old but some are already getting that coating of urban grime that scrubbing and bleach can't touch, which says more than anything else about what goes on in a place. I believe the police station was built two years ago, but its walls and floors are already grey.

'Your friends Mr and Mrs Banks,' the officer opened in Spanish, 'was it a good marriage? Were they happy together?' He was young and large eyed, with black hair cut short like astrakhan fleece.

'They had the usual stress of moving to a new country. They were married four years ago and decided to live here, but she says he didn't adapt to the life well, he changed. But I don't know how serious she was.'

His pencil, poised over a plain student notepad,

descended slowly and wrote this down. 'Two marriages,' he observed, turning over another paper to
check.

'Yes.'

'How many years have you been friends?'

'Fifteen years.'

He nodded as if he was impressed, maybe by the
length of our friendship, more likely by our looks relative to our ages. Stella definitely looks like a woman
six or seven years less than she is. People say the same
of me, although I think they do it because Matthew
is younger than me. 'You knew her other husband?'

'No.'

'What went wrong with him?'

'They got married very young. When he lost his
job he decided to go to Australia.'

'How did she feel?'

'Unhappy, of course.' The pencil wrote again.

'Her business here, is it successful?'

'I think so. She's an agent, she finds properties
for people to buy, she hasn't invested herself.'
Actually, I knew the Residencias was making good
money but Stella had asked me to keep the faith.
Until I knew which faith I was supposed to be keeping, it seemed best to be cautious. 'What's this
about?' I asked, not expecting an answer.

He ignored the question, but it was an effort for
him to do it. 'Mr Banks. Was he in good health, did
he complain of anything, any health problem?'

This was difficult, because Tom had made a career out of health, his own and ours as well. He lectured us and devised regimes for himself with a slightly resentful enthusiasm, trying to guilt-trip Stella for not mothering him in that way. He was Islewyn's most loyal patient, he saw Leif twice a week, and even they tried to make him talk about something else. He entertained himself with books on nutrition as Stella did with interior design magazines.

Tom's rationale for living on the island was the unpolluted ocean and its fish, free from environmental oestrogens. At the time of his death he had been taking Qi Gong classes, food-combining and trying to beat the blues with St John's wort.

'Personally, I don't think he had any real *problems*, but he worried about his health all the time. He took a lot of vitamins, he went to a naturopath for them and he went to a chiropractor quite often because he had back pain, he had migraines sometimes . . .'

He asked for their names and I gave them. 'Was he depressed also, Mr Banks?'

I remembered Tom as I first met him, fretting to assure me that he was not at all the kind of man who left his wife and family even though that was what he was about to do. 'He could have been. It's hard for me to say. Life's not the same here as it is in England.'

'Was he nervous, a nervous man?' In Spanish this

has a subtext; he was really asking if I thought Tom was neurotic.

'Not really.'

'Did he see a psychiatrist?'

'I don't know. Is there a psychiatrist on the island?'

'I don't know.' The officer shrugged, but our ignorance formed a basis for cooperation. 'And sleep? Did Mr Banks have problems sleeping?'

'Yes, he often said he couldn't sleep here. He said it was very quiet up where their villa is, and if something happened, like the dogs started barking in the night, it would easily wake him up.'

He wrote this down on a fresh line. 'Did he take sleeping pills?'

'I don't know. He liked natural remedies.'

'Did Mrs Banks take sleeping pills?'

'I don't think so.' If Stella had trouble sleeping, she stayed awake. If she actually wanted to sleep, she hit the brandy. 'Why do you need to know?'

This was the lucky question. The officer looked at me as if he were trying to judge my fitness to be told, then pushed his cap back and spilled the beans.

'Because the report we have from Las Palmas says there were both alcohol and drugs in his blood. Barbiturate drugs. Actually, it suggests that his injuries in the crash were not so bad and not the cause of his death. He died because he was narcotised. It is possible he died even before he was in the car.'

'He looked pretty bad.'

'You saw him.'

'I went with my friend to the hospital here. So you're thinking of suicide?' Again, I didn't expect an answer.

'It's possible. And murder is also possible.' He nodded at me, implying that the official opinion was that murder was actually probable. I started to rearrange my interpretation of what happened the night Tom died. It was possible, if he thought Stella was leaving him, that Tom might have wanted to kill himself. He was probably the only person on the island who thought she was still in love with him.

But nobody had a reason to kill Tom, not even Stella. She said that she could kill him quite often, squeaking the outrageous word. I always took it as one of her provocative jokes. She used to say the same about most of her men. We had never taken her seriously.

At the top of my mind was one outstanding fact. Whatever had happened to Tom, Stella and Matthew were the people standing closest to him at the time.

* * *

3 **November:** *Soon after I began the Mass this Sunday morning the noise of a cannon fired at sea was heard in the silence of the church. Fearing*

corsairs, some men ran to the tower. At this time the church tower was the highest point of outlook, giving a clear view over the fields of the plain to the coast and the sea. They soon came down saying that no vessel was in sight, but I noticed two boys slip out of the church, no doubt to run out to the cliffs from where they could keep watch over the whole strait between our island and the next.

In the north of our island, where the land is mountainous, the settlements are protected by the old Moorish fortifications which gave us our name of Alcazares. My people in Yesto, where the land is low-lying and offered no natural defences, often suffered attacks from pirates.

I continued the service and another single shot, again soft, as if from far away, was heard during my address. People became restless; corsairs, when they have attacked Puerto de la Frontera, skimmed around the reefs until they were within range of the harbour, then fired repeatedly on our simple defences. It was more likely that those single shots fired at intervals denoted a ship in distress, making this use of her ordnance in the hope of attracting help from local fishermen.

As I elevated the host yet another distant noise was heard and a few of the young men who stood together at the back began to shuffle and murmur. Some older women tried to silence them, and a dispute ensued in a manner that was barely

*reverent. Finally Don Andres himself turned
around and ended the argument with his fierce eye,
then turned back and gave me his attention in front
of all the people.*

*Don Andres was the father of our province and
people took their lead from him in everything. There
was no more restiveness and the office proceeded
normally. The youths who had dared to think of
cheating Our Lord of his proper worship kept their
eyes on the ground, although more cannon shots were
heard.*

*They had the doors open the instant I uttered the
last syllable of the blessing and many people left as
quickly as they dared to run for the shore, no doubt
hoping for a wreck. Ships foundered several times a
year on our rocky shores. It saddens me to say that
the merciless existence of these islanders does not
inspire great compassion for shipwrecked sailors;
instead, they look upon wrecks as their lawful
bounty. When a ship is lost half of Yesto runs out
to the shore to drag whatever they can from the
waves, often fighting the folk from Puerto de la
Frontera who come up in their boats for the same
purpose. Wrecks bring us all the necessities which
the soil does not yield. Your Excellency knows that
many trading ships come into our ports seeking
water and food; some, when they see the simplicity
of our way of life and understand that there is not
one cannon to defend Puerto de la Frontera, offer us*

only sword cuts and broadsides in exchange for
what they need. The people judge a wreck as God's
recompense for these sufferings, arguing that the
winds and the reefs were created by Our Lord.

Every house in Yesto was built with the timbers
of lost ships. I believe every nail and hook and iron
cook-pot was saved from the sea. The brandy used
to make our sweet wine is often also a gift of the
waves. All the island believes that off
Punto Grande, where the sea bed falls away to
depths beyond measuring, a great hoard of gold
from the Indies lies scattered over the bottom.

I can find no wrong in taking what is given by
God in that way, but it is undoubtedly a practice
which enlarges men's savage instincts. Five years
earlier Don Andres sent to Ubrique for hanging,
three men and two women from the same family in
Puerto de la Frontera caught setting false lights on
the shore to lure ships to disaster. I have heard that
there are those who help the drowning sink by
clubbing them with an oar's end from the boats,
especially at times of drought when the aljibes run
dry and we are forced to buy water in barrels from
Fuerteventura.

Cruelty is to be expected when lives are hard, yet
there is much kindness here. I find a generous spirit
wherever I go; although there are hardly twenty
men able to read and write in the entire island,
and most of the inhabitants are as humble as the

farmers and fishermen Our Lord chose as his disciples, they welcome all who come in peace, readily sharing their meagre supplies. I find here an honesty surprising among such simple people.

As was usual on Sunday, I had the honour to dine with Don Andres and his family. His white camel had given birth to twin calves. On the summit of La Negra, the highest peak hereabouts, the gentians were in bloom early. These are plants with bell-shaped flowers of a vivid blue similar to the mountain gentians which may be familiar to Your Excellency, but perhaps a quarter of the size because of the dryness of our climate. Their colour, however, is even more intense and on La Negra they are plentiful, so to an observer a couple of miles distant in Yesto they look like a blue shawl thrown over the bare shoulders of the mountain.

These are sure signs of early rain and give us good hope of another fruitful year. Don Andres has ordered a double crop to be planted. The soil of this region is extremely rich and the air always warm where shelter from the wind can be achieved. The people are not afraid of work. All that is necessary is enough rain and two plantings of wheat can be harvested, one in late summer and another in the spring.

4 November: From time to time, cannon fire can still be heard. People reported that off the north coast the sea was very rough and had broken the sea wall and flooded the outer salt pans at Jimena. At Vespers I offered special prayers for those in danger at sea.

5 November: *After two days the wind had changed and the noise of the cannon had subsided, suggesting that the ship was out of danger. But as the first of those who had watched for a wreck dragged their tails back to the town this morning, claiming to have found nothing, the current began to carry splintered timbers into the shore by the salt works. In a few hours all manner of goods and debris appeared on the waves, including chests of fine leather of Moorish style, spices and silk cloth, suggesting that the lost ship had left a port in Africa.*

6 November: *The waves have now brought in the body of an African, much battered by the wreckage. The body carried no sign that the man had been of our religion. The corpse was therefore interred with proper ceremony but outside our burial ground.*

The wind has moved to the east, the direction which most often brings rain. No cloud is yet to be seen, but my housekeeper claims she can smell the rain already. It is true there is a scent in this wind, something sharp which almost irritates the nose. I thought she was mistaken because to me, the smell of rain is soft. If there is rain, young plants are set while the ground is soft. Planting is a task for the

*women and my housekeeper asked if I could spare
her for a few days to help in the fields.*

'She was trying it on,' said Eva, reading over my
shoulder.

'He didn't dare to argue with his housekeeper. Or
he was too dumb to realise what she was up to. He
must have been really young,' I deduced.

She pinched my ear. 'But we don't know what she
was like, do we?'

* * *

After the bus came the scene in which Matthew said,
'I don't want to have an affair with you.'

After four days we were in a firestorm of emotions. I was like a teenager, I kept looking in
mirrors, amazed that I looked the same when I felt
so different. When he said that it set off all kinds of
reactions. I felt rejected, of course, also cherished, a
strange new sensation; I was suspicious, because he
seemed so knowing. There was fear, the fear of losing
him, appearing now for the first time. Most strongly
I felt relief because I was not in the habit of adultery.
I was afraid sex would be the beginning of the end of
the dream.

Suspicion was the feeling that I chose to let out. I
was so afraid of the answer that I could hardly do
more than whisper. 'You've had other affairs?'

'I was in love with a married woman for five years,' he told me, and as he said it I saw pain ricochet through his eyes. 'I never want to do those things again. I don't want to have an affair with you. I don't want little pieces of your life, I want it all. I want to be with you. This is everything to me. I want you to leave your husband and get a divorce and marry me.' He had been holding my hand, stroking the fingers, and now he squeezed it, trying to crush belief into me.

'Why are you saying this?' Now I was angry with him. 'It's just words, isn't it? You can't love me, you don't know me. You're just saying it, you're playing some game. For God's sake, we've known each other four days.'

We were in the traditional venue for forbidden passion, a car. Nothing original about us, just as I promised you. You see the same scene happening everywhere, those intense, wretched couples who have parked in a discreet place and sit there framed in the windscreen like actors in the cinema, separated by handbrake and gearshift, trying to square their circle of deception.

It was the Sunday after the bus. Our life was going to leap forward long before I was ready to move; already events were setting their own pace. Matthew was an actor, touring with some ridiculous Restoration comedy which played a week in each town. I had been to see the show the previous evening, taking Liam, my son. He had never seen men in wigs, beauty spots and satin breeches before. The flourishing dialogue confused him; he withdrew into good manners.

In Matthew's dressing room we were three awkward figures trying not to see themselves in the very large mirror. Stella calls him handsome. I never saw that. He's Matthew to me, not an adjective. He is tall but slighter than he appears. He could be Latino but there is also something Celtic there: his eyes are too round, too open, too innocent to be true. He can easily look sulky, which he seldom is. He can easily look as if he's spinning a tale or shooting a line or winding you up, which he may be.

When he chooses to be, Matthew can be a magician. Now I run back our tape and try to see if he turned on his brilliance to seduce me. On the stage it came across simply as presence. The first time I saw him I was bedazzled. I was awed, I was proud that the little knot of women queued for his autograph at the stage door. I was jealous of the skinny, chain-smoking actresses who shrieked along the backstage corridors and told him they would wait for him in the bar.

The next morning I booked the marital car, Conal's company Rover, and said I was going for a walk. So there we were, in a picnic area at our neighbouring woodland park, and it was still raining.

'I love you.' He was desperately stubborn. 'And

you love me. From that moment on the bus. Whatever this thing is, it just appeared from nowhere, it's there like a mountain. Sure, we can say it never happened, but we know, we know it did. If we split up now, if we go away and never see each other again, it will still be there. We'll just be living as half of us, wherever we are, whoever we're with.' He was trying to hold my eyes with his, but I looked down at my hands, holding on to the steering wheel for support.

'I'm not ready,' I answered him. 'This is all new. I can't believe it, I'm sorry. I need more time.'

'OK. But I don't need convincing here, Kim. We might have known each other a thousand years. I can't even say you're the one. Nothing else exists, nobody else. This is my life.'

There was a new feeling coming in, a feeling Matthew gave me constantly in those early days, a feeling I liked even more than the sensation of having found a person who completed me as perfectly as a missing skein of my own DNA; it was the feeling of power. Truthfully, I loved him but I loved him loving me even more. So you understand it was not really my husband I was betraying here; it was Matthew.

'Look,' he said, 'I know I'm young.' We had established that he was six years younger than me but whether his soul was younger than mine was something else. Spending my time with children made me feel not just older but actually senescent, because I had never had the clear optimism that is supposed to be youth's birthright. On the other hand, having my own child made me seem mature to Matthew; at times I felt he identified more with my son than my husband. Then again, he was sophisticated. He used words I had never spoken, even with Stella, words I had only ever seen written; he asked me questions too complex for me to answer straight out. With Matthew I was already living at a higher level.

'I know I'm young,' he repeated, 'but I know some things. I do know that you're never ready. Whatever it is, you are never ready for it. If you wait to be ready, you'll wait forever. I believe you have to do what you must do in your life. Just do it, ready or not.'

'Is this your way of saying goodbye?' I was living in the future, a mother's habit. I was counting our hours because we had established that he had to pack up and move on to the next town on Monday, leaving no later than two P.M.

'God! No! Jesus, God!' He hit the dashboard in frustration, then got out of the car and started walking about, slipping on the wet dead leaves. It was raining only lightly, the drops pattering on the woodland floor.

I sat for a while watching this violent figure striding around under the bare trees, his head hanging in agony. My emotions were good and bad together, and my mind was lecturing me that this was impossible, that this man was dangerous, that what he said was irrational, that it was all too soon, too random.

I don't believe in relationships, I believe in love. A relationship is expedient, inauthentic, dead. Whatever I had with Conal was a relationship. My theory is that a relationship is a temporary fence people throw up around their loneliness. Love is something that happens of itself. I didn't want a relationship but I could not believe that this was love. When I tried to see our future there was only mist.

Then I was out of the car, walking towards him, feeling the rain falling like needles of ice on my head. He threw his arms around me. His face was wet, there were tears in his eyelashes. Matthew cries much more readily than I do. We walked together in blind panic, a few steps this way, a few steps another way, the what-to-do tango. Where our faces touched we were warm. Until that moment we had not even kissed, we had stopped ourselves touching very early in the sequence. I didn't know what I was afraid of, the beginning or the end, or just of change itself.

His lips were drinking raindrops off my face and his tongue was hot. He tried holding some of his coat over us to keep off the rain, his other arm tightening around my waist, under my coat. I was thirty-six years old, I was a mother and I had never felt desire before then.

On the ground he lay over me, the rain falling on his back, running down the sleeves of his coat, trickling over my bared skin. He was so light. After being crushed under the weight of Conal he could have been the fairy quilt of fallen leaves that blew over Hansel and Gretel. We were wet and awkward and stupid; we laughed. When he was inside me we were indivisible. From the corner of my eye I saw the blades of grass beside my face; a brown leaf upended in the distance, blocked my view.

'I don't want this,' he whispered sadly in my ear, 'I want a big white bed that's our bed.' But when we went back to the car and kissed in the dry I made sure we stayed there a while longer and steamed up the windows.

The car was in a state, with mud on the seats. 'Somebody designed that,' Matthew ran his hand over the tan textured vinyl seat cover in an interlude while we were resting apart. 'Somebody drew this, somebody who studied art and probably wanted to be Brunel or William Morris or somebody. He actually drew this piece of plastic, you know, and made sure it was manufactured just the way he saw it, with all these little holes. Waste of a life.' I took his hand off the car seat and put it on my body again.

Matthew got angry when we parted. The rain was falling much more heavily by then, a real downpour.

'The sky's crying because we can't be together,' he alleged.

'That's crap,' I answered drily. 'It was crying when we met.' He was distraught and I felt quite omnipotent and guilty because of it.

My message to Conal was the state of the car. He was, of course, the kind of man who worshipped his vehicle. It was the supreme token of his status, at that time the only one he had besides his son and wife. He sponged it lovingly of a Saturday and sniped at us if we dirtied it. It occurred to me to clean it up, as I drove back home with my feet trembling on the pedals, and I decided not to. If Matthew had the courage to ask for me, leaving some smears of our mud in my husband's car seemed the least I could do.

CHAPTER 5

Visions

Our campus was mesmerised by Stella. If she was in the bar, at a party, even in a shop, people would say, 'I saw Stella Mahoney there,' as if it validated them to have been in the same room. We didn't know each other. She would probably never have noticed me if she hadn't changed my life by accident.

She was small and vivid, poised on half-point in her silly shoes as if she were about to take flight. She didn't move, she burned along a random path of excitement. When I was teaching seven-year-olds a class called Science Magic I always thought of her when I did the experiment with a grain of sodium dropped into a dish of water. The sodium is so reactive that it fizzes all over the surface until it burns out.

Now I know Stella's history, I understand that she had been fired by death, by the death of her mother that summer. She didn't tell anyone; Stella gives compassion but she doesn't like to receive.

A lot of us, women and men, thought she was beautiful. She has a round face, nice skin and thick straight hair, very dark brown. People often say she looks like a cat, because of that delicate chin and the fact that her nose is slightly flattened, and because there is something else feline about her which is hard to identify, something diabolical in the way she stirs up feelings people never knew they had.

She was at the party to which I went although I could feel the wretched fever creeping up again. My boyfriend wanted us to go, poor fool. We had paired off in freshers' week and had clung together ever since, feeling superior to people who were still unattached although we were both reserving our positions on becoming a serious couple. I liked him, but I didn't feel any great connection to him. He had a girlfriend back home. It seemed wrong to push him when I wasn't sure I wanted him. So there was no reason for me to use contraception that night.

Stella says she can't remember bringing Conal to this party. Crazy, but I'm still proud that she has registered me, after that night when our lives were spliced together and she never noticed. She had so many dates then that remembering any one must have been difficult. But I remember her, wearing a trim pink dress, laughing and snorting cigarette smoke out of her wide nostrils.

I can hear her voice swooping through the babble of the room. As always, she was the centre of a group. Conal was beside her; he was a stranger, definitely not one of our crowd. He wore a suit, while all the other men wore jeans, and he stood around uselessly the way he always did, with a smile that was supercilious but ingratiating, like some idiot bishop conferring an unwanted blessing.

I can't remember much else, except that the party was in a dilapidated but very grand house, with ragged velvet curtains at tall windows and blistered plaster cornices. Apart from that, picture the usual student thrash, people treading through a lake of beer on the kitchen floor, people tobogganing down the stairs on trays.

I know I had one drink, because afterwards when my brother gently implied that I might have been drunk I took care to tag that memory before it vanished. I had one drink, one glass of sickly white wine. It was hot and I started to feel faint. My lips were blistering. The fever was back. In another hour or so, I went into the bathroom and was sick, very considerately in the lavatory, which I cleaned afterwards and left as I would have wished to find it.

Then, because the poor fool was enjoying himself getting boozed up with his mates, I went into one of the bedrooms to lie down until he felt ready to take me back to the hall of residence.

I don't know what time it was when Conal came into the room. He stopped in the doorway. He was tall, heavy and square-shouldered and he seemed to fill the rectangle of the door frame. The light from the corridor caught his white face. As soon as I saw him, I was afraid. I tried to sit up but already I was too weak to do it. All I managed was a movement that must have told Conal how weak I was.

He came in and lay on top of me, trying to kiss me. There was a disgusting smell of beer and sweat. I was strong enough to turn my face away and I must have called out because then he put his hand over my mouth and leaned all his weight on it, so I was pinned down to the bed by my head. Then I remember struggling with my clothes, my legs and the sheets, tangling them, trying to stay covered, to put any kind of barrier between myself this huge, heavy man, who was systematically tearing my protection away. I remember the door opening more than once during all this, and I curse whoever it was who came in and never thought to help me.

His penis stabbed me in the groin. I felt the tearing of the dry skin, and heard Conal swear. He knelt on one of my thighs to keep me still. That was hugely painful and an enormous bruise came up the next day. The memory of the actual rape is buried in the pit of trauma. When he'd finished, he threw the sheet back over me and left. Apart from swearing when he couldn't get his cock in me easily, I can't remember him saying anything in the whole process.

That event was as surreal as fever dream. I'm sure I wished I had hallucinated the whole thing. The virus pulled me down and I had to go home. I was ill for two months. In my childhood bed by the butter mark on the wallpaper I had to tell the doctor I had got to know so well, the same doctor who had seen me through the broken arm when I was seven and the acne when I was thirteen, that I had not had a period since before my illness had recommenced.

The vacation was over by then; I should have been into the summer term; my real mind had returned in place of the fuzz that fills your skull in a fever. I could not eat and I felt nauseous all the time. Lying idle in bed, I had been counting up days and getting a scary result.

I was not at all ready for this. Being ill again had sent me back to being a child. I had romantic day-dreams, I was fantasising tentatively about falling in love, crystallising my hope for one special person.

For a while I had achieved what I called a real boyfriend in spite of my illness. Ours was a sweet, six-week holiday thing. With the grave caution of two well-educated virgins we went into our affair for that specified duration pledging to use as much rubber as two lovers can. So this was my first pregnancy scare.

I went on the facts. I computed the data of text-books and the calendar. I sat up in bed and fitted my bra cups over my breasts, finding a distinct expansion. I lived on toast and water for two days and started vomiting. It's amazing how unreal it feels to be pregnant.

'They always were irregular, weren't they?' the doctor tried this in a hopeful tone.

'Three weeks, five weeks – nothing like this.'

'I'm sure it's just the fever,' she resisted.

'It's been nearly three months,' I insisted.

'And it's never been that long before?'

'Never.'

'Have you done any of those home test things? Because they're not very . . .'

'I can hardly get up, I can't go shopping. I can't ask my father to pick up a pregnancy test for me on his way home from work.'

'You haven't mentioned this to your parents?'

'I have to know what's happening to me. I'm being sick. My temperature's normal.'

'I thought it was still a little elevated.'

'Please,' I said, suddenly ready to cry. 'I haven't had a period for at least ten weeks. I'm throwing up. My bras don't fit. If I'm not pregnant, what else can it be?'

'Lots of things,' she said stoutly. I realised that she did not want to find me pregnant because she did not want to be part of my tragedy. There was nothing for it but to use *force majeure*.

'I must know,' I begged her. I could feel tears

coming into my eyes. 'Something awful happened to me. I got raped. When I was coming down with this again. I keeled over at a party and I couldn't stop it. I've not had a period since. Ten weeks, I'm sure of the date.'

'It would be a terrible coincidence . . .' she held out.

'Yes it would, but I've got to know, don't you understand?'

She was foxed; for a moment she didn't know what to say. I thought of her as an old woman, but she had a very fresh complexion so perhaps she was only in her forties. There was an absence of vanity about her. She had thick white hair worn in a schoolboy crop. It had made her feel bad that she had not been able to defeat my illness. But she was kind, she must have been or she would not have argued with me. In the end she managed to get out some suitable words. 'Of course,' she said, 'I'm so sorry, I just didn't . . .'

'I've got to know as soon as possible. I can go back to uni next week, you won't have to be involved any more.'

'A viral infection . . . are you aware . . .' She was clutching at straws. 'Even if it should be positive, a viral infection is often associated with an early miscarriage. During the first trimester. The first twelve weeks.'

'You know I can't wait,' I insisted weakly. I had

learned something useful in sex ed after all. 'I could be twelve weeks already. You know I have to find out right now. It's almost too late as it is.'

So I struggled to the bathroom and peed into a plastic tube. She called in the next day to tell me I was pregnant. I got out of bed, fear overriding weakness. There was shock and shame in that weakness as well as the fever.

All I told my mother was that I was going back. 'Are you sure, dear? You still don't look well. You really are dedicated to this studying.' She tried only half-heartedly to stop me because she wanted to be alone with my father. I felt terrible in front of her, knowing I was pregnant.

There was no vision of a baby before me, only of a huge black disaster walling me up in the tomb of failure from which I had only just been raised. I packed up and went back to the hall of residence. The plan was to see the student counsellor, to tell nobody and to get referred to one of those clinics that processed unwanted pregnancies a dozen a day. I had been out in the world long enough to have seen the leaflets in the students' lavatories and I knew what I had to do.

Everything was working fine until the counsellor said, 'There'll be a fee.'

It was more money than I had. 'Look,' the counsellor offered. 'We can contact this man. We do it discreetly, people don't have to know anything. You don't have to see him if you don't want to. Usually they're happy to pay. He's responsible, after all. He doesn't know that you don't want to press charges, does he?'

'Nobody knows anything,' I said.

'And you are quite sure . . .'

'Oh, yes.' I'm not the right-on kind; I hid if I saw the college women's officer coming and I had no ambition to be the star of a big rape case. Although the idea of Conal being called to some account definitely appealed.

'Give me a name and address and leave it to me,' he promised, that nervy, sexually ambiguous little male with the best of intentions, the best available substitute for a knight in shining armour.

Stella has a favourite quotation from Oscar Wilde: no good deed goes unpunished. It works for both of us. I found her easily since everyone always knew where she was. It was in a gloomy, newly tarted-up pub, quite empty in the early evening, with fruit machines winking in the middle distance, that I put on a bold face and asked her where I could find the man she had brought to that party last term. 'We had a really good conversation.' I was trying to force the blood out of my cheeks because I was sure I was blushing. 'He promised he'd lend me some books.'

'Baby, I wish I could help,' Stella dragged on a cigarette, obviously thinking I had taken a fancy to her discarded date. 'I got so blind that night I can't remember him. What did he look like?'

'Tall,' I bluffed, because I couldn't remember anything useful about Conal either. 'A big guy with a white face.'

'Oh, *him*. Did he have an Irish name? Business school or something?'

'Uh . . .'

She was looking at me with encouragement, her eyebrows arched. No, after he raped me he did not take the trouble to tell me his name. 'Uh . . .' I tried again, slapping on what I hoped was a daffy smile. Later she did remember me asking her this; she really admired my guts trying to track down another woman's date so boldly, having hardly spoken to him at all. She thought I must have fallen in pop-song love across a crowded room.

'I remember him.' Somebody else in the circle spoke up, on the same note of admiring surprise. 'I play squash with him. His name's Conal McEverdy. He's at the business school.'

So Conal was found.

'He really would like to see you,' the counsellor said. Now he looked at me with mistrust, and I knew that somehow my knight had been recruited by the enemy. 'I would advise it. I think you'll be quite surprised by his attitude – in the best way.'

Almost at the instant I agreed, the door to the counsellor's room crashed open and Conal came in with his arms wide and all his teeth bared in a smile that even then seemed to me to be crazed. He leaned over and dabbed a revolting, reverent kiss on my forehead.

'This is great news,' he said, his voice vibrating behind his striped shirt. It was one of those wide-striped shirts chosen by men who buy how-to-succeed-in-business manuals at airports.

'Why?' I demanded.

'You're going to have a baby. That's wonderful.'

'It's not wonderful and I'm not having a baby.'

'We should talk,' he answered, his tone sinking to menace.

Instead of paying a reasonable sum to have his crime forgotten, he decided to spew himself all over the poor bud of my life and smother it. His shame would be transfigured while mine was made flesh. That was the end of me for seventeen years. And maybe forever.

* * *

The Cura's journal is the only eye-witness account of the creation of the island. I have two versions of it, both in Spanish, neither of them original or complete. One is a smudgy, dog-eared typescript, an awkward retranslation from a German thesis. The other is a much older document, handwritten in looping copperplate in a leatherbound book which is dried out and falling to pieces. The pages have been sewn together with thread which has broken in several places, so some sections are missing. This version, Eva says, is in archaic Castilian, and is occasionally punctuated by naïve exclamations – 'What a disaster, Excellency! What a din, Excellency, what a ghastly racket!'

The events that interest me, and Milo, and possibly *Nature* magazine, occurred between 5 December 1792 and 27 May 1799. Both the accounts I have were written in the last century. The German version was based on a document found in the episcopal archives on Gran Canaria by an amateur vulcanologist from Heidelberg. The Spanish version is one of a bundle of thirty-seven original documents from the regional museum on Gran Canaria. It includes some maps which are surprisingly accurate for their supposed date.

The Cura seems to have been more than a bit of an anorak, but it is his nitpicking detail that now makes his diary so valuable for Milo's report. I have established that the older text is still not the original; it was extracted from whatever day-to-day account the Cura originally wrote and it is dated 1801, thirteen years after the events began.

In the Spanish text the Cura shows affection for his *conejeros* in long defensive explanations of island culture. His account is dedicated to the Most Illustrious

Señor Don Juan Francisco de la Guillen, Bishop of Canaria, and he is clearly anxious to commend his simple parishioners to this grand personage.

I don't feel Fr Rosario was a particularly educated man and the style of the older account, which often breaks down into a torrent of phrases that are bare of verbs for several lines, makes me think that the original was not in Latin. Even in the old Spanish text, every now and then I come across a word that seems out of place.

My profile, the product of all the assumptions I make about him while I'm working, is that the Cura was a *conejero* himself, but educated at a seminary in the north of Spain, maybe at Compostela. I think he wrote in the old Canarian speech, a dialect of Spanish salted with words from the races which have made landfall here: the creole of the West Indies, the Arabic of the corsairs and all the tongues of north-west Africa.

I think Rosario spent time in the north because he seems to be familiar with mountain greenery, but he refers to the birthplace of his mother on the island. So a Canarian girl perhaps married a seaman from the north of Spain.

That would also explain how he came to be here. Los Alcazares has only recently been a dream destination. For most of its history the island was a favourite for the title of armpit of the universe. The old names of the villages mean things like 'flea-pit' or 'devil's arsehole'. People were born here or they were marooned here.

There are still little communities of dark-skinned, fine-featured, Arabic-speaking islanders, descendants of the traders who ran spices and slaves up and down the African coast, nomads of the sea who one year failed to move on. The prehistoric remains which have been found in burial caves suggest the earliest islanders were racially similar to the Berbers of north Africa. Occasionally perhaps a conquistador would be left behind by comrades who decided to ditch him because he was trouble; the islands were the last landfall before America. For most of the human race, Los Alcazares was a place to avoid.

I can't find any vice in Rosario: he can be pedantic, he's quite intelligent and he's as innocent as the Holy Virgin. My man was not exiled here for any crime other than perhaps extreme uncoolness. I think he wanted to be here; he felt his vocation was to look after his own people.

14 November. On this day, Don Andres' steward called me to the great house. A strange illness had struck both his eldest daughter and her maid, recently returned from a journey to Ubrique to visit her fiancé and his family and to buy linen. Dona Maria Caterina is betrothed to the Señor Alfonso José Ducque Muñoz, the second son of our Governor, Don Jaimé Ducque Muñoz.

To save their laden mules the women, who were accompanied by an older woman as duenna, and had two of Don Jaimé's men with them, had taken the coast road through Viera. A mile or so north of Yesto, when they were nearly home and about to turn inland, the two young women and one of their male servants saw a very large ship out at sea.

All three described it as a galley of the ancient style, propelled by three banks of oars, with a square white sail and pennants which appeared silver in the sunlight. They could not see any marking on the flags or the sail. The sky was clear and the sun brilliant, and this pale trireme was such a majestic sight that they lingered to watch it and reported it with excitement when they reached home. The other two travellers did not see this ship; the duenna was riding ahead and the other man was occupied securing one of the animal's loads.

That night both young women seemed tired, which was to be expected after their journey, but the night's rest left them no better. By the end of the next day both were so weak they could not stand and Don Jaimé's man was also affected by trembling and faintness. None of the three had been able to eat or drink and the family was alarmed. Dona Maria is Don Andres' eldest daughter, a fine, strong woman of sixteen, whose wedding the next summer he intends to be the most magnificent celebration Yesto had ever seen.

There is a legend among the fisherman here of a ghost ship which appears at sea when a crew is doomed. They believe that this ship is sent by the devil to take souls to hell and any man who looks at it will die soon afterwards.

Throughout these small islands people have a great fear of the ocean. Even though many of them live by fishing, they are not seamen and are afraid to voyage out of sight of their own coast. The native islanders discovered by our first settlers were extraordinarily tall and gentle men who had no knowledge of shipbuilding or navigation.

As we rode to the great house I asked the steward what the common people were saying. He replied that the story of the ghost ship was already well remembered, and the more credulous were already declaring that this ancient trireme was indeed that ship, and Dona Maria and the two servants would die, while the duenna and the man who did not look up will live. Indeed, I found this man later as healthy as a horse and ready to tell anyone who would stand him a drink how terrible and ghastly was the vision his companions had seen, with a death's head carved under the bowsprit and flocks of winged demons flying about the masts. I take this to be the product of his own imagination since Dona Maria has not mentioned these things.

I found Dona Maria lying already as still as a corpse, her hair soaking with perspiration and her skin sunken on her bones. She could speak and opened her eyes as I prayed over her. The maid, a girl who at best was always skinny as a chicken, was in an even worse state while the man was less affected, but quite incoherent with fear. The vision, as he related it to me, was certainly strange for he was emphatic about the oars although no galley has been seen in these waters in recent memory.

I examined the duenna at length. She had seen nothing and believed Dona Maria was pretending lovesickness in order to persuade her father to bring forward the date of her wedding. Before I could enquire, she swore that in Ubrique she had never left the young woman's side and had slept in the same room with her every night. Many had observed true affection quicken between Dona Maria and Don Alfonso whenever they met, but Don Alfonso's character was most honourable and prudent. None had the opinion that the couple had improperly anticipated the joys of their union.

I advised Don Andres to send to the anchorite of Guanapay a wise healer who could infuse his remedies with special prayers as a result of his holy state. Two of the fastest riders were sent at once with a letter in which I fully described the circumstances. I said a special Mass for the household every morning, and sent the figure of St Catherine from the Church to stand in the room where Dona Maria lay. I know people find it hard to understand Our Lord's purpose when he allows the death of a pure and lovely young woman.

CHAPTER 6

Inquisition

They brought Matthew down to the police station at about nine P.M., just as my interview was finished. I guessed that the guardia had just staked out our apartment and waited for him to come home.

He walked in between the two officers in his old stage stride. I hadn't seen that in a while. He looked relieved when he saw me and I felt a wrench in my guts at the sight of him. We said some awkward nothings to each other before the guardia took him off behind the white-painted partition hiding the corridor to the captain's office and the interview rooms. I went back to the bench.

Out here, Matthew had taken the lesson from Tom and put a lot of energy into finding his feet. He latched on to Sam at Radio Angeles and sold him on an after-midnight show called The Red Eye. They record fourteen hours, the whole week's output, in one day. Radio Angeles is high tech and low maintenance. Round-the-clock radio for English-speaking ex-pats is created by Sam or another guy doing two live shows and leaving the rest to the computer. The studio is the small bedroom in Sam's apartment. The other guy is like Sam, skinny, hyper and too old to be credible in this job back home. They keep Matthew strictly at arm's length because he is talented and a pro. That's not love talking, it's about the only truth out here that is held to be self-evident. And he gets fan mail, sometimes with G-strings in it. Mostly from women.

With four days a week to spare, Matthew created a job for himself at the international school, teaching drama. I was not ready for that. There's something claustrophobic about my lover going into my old profession. I think he has changed here. He is brighter, louder, more insecure. This is half-life to him and he feels unstable.

His agent won't give up. She faxes him sometimes about parts he could fly back to read for, but Matthew says, 'I told her the deal. I was coming here with you and I'd take whatever time we needed. She knows that. If she's angry about it, that's her problem.' His old apartment is rented and money is not an issue.

The school isn't big. Most of the Brits here are either young and free or old and free of their families.

There are only about thirty English-speaking children between the ages of five and thirteen.

Matthew takes the work very seriously. My teeth set on edge when he says teaching is so much more rewarding than acting. He loves something about it, but whether it's the work, the children, the opportunity to regress or the pose potential I couldn't say. The children adore him. He puts in such long hours that he's making the full-time teachers uneasy.

We can't sink into the real island life because we are working a mainland schedule. It is strange to be stressed in the sun. The school is an hour's drive away from the Instituto. Siesta time is not for us. Matthew is always calling in late because he's preparing classes or supervising the extra rehearsals for the shy kids, or painting scenery, or rigging lights or talking one of the mothers into running up a costume. At least, those are the things he says he is doing. How would I know?

So far, Matthew has produced *The Wizard of Oz*, *James and the Giant Peach*, and *Grease*; he is now working on *A Midsummer Night's Dream*. I can't quite believe that my perfect lover is content spending all day with small children. The old Adam isn't dormant either – those costumes get sewn too well and even the youngest of the little girls goes wriggly around him.

In the police station I sat upright on the bench and tried to meditate to pass the time, but my brain was buzzing. Meditation is like painting: it's one of those dream-scene things people are inspired to do on the island and imagine they will have all the time in the world to perfect when they live here. Carole gets frustrated because people join her group, come a couple of times, then drop out. 'How can people come here and not want to tap into this incredible energy?' she complains. Stella went once and said the meditation room smelt of damp.

An hour later another squad of guardia brought in Terry, who looked plain scared. He was also taken behind the partition but came back out again a few minutes later.

'They've impounded the boat, the bastards.'

'That's bad,' I said.

'Too right, it's bad.' He looked miserable; his boat is his life. 'I've got twenty-three punters booked for tomorrow. What am I going to do with them?'

He threw himself on the bench next to me. 'What can I tell them? I wish I could tell them more. Stella came down to the boat with Matthew sometime that night. It wasn't late, midnight or so. We had a couple of brandies. She said Tom was going nuts, they'd had a row or something. I'm not speaking ill of the dead, but – well, he didn't know how to manage her, did he? He let her get away from him, didn't feel the wind change. We sat around, had a bit of a chat and then they left. That's it, that's the whole thing.'

For all that he has lean muscles on a wiry frame, isn't much taller than Stella and seems to have led a very limited life until recently, Terry is made in the mould of the old Hollywood heroes. He's as growly as John Wayne, he grins like Kirk Douglas, he's got that Burt Lancaster spark in his eye. All his features are overlarge – hands, ears, teeth, feet. He wears a faded Levi's shirt that is never buttoned up very far, so there's always a fine expanse of sinewy brown chest on view. Matthew swears he shaves it.

He takes the sun well, best of all us Brits who tend to get the boiled-lobster look in the long term. Only the grey in his hair, which is fine and curly, suggests his age; that and the spots on backs of his thick hands. He has a black elephant-hair bracelet on one wrist; it looks almost degenerate with all that salt-streaked masculinity.

'I like Stella,' he went on. 'Don't get me wrong, I know she's your friend, I genuinely like her. But she's not handled this right. She's too – too open about it all. Like she's got no respect. She should have waited for the family at that funeral. Sent the body back to England, I don't know. It just doesn't look good. She's still talking Tom down. I haven't heard her say a word about how sorry she is.'

'Nor me,' I agreed.

'And she's buzzing about, talking about business as usual from Monday. Maybe she is glad he's gone, but she ought to pretend.'

I agreed with him. 'But you know Stella, you can't tell her anything.'

'Oh yeah,' he said with a laugh, 'I know Stella. That's for sure.'

In the weeks that followed, I had that conversation everywhere I went. 'I like Stella – but . . .' became what people said after they said 'Hello.' It seemed that while we were in the hands of the guardia the whole island had found out that Tom's death was probably not a simple case of drink driving, because those conversations began the next morning. People were in a great hurry to distance themselves from Stella.

'They want me back here tomorrow. There's a CID man coming out from England – did they tell you that?'

'No. Just that he'd taken drugs.'

'What drugs?'

'Anti-depressants, sleeping pills – I don't know.'

'That was it, was it?'

'Didn't yours tell you that?'

'No. Just that the British coroner got the autopsy report and decided to send out a cop to check things out.'

'Mine said there was alcohol and narcotics in his blood.'

Terry sucked in a deep breath through his Kirk Douglas teeth. 'So that's it, is it? They mean sleeping pills? He was a bit careful of his health, old Tom.'

'Hypochondriac.'

'Yeah. Vitamins and that. If you shook him he'd rattle.'

Normally, trashing our fellow castaways is a great sport, but we were not really in the mood for it. The police station had livened up. Telephones rang more often and the guardia brought in a couple of sulking mainland-Spanish youths. The two cops in dayglo jackets who direct the night-time traffic in Angeles strutted out, full of the importance of their office. Playa de los Angeles is busier by night than by day now. The strip along the beachfront is a river of headlights from six P.M. until past midnight. One of the cops gesticulates at the junction outside the Hotel Las Rocas, which marks the western end of the beach. The other cop has a little podium at the far eastern end of the strip, outside the Aloha Hawaii Cocktail Lounge.

Stella was released at about half past ten. The captain escorted her out, so her voodoo had worked on him. Terry and I got to our feet as she approached us, not smiling.

'Let's get out of here,' she muttered, as if she didn't want the police to overhear. 'Have you waited all this time?'

'They talked to us, too,' I told her.

'Why?' She was looking in her handbag for cigarettes. 'They shouldn't be hassling you. You weren't there.'

Terry offered her one of his Marlboros. He kept his pack in one of his shirt pockets, and his wallet in the other, giving the illusion of the pecs he hadn't got.

'I can't smoke them, they're too strong,' she said. 'Come on, we can get some on the road.'

'I'm waiting for Matthew,' I told her. 'They brought him in a couple of hours ago.'

I paid attention to the way she took that news. Her face darkened. Then she stretched her hand out to stop Terry putting away his Marlboros. She took one, let him light it for her – which Stella cannot do without catching the man's eye over the flame – dragged deep, pulled a face as she exhaled and said, 'I suppose I should have expected it. They're not wasting any time, are they?'

'A CID guy's coming out from London, that's what they told me,' Terry said.

'Did they tell you about what they found in his blood?' she asked us both.

'Booze and pills.'

'Yeah.' She blew out smoke. 'Well, I told them, that was Tom. Him and his remedies. Pills for everything.'

At that moment Matthew came out, and she went to him at once and hugged him around the waist, saying, 'God, I'm sorry. I'm so sorry. This is such a mess. Bastard mess.'

He had to get free of her to come to me for a kiss

hello. The hello and goodbye kisses he does without thinking. In all the years with Conal every touch was calculated to show his ownership, the hand on my back pushing me into his office party at Christmas, the large grab for my luggage, those vestigial kisses he estimated that I could not avoid. It is heaven now to be with a man who just kisses you because he likes you. Call me mushy, but when we aren't together, it's nice to have his kisses as hostages.

'Are you OK?' He kept hold of me by the arms.

'Yes. They didn't have me in there for long – there isn't much I can tell them. You?'

'Why did they even talk to you? You aren't mixed up in this.'

'Don't get angry. I was with Stella when they picked her up.'

'They shouldn't drag you into it,' he said. I could feel the tension in his hands. His shoulders were tight and he kept shifting his weight from one foot to another.

'Stay still,' I said. 'You're bugging me.'

'Let's get out of here,' Stella suggested.

We decided to drive Terry back to the marina to pick up his stuff from the boat. I told him he could cram into our place for the night, and sort out somewhere else next morning. In the car, Matthew sat beside me in silence and Stella looked out of the window without speaking while Terry talked himself through the logistics of the next day's trip.

Crawling cars, glaring neon, thumping techno, disco, house, reggae, flamenco, whatever – I hate the strip by night. I turned off and cut in and out of the back streets, avoiding the tourists who straggled off the pavements. Keep the faith. If the boys left us alone, I could ask her what she meant. Matthew hadn't mentioned taking Stella down to the marina.

* * *

The night Tom died we started out as six – Stella and Tom, Matthew and I, Maryse and Jesus who is her lover and keyboards player. They teamed up a couple of months ago and toured the hotels with greatest hits by Eternal and Simply Red.

We met at the Macarena and I came from the Instituto, the last to arrive.

Since that night, I replay my arrival at the Macarena a lot. How did Matthew react, where was he sitting relative to Stella, what was passing between them? He was next to her, leaning back, looking into his glass, looking stressed. Stella was slating Tom for wanting to drink sangria.

'You're not a bloody tourist, for Christ's sake,' she said. 'You live here now. You're a resident. When in Rome, darling. Have a beer, can't you?'

Then Tom started. 'What I'd really like, since it's a nice warm evening, is a Pimm's. Of course, I don't suppose they've got any here. If they had, they wouldn't know how to mix it. Cucumber skin, that's my secret. Plenty of mint and just the skin of the cucumber. I could show them how it's done.' He was genial. He was quite unaware that he and Stella had moved into that territory where nothing could go right between them again. Her snippy remarks he interpreted as humour. He was sitting in that way in which, as Ian Fleming observed, only Englishmen ever sit, with the ankle of one leg casually resting on the knee of the other. Because he thought the ex-pat thing was the thing to be doing, he wore a V-neck cricket sweater over his shirt, and had his sunglasses hanging over the point of the V.

'Don't be a prat,' Stella suggested.

Matthew pulled out a chair for me. He ordered another beer, so did Maryse and Jesus. Stella and I had gin and tonic. Tom demanded his Pimm's and went up to the bar to supervise its composition.

After a couple of rounds we started deciding where we wanted to go for dinner. This is a nice choice, because in Alcazares we have a restaurant or ten from every culinary culture in the world so you can pick the precise eatery for your mood of the moment. Cheap and cheerful – El Pescador on the harbour in Angeles; posey at La Nôtre Dame on the Costa Ubrique; politically illiterate at the Chino Tiananmen; nostalgically right-on at the Vientiane in Villanueva. For birthdays and fiestas, we book at the Casa Alcalde in an old mansion in Ubrique, German-owned, Australian-designed, with a Catalan chef. When we feel a sentimental yearning for urban fast-food we make for Wok-Wok-Wok on the strip, which is next to the Cutty Sark Carvery, favourite for the xenophobic British Sunday blow-out, although the roast beef comes directly from Argentina. We do not, however, have a Mcdonald's, a Burger King or a KFC. It's probably only a matter of time.

Stella has dictated that we should favour the small, authentic Spanish-owned places. There are scores of them but that night nothing anyone else suggested satisfied her. 'It's time to go,' she kept saying, meaning time to leave the island. 'It's all gone, the magic of it. It's had it. It's over, the scene's moved on. Why are we staying here, when we don't have to stay, huh? We can be anywhere, can't we?'

In the end we went to a place Jesus suggested, on the main street in Tamiza. This is a village north of Angeles which will shortly be consumed as the resort expands up the hills. Tamiza is one of the island's five regional capitals, like Yesto, Ubrique, Villanueva and Aranda, and the only one not to have a communist mayor.

The mayors are one reason why the island is still beautiful outside places like Angeles, which they designate for exploitation. They're stubborn and fanatical.

The people of Los Alcazares, having no water,

looked on enviously for decades while thousand-bed, twenty-storey hotels disfigured Tenerife. Then a desalination plant was built here to make fresh water from the sea. The mayors of that time got together and framed the most ferocious zoning legislation in Spain. They declared Tarfaya, Punto Grande and all the land north of Aranda national parks. They hired architects from the Catalan school to design the entire island, the airport, the tourist sites and all the public buildings. This was also the politics of revenge, because while the tourist trade developed, the island's fishing industry was killed by edicts from Brussels.

Now every tourist hot-spot is an architectural miracle. The thousands who fly in and out by jumbo jet look down at the craters and lava fields and can't distinguish the huge white-walled bar-restaurants and the acoustically perfect conference suites from the rocks around them.

All new building is severely controlled: two storeys is the limit and a million-peseta bribe won't buy you permission to paint your front door anything but white or green. The mayors' chief amusement is to trick some multinational capitalist octopus into heaving up a concrete high-rise, then slapping on a zillion-peseta fine and condemning the building to be bulldozed.

Corruption is nickel-and-dime stuff but it's growing. 'Look at all that,' Stella gestured at the row of young royal palms landscaped down the centre of Tamiza's main drag. 'You'll never make this place the Champs-Elysées. It's a scam, all these civic amenities. We know the mayor's brother's got a construction company, we can guess who got the contract. We're going the same way as the rest of the world. It's all over. It's so sad.'

'What did you expect?' Tom countered her. 'People are the same, the world over . . .'

One time Stella and I wandered into El Toro, the bullfight bar, where they show the corridas on widescreen TV. We watched a young bull who was so hellbent on stomping the matador he practically ran onto the sword and killed himself. That's how Tom was that evening. He argued with Stella over everything including the fat content of the stew and the number of years *M*A*S*H* had been screened. Then he sat and spooned up his chocolate ice-cream to the final dregs while the rest of us quivered from the violence of their argument and Stella smoked furiously and stared into the distance. Matthew, I remember, was sitting next to Stella and stretched his arm along the back of her chair as if he wanted to protect her. Jesus took Maryse away before the bill came.

Tom got up, walked out into the street and fell over the kerbstone, which was when we realised how drunk he was. So Stella asked Matthew to drive them, saying he could take her car back to our place once he had dropped them at La Pasmada. So I drove back to our place by myself, angry. And Matthew says he drove them home, had a coffee in the kitchen and came straight back. Terry now says he took her down to the Marina.

I know exactly what time Matthew got back because I lay in our bed in a ball of rage, trying not to look at the clock. He came in at 2.32 A.M.

I pretended to be asleep. When he slipped his arm around my waist, I cringed away, muttering that I was hot. That was so much like being married to Conal that I wondered what curse was on me; having lost so much to share a bed with a man who loved me, I was turning that loving bed into the barren place from which I had paid such a terrible price to be free.

Matthew would never let me get away with that stuff. He got up and asked me if I wanted some tea. He moved deliberately about the apartment, which is only two rooms, until I felt my bluff called and got up to join him. We sat on the sofa and looked out of the window into the night. In darkness, the mass of the land is so utterly black that all the lights are piercing. Angeles was a great smear of colours. Out across the sea a village on Fuerteventura was like a galaxy far away. We watched the headlights swooping up the road to Yesto, like dancing ghosts, up to the point where the road slips between the rising mountains of La Mora.

After a while I moved closer to him. He pulled me into his arms and held me as if I were a child. 'Tonight was bad, wasn't it?' he asked. 'Tom and Stella fighting.'

'Can we leave it alone?' I didn't want him wading in to catalogue all my feelings when I could hardly recognise them myself.

'You're unhappy,' he reasoned. 'I want to make it better.'

'Then tell me why it took you three hours to drive them home.'

'I thought you'd be asleep.'

'I was waiting for you.'

'I was afraid to leave them. He wouldn't let her alone. They were fighting like . . . I don't know what. I don't know whether I was more afraid for him or for her. Why's he so mad at her?'

Now, of course, I wonder if Tom had also sensed something between Matthew and Stella. I wish I'd asked him before he died. I said something about men falling for Stella because of her weaknesses, then coming to hate her for them. Because that's how it's happened in the years I've known her.

'She's the stronger one,' Matthew said. 'I didn't see that at first. I thought she was like a lost kitten.' And he laughed. 'But she did love him?' I was afraid to ask him why he wanted to know.

'Yes, she loved him. She likes to take care of people. She's not romantic like hearts-and-flowers but she meets someone and starts this dream about them. Or about what they can be, with a little love. And the man likes the dream and fits himself into it and the whole thing works. But she doesn't stop dreaming – she wants more, and then suddenly the man can't change any more. So she's disappointed. She thinks she's failed.'

'Witch.' He said this with wonder, as if he too was spellbound.

I couldn't say anything. Stella had done the same with me, showed me the mirage of our friendship, of two free hearts against the world. I had walked into that and now it was our reality. Then I had introduced Matthew, and he didn't fit the picture.

'Did you fight with Conal?' Matthew asked. Since its end, he had never asked me about my marriage. One day I may be able to talk to him about it, but up to now I have been gagged by guilt. It's suffocating. I would like to be free of it. Stella's absolution wasn't enough this time. So I tried with Matthew.

'You couldn't fight with Conal. He could have been in a parallel universe.' While I was saying this, I felt his interest fade. He started slowly flicking his fingertips, lost for words. The weight on my soul did not lift. So I sent the conversation off on an easier track, saying, 'I'd have given anything to be able to scream at him the way Stella can scream at Tom.'

'Tom doesn't hear her, though, does he? He just smiles and smiles and thinks she's brilliant because she's a spitfire. He actually said that. I suppose that's the problem now – he can't maintain his illusion of masculine supremacy.'

Matthew is sophisticated with feminist theory, which makes me uneasy. My concept of feminism was never that elaborate. Once I had found a rationalisation for Conal, and as long as I could have my own life, I didn't really care about sexual politics.

All I could think of at that moment was Matthew and Stella. My mind was running a sequence of Tom passing out and Stella sitting with Matthew just as I had sat with him, and then moving in for her kill. I had seen her seduce. She would be provocative and pitiful by turns until the man was paralysed with fascination and she could drop her veil of enchantment over him.

I touched Matthew's face. The night around us was empty. We were two tiny figures, microscopic dots of life on a rock in the ocean. I was scared. I felt bad that I had mistrusted him, so I let Matthew try to comfort me, although I was beyond comfort.

* * *

When we reached the marina, we found Terry's boat laced about with police tape and a solitary guard strolling up and down the jetty. Terry gave him a few hundred pesetas and went below to get a bag together with his clothes, phone and diary. They did not seem to have thought about his car.

Back at our place I threw some food together while Terry took his phone out to the terrace to make some calls in private. The twenty-three Hemingway acolytes booked to go sport fishing on his boat were not the major problem. He could hire another boat for the day. The major problem was his women.

Terry was some kind of engineer who had retired early, built himself a yacht in his suburban garage, rolled it down to the Thames and sailed away, leaving his sick wife and his daughters with everything else he had. He says that when his wife was diagnosed the doctors expected her illness to progress rapidly through paralysis to death. Instead, it went into remission, with only the occasional scare to keep them on their toes.

Terry says he has put in twenty years of hovering beside his suffering wife, planning for the day she would begin her lingering and tragic death. Now, with the best will in the world, because he seems to have a good heart, he thinks he has never lived and wants to make up for it. He intended to sail around the world. One day he put into the new marina at Puerto del Ducque, liked the island and made an excuse to linger. The excuse is that he's looking for a crew.

People ask after Terry's crew with heavy innuendo. Screw, not crew, is what he'll say he really
needs, a nice sexy woman who wants to fuck her
way over to Barbados with him. Terry, as I've indicated, is not at all without charm and Alcazares is
heaving with overheated females ready for adventure. Once a week he runs an all-day cruise and
barbecue to the beaches of Punto Grande. The bow
cabin on his boat has seen a lot of action, but Terry
just hasn't found the right crew yet.

That night, I was never alone with Matthew or
with Stella. It was nearly one when the four of us
went to bed in our little apartment. At first only
Terry slept and the rest of us heard him snoring.
Matthew held me, but his arms, normally so still,
were trembling. He had figured out the fact that
was glaring at me. If Tom had taken a sleeping pill
and passed out, Stella alone could not have carried
him to his car, put him in the driver's seat and got
the vehicle on the road. Somebody stronger must
have helped her. And Matthew had been there,
Matthew had been the only person with them.

CHAPTER 7

In at the Birth

Positive. That word sounds as big as the Big Bang when it's the result of your pregnancy test. I was catatonic with shock. Even though my breasts tingled, I felt constantly nauseous and threw up sometimes, I could not begin to visualise a baby. All my mind was occupied just trying to understand that I had conceived.

'We should talk,' Conal said in the campus counsellor's office. My knight in shining armour had left me alone with a towering, grinning stranger. He wore spectacles with thin red frames and large, thick lenses that magnified his eyes.

'Let's sit down,' said Conal, pointing to the interview area in the office, some worn seating units grouped around the token coffee table which was supposed to give a domestic feel to the area. 'This is . . . great news. Great.'

'Not for me.' My mistake was trying to make him understand.

'But it can be great, it can be. Look, I'm not running away from anything, OK? I'll stand by you, of course I will.'

'Good.' Optimist that I was, briefly, I thought he meant he would pay up and go away. 'Then you can just give me the money and that's the end of it.'

'No, no. You don't understand. I mean, I'll take care of you.'

'I don't want taking care of. I want my life back like it was before. I can't possibly go through with this.'

'Anyway,' he set off on another tack, 'they won't give you a termination just like that. I found out. We met thirteen weeks ago. That's too late for a termination without all kinds of special consultation, procedures . . .'

I felt cornered. This was not a deranged impulse; he had actually researched the mess I was in. 'We *met*!' I lashed back at him. 'You don't remember . . .'

'Yes, I do.' A glance with a huge load of implication, as if we had an all-time cosmic sexual experience. He was ready for me on this ground, too. 'I'll never forget, Kim. Of course I remember. We'd had a lot to drink, but I do remember. Oh, yes.'

'Well, then, you'll remember that you raped me.' I was so angry that the word burst out, even though I had hardly said it to myself.

'That's an ugly thing to say.'

'Ugly and true.'

'I don't think so. Not to me . . .'

'Consent. Consent, that was what was missing. My consent. That little word, "yes". Don't tell me you remember that.'

'Look, it was a party, wasn't it? We were having a good time . . .'

'I never even spoke to you.'

'I was with a friend of yours . . .'

'I don't know her. I didn't speak to either of you. I came with my boyfriend and I went to lie down because I was ill.'

'We'd had a lot to drink . . .'

'Not that kind of ill. You were drunk, I wasn't. Glandular fever, I've been ill for years, there are records, medical records, my doctor's got them . . .'

'I had no idea.' Now he made it sound as if I were revealing some wondrous statistic, newly researched. 'Will it . . . does it . . . affect the baby at all?'

'I wish it did.'

'You mustn't say that.'

'Look, I can't have a baby. I'm nineteen. All I know about you is that you . . . well, you know what you did. I want a termination, and all I want from you is the money to pay for it.' I still thought that the truth would save me, that because I knew what had happened between us we were bound to reach the right outcome in the end.

'You don't understand. We could get married.'
He said it with a huge expression of triumph, as if
he were putting down the ace of trumps on top of
the king.

'I don't want to.'

'But I want to,' he urged, his eyes excited behind
his lenses. 'Don't you understand that? It's my baby
too.'

There was a tap at the door. Our forty-five minutes of counsellor-time was running out. 'Come in,'
I called, relieved to be interrupted in this madness.

'She's going to think about it,' Conal told him at
once and actually reached out to clasp my hands in his.

'No,' I said at once. 'There's nothing to think
about. If he won't give me the money, I'll borrow it
somehow.'

'Shall we make another appointment?' The counsellor stood over his diary and looked at me.

'No,' I answered.

'Yes,' said Conal. What a sick discussion they
must have had, Conal's ego already engorged with
the proof of his potency and that lousy little closet
misogynist massaging it for all he was worth.

'Shall I pencil you in for the day after tomorrow?
And then you can think about it. I should see you
again in any case.' This again was to me.

I walked away from Conal outside the door, but
he followed me wherever I went, arguing on until I
was crying with fatigue and anger.

That evening I was called to the telephone. 'This is such wonderful news.' It was my mother's voice, jacked up to the pitch of acceptance which she felt was right for these different times. Conal had called her. I guessed that he had copied down my parents' details from my form; perhaps the counsellor gave them to him.

From my mother I learned that we were a major item. He adored me but had not dared propose because I was still only a fresher and he was graduating that year. But now that I was pregnant he was overjoyed and wanted to get married.

Conal had painted this picture in such colour that my parents believed it entirely. My feverish little voice, denying, staking my claim to the right to make the final decision, was drowned by their enthusiasm for my marriage.

I did succeed in seeing the counsellor by myself, to find that Conal had spun him the same yarn. The man paused briefly over my insistence that all our relationship amounted to was a two-minute crime in a strange bedroom, before saying, 'It is his baby too,' and coming back to the idea that I should 'think about it some more.'

'If I think any more, it'll be too late,' I pointed out, appealing for help for the last time.

'That wouldn't be so bad, would it?' was how I was dismissed.

Conal then swept everyone before him, trawling

up my whole life in his phoney embrace. To make things worse, I was sick more and more often. Soon I was throwing up all day. In the end I found myself in hospital being nourished by a glucose drip. I lost weight, lost strength and lost the will to struggle. All around me people – nurses and doctors – were walking on eggshells for the sake of the entity they called 'baby'.

Failure was so familiar. When I thought of the lectures I had missed and the essays I would never be able to write, the idea that I would never graduate anyway grew powerful. The memory of my mother's jealousy reproached me: I would never be big enough for the role of first university-educated woman in the family. In our marriage, my parents saw their freedom. Their last child would be settled with a good provider with a business degree. They took his side. My tutor saw a scandal evaded and advised me to drop out and get married, assuring me that my place would always be there for me if I wanted to come back as a mature student. My counsellor, in the end, told me flat out he thought I was lying.

So it was a shotgun wedding, but the bride was the one who was forced into it. Through all the traditional processes, the arguing, the lying, the vomiting, the weeping, the wedding and the pregnancy, I walked on like a zombie, my soul already damned because I had refused to be grateful for my husband.

My only true companions were the sad spirits of every girl sent pregnant to the altar since the dawn of civilisation. They gathered round me, these ghostly girls, and at times, in the hot, breathless discomfort of the last trimester, I thought I could feel them crowding me, shoving me about, buffeting me in their anger.

Even when we were alone, Conal would never talk about what he did to me. 'We don't need to discuss that now,' he said. 'It's all come out right, after all. We can just put it in the past.'

My brother, when he came home for the wedding, was my only believer. 'My little sister,' he said sadly, holding me in his arms in the corridor outside the farce of our wedding reception, while inside Conal floridly impressed my uncles. Rob was living at a training camp in Texas then and he had acquired a faint cowboy drawl. 'I can't bear to see you . . . sold off like this. It's your body. You should have the say here. This is like the middle ages. I can't believe our folks are doing this. This really sucks.'

'Haven't you seen our mother's face?' I answered him. 'I've never done anything that pleased her so much.'

Then I became Mrs Conal McEverdy, big-time. I never used my own name unless I had to. That was another way of preserving my self. Kim was for my friends and my brother. Everyone else could see me as whoever it was they needed me to be so badly.

On my plastic wrist-band in the maternity unit I was Mrs Conal McEverdy, and Liam was tagged in the same style, boy of Mrs Conal McEverdy. Having him was hell. The birth was your classic nightmare of obstetric intervention beginning with a full-day trial of labour and an epidural which only worked on my left side. My clearest memory is of lying in the delivery room watching the contractions on a monitor, trying to fight down the hysteria every time I saw the trace start moving towards a new peak.

Conal told everyone he would be present at the birth. I went into labour alone while he was on his way to work. He was then in his first job in a merchant bank. He telephoned when I was on the delivery table, curled as far as I could manage into a ball while the anaesthetist was sticking his tube through my backbone into the space around my spinal cord.

'I hope it all goes well,' said the husband for whom I had been forced to give all that I had. 'Keep smiling, eh?'

The nurse was holding the receiver to my ear. The anaesthetist was running the numbing fluid down his tube. It wasn't painful, but it was weird, suddenly being made aware of that secret space in your body in which any mistake could cost your enjoyment of life. With the tube through my back, I also had the impression that my vertebrae were going to pop from their ligaments and cannon across the room. Another contraction was building.

'Aren't you coming?' I asked him. I wanted him there not for any comfort – because seeing him still chilled me – but to put a good face on my shame. Not logical, captain, but I could never get out from under the shame of having been raped. That as much as my illness sapped my will and sent me unresisting into my marriage. Between the two of them, I was just too weak to care what happened to me. It felt better if Conal whitewashed our sepulchre and went through the motions of being a husband. It seemed the least atonement he could make.

'What for?' He responded, sounding quite triumphant. 'I'd only be in the way.'

At this moment, with the contraction imminent, the trickling liquid over my raw neurones felt so bizarre that I must have screamed. The anaesthetist stopped whatever he was doing and sniffed with annoyance.

'What's the matter?' Conal demanded indignantly, loud enough for the nurse to hear him.

'She's having a baby!' The nurse snatched away the receiver and took it outside the delivery room. She came back with a face of pure contempt. I think Conal eventually arrived after leaving work at his usual time; by then I was unconscious.

After his call I had an haemorrhage, after which a bad-tempered consultant admitted at last that a

Caesarean was the only way out for my boy. That went on under a general anaesthetic, which was the only good thing about the whole experience. My mother – my parents were called when it seemed possible that I would die alone and somebody might then sue the hospital – told me that the consultant took them to the end of the corridor by a drinking fountain, filled a paper cup with water and tipped it out, saying, 'That's how fast your wife is losing blood and we haven't been able to stop her.'

'Conal was so disturbed,' my mother told me. She persisted in trying to show me that I was mistaken in Conal, that he loved me, that he was no more vacant emotionally than any other man.

'Maybe he didn't like the idea that he might be going to kill me as well as having raped me,' I suggested. Nobody ever wanted to hear that burning word. I would not have my struggle to say it go for nothing, so for a while I said it as often as I could.

'You put things so harshly,' my mother complained.

'That's the way they feel,' I told her.

'You girls.' She sighed. She was angry but swallowing it down. 'You girls and your feelings. You make so much of them. Feelings are nothing, they're just not important.'

'My feelings are important to me.' But even offending her was no use. My parents were so anxious to close the ledger of family responsibilities that at that time nothing would have made them accept that they had been wrong.

'Kim found having Liam quite traumatic,' Conal would tell people. He said that with an air of vague bewilderment, as if he had never realised there was any pain attached to childbirth. 'So we decided we didn't need any more children.'

Again, I reserved my position here. I could have hassled some doctor somewhere into tying my tubes, but I didn't because somewhere below the threshold of hope lay buried the dream of a child I would want to conceive. I suggested a vasectomy to Conal. 'Why should that be necessary?' he countered. So I made sure I had an IUD, and submitted to sex as infrequently as I could without actually jeopardising the marriage while I still needed it.

Liam was not easy. He was small and tense and seemed to want to stay that way, because he gained weight only very slowly. Until he was more than a year old, he never slept for more than half an hour at a stretch. He cried desperately for long periods, his whole body shaking, his small fists clenched so their nails cut his palms. Nothing anyone could suggest calmed him. And I, of course, with my abdomen sliced open and the pain marking the entry point of the anaesthetic like a rapier stabbing my back, woozy with assorted drugs and spinning in an endless panic over my lost life, sank into despair.

My mother looked at Liam with surprise and said,

'I can't be much help to you. You were both wonderful babies, I couldn't have asked for more perfect children. I've no experience of this sort of thing. He's sure to settle down, they always do.'

'He'll be right when you're right,' was the verdict of Conal's mother, who always looked at me as if she were afraid I was about to spill the beans about her son. She went with me to the baby clinic and demanded attention for both of us. Liam was diagnosed with multiple allergies including to his own mother's milk. They gave him hypoallergenic potions and he smiled and got fat. Whatever was wrong with me responded to Prozac, so I cruised through a few more years in chemical good humour.

When I was myself, I fell in love with my son. It happened without warning, the same as with Matthew. On a normal afternoon I went to the kindergarten to collect Liam. The door opened and twenty children ran out but I saw only one of them, this shining boy in a nimbus of life. I held him in my arms. I forgot how heavy he was and tried to pick him up and I wanted to cry. He struggled because he wanted me to put him down so he could run around. He was a new soul without any past life. I let him run, and looked sidelong at the other mothers to see if they had noticed that a miracle had occurred. They were all busy with their own children.

* * *

Stella offered Terry her spare bedroom and they moved back to La Pasmada. When people drove along the Yesto road they looked up as they passed the turning that led up to it and thought about her up there with her memories and her fears.

Tragedy gets rid of friends pretty fast. When I left England I didn't leave anyone who wanted to associate with what had happened to me. Now Stella got busy, binding people to her with promises, demands, commissions – and who could decently refuse to help a widow? Matthew and I had her company almost every night. She took to going out with Terry if he had trips on the weekend. She went to church every Sunday.

People talked about her constantly. I got tired of my role as chief oracle. I started to work later. Matthew said he was doing the same. I got my own proof that he was spending time with Stella when I went into Tamiza for late-night groceries on my way home once and saw them together in the far corner of a bar. I walked on.

Sometimes I saw Matthew watching me as if I were hurting him. I had a strange encounter with Sam, who doesn't normally bother with me or any of Stella's set but got me on my own at the Lumumba and said flat out: 'D'you reckon your old man was up to something with this crash business?'

'You mean, do I think Matthew was involved in Tom's death?'

'No,' he backed away at once, 'no, not like that. But, he was there, wasn't he?'

'He was home with me when Tom actually died.'

'So you don't reckon he was mixed up in anything?' Sam was, as usual, strictly focused on himself. He'd been sitting in his crow's nest above the marina worrying that he was sharing his microphones with a murderer.

'You mean, you'd look a bit of a prat if he were mixed up in something and you didn't know?'

'Don't get feisty,' he protested. 'It's a fair question.'

'Ask Matthew, why don't you? He'll straighten you out.'

'Could be that's what I'm afraid of.' He winked to tell me he wasn't serious, not at all, not about any of it. I was wondering if I knew the man I was sharing my life with, but it wasn't a problem I wanted to open with a man who had classified women as a waste of space.

Stella appealed to me. 'Come and help me, Baby. There's so much to do.' I went to help her clear out the cupboards in the villa. She seemed in a hurry to remove Tom from her life. 'I want to send his clothes down to Father Martin. He says he can use them for people in distress. You know, sometimes the airlines lose the luggage or something.' I folded and packed, while she sat on the bed sorting through the rest of Tom's possessions and packing what she did not want into a crate for his children. Nobody has much personal baggage here. It's a sweat to bring more than twenty-two kilos of your history with you.

The crate filled rapidly. She did not seem to want anything. Wallet, cuff-links, watch, photographs, CDs, the heavy mock-Regency silver table lighter and some tarnished sporting cups, the trophies from Tom's life before Stella.

'What are you going to do now?' I began.

'Do? I'd like to sell this.' She indicated the villa. 'Thank God he didn't die here. Still, I won't get much of a price if I sell now, will I? Best to rent it, I suppose. I don't want to live here much longer.'

'So – where?'

'I can't *go* anywhere, the bastards have still got my passport. I'll have to stay here until it's all over. It's so stupid. It's obvious it was an accident – why can't they just accept that?' Fretfully, she started opening drawers and pulling out their contents. 'They might as well know what a bloody hypochondriac he was.' She tossed some plastic containers of Islewyn's remedies into the crate with the rest of Tom's souvenirs.

This was the first time we had been alone since I found her note in my jeep. 'Keep the faith,' I asked her, 'what did you mean?'

'I meant keep the faith, Babe. Stick by me. I need you.' She was lying, she couldn't hide that from me. I waited for more, so she added, 'Because I knew it was going to get rough. When they pulled me in.

They don't bother unless they're serious, do they? I had no idea it was going to get as complicated as it is, mind you.'

'I can't get over him using regular drugs,' I said, seeing another line of attack. 'Did they ever find what it was?'

'Don't tell me *you're* running that trip. You, Kim. My best friend.' She was more than fretful then, she was scared. 'Hasn't Matthew told you? I thought he would have told you.'

'Matthew told me he left before it happened. Didn't you both go down to the Lumumba? I don't know what to think, do I?'

'You never asked him about the pills?'

'Why would I? I was more interested in what he was doing with you.'

'Well, I'll give you the answer, Babes. We were taking Terry his charts. Tom was rolling around the kitchen whining at me, being drunk. I wanted to get away from him. I'd got Terry's charts, I'd copied them for him in the office, I saw them lying on the table, I know he has a panic attack if he hasn't got them, so we decided to leave Tom to stew and go down to the marina. Matthew did the driving, we had a drink with Terry and then he dropped me back here. I went to bed. I didn't see Tom. I assumed he was passed out somewhere. Matthew went home to you. And then the police woke me up to tell me Tom was being scraped off the rocks. That's it.'

I said nothing and I looked at her. She came over and hugged me. 'Not you too,' she said. 'Not you, Kim.'

'Everyone's got a theory about it, you know. People are always laying their theories on me,' I offered in mitigation.

'So,' she said quickly, 'what's your theory?'

'How do you do that?' I demanded, holding her off at arm's length. 'How do you twist things around, so whatever someone intends to say, you make it come out different?'

'Don't be stupid. I don't twist things.' She pulled away from me, folding her arms more as if to hug herself than to defy me.

'The general theory is that you and Matthew are having an affair.'

'Oh, and presumably that together we doped Tom up and murdered him?'

I wouldn't answer her. Safer to stay with jealousy than go all the way to that end.

She was angry, her voice was rough. 'And you think that? That's what we've come down to?'

'I don't know,' I retorted. 'You tell me.'

'How can you do that to Matthew? How can you do that to him? Suspect him like that.' I didn't answer that either, but I thought of Matthew and I wanted the whole thing to be over because the doubt was killing me. 'I suppose you're sitting there thinking that I would say that, if I were in love with him.

Jesus! He gave up his life for you, Kim. He gave up everything. To be here with you and get you through your stuff. Hello? Are you hearing me?'

'He said he was glad to do it. He said he wasn't giving up anything that was important to him.'

'Anything more important than you, that's what he meant. I think he gave up a lot, Kim. I really do. And you can't even give him your trust.' She went out to the living area where her cigarettes were and came back blowing out smoke. 'Well, I am jealous. I will own up to that. I am jealous, because I don't think that any man will ever love me the way Matthew loves you. And I'm jealous the other way, always have been, because he loves you more than I do, and you love him more than you love me, and he took you away from me. And I did try to be nice to him for your sake, so we could all live here together and be happy. But three's a bad number, isn't it?'

'It's just a number.'

'No, it's a bad number when you're counting people. Three is always a two and a one. When Tom was with us – I mean *with* us, before he curled up and died which is what he did before he really died – we were four. Two is perfection. Four is OK, four is quiet. Three isn't. Three is a hand grenade with the pin pulled out.'

'It's just a number,' I said again. 'You can believe what you like about it. When it was you and me and Conal we were three.'

'Two. Conal didn't count.' She was walking around the bedroom taking short drags at her cigarette. The shutters weren't closed. It was early evening, the sky was still amethyst and there was enough light to make the walls of the houses glow living white against the dark earth.

'I can't believe this,' she said. 'I thought you were my friend. I thought, you know, with what we shared, nothing would ever be able to spoil it for us.'

I said something about us all being stressed. She bought it and we backed out of the danger zone. I folded the last of Tom's too good, too clean T-shirts and took the bag with me when I left, to leave with Father Martin at his customary bar near the church before going home and putting my key in the lock and finding out how that sounded.

CHAPTER 8

Escapes

When Liam was small his cheeks were as smooth as petals and his eyelashes rested on them when he was asleep. His eyes reflected my regrets. Once I could love my son, I started to understand things.

I understood that Conal was, as Stella put it, a few glasses short of a party.

Sharing a life with him was like dancing with a deaf man. He wasn't able to perform the full range of ordinary human behaviour.

He seemed to think that our son was an object, a thing with no needs. He never talked to him. If I asked him to feed Liam while I was out, I would come back to find a hungry child and Conal saying, 'I didn't think he needed anything to eat.' When Liam went places with him, whoever they met would make a point of telling me that Conal had let him stray into the road or wander away and get lost.

When I questioned Conal about these things, he would say, 'I don't see that at all.'

Whatever was needed, whatever we asked for, he refused it and the refusal came from some cross-wiring on his mental circuit-board. I think he was aware of a fault but instead of trying to learn or to compensate he just denied it with an arrogance that was almost hysterical. This was not an innocent disability. Conal was perversely perverse.

The ideas I had about happiness and sadness, about a baby, a home or a family were beyond him. He made all the wrong moves and at first I blamed our history. Only very slowly did I realise that the blame belonged to him.

His mother gave me the clue. She seemed grateful for me. Conal was her only child. We all knew that I would be his only chance.

We started out in good style. My parents found money for all kinds of necessities; that was my bride price. So we had a flat, and we had our wedding presents, the great flashy food processor like a space-craft docked in the kitchen, dozens of matching plates and cups, knives and forks. We had curtains and a sofa. I asked for a bookcase but, like Conal's vasectomy, nobody saw the need.

I find it ironic that whatever was wrong with Conal made him good at making money. To do this he travelled, three different European cities every week. His travelling meant that I could see very little of him if I worked out my sleeping right. Perhaps that was another reason why it took me so long to guess the truth about him.

For Liam, I was the dream mother other boys wanted. To shore up the bad foundations of our family, he had the fanciest birthday cakes and the flashiest trainers. His bedtime was totally negotiable. With gangs of friends we whirled into the drive-thru' McDonald's, the skate park and the multimedia exhibition. I watched through a screen of guilt for signs of Conal's problem but saw nothing. Liam wasn't remarkable, except to me. When people talked to me about him, they called him nice. His teeth were late, he learned to read in the end, and he clung to me like a little octopus until the time came for him to let go, stand alone, stop taking notice of adults and be a boy.

Conal's hair thinned drastically and he gained weight, so he looked like a man twice his age but with a strange baby face. He announced, 'Nobody expects you to go on in banking forever. It's not a man's game. I'll be getting out soon. You can't make real money unless you work for yourself.'

He resigned his job and took a lease on a marble-walled office suite uptown. He liked spending and wanted me to do it too, but I had no interest in furnishings or clothes or anything that might be collected, all of which he acquired for himself in quantity. He bought whatever cost most. His car cost more than our first flat. He took up shooting, because it was the most expensive pastime and bought a pair of famous-name guns and a gun case in which to display them.

I asked to travel. I didn't want to go anywhere in particular, but I wanted to stay in a hotel. A hotel room seemed full of possibilities. Pain can be comforting, and I still needed mine, but the instinct to put water between us was growing. Conal pretended agreement but imposed rules to defeat what he assumed was my purpose. I had to travel alone and in the winter. Carole would call all this karmic, intended to lead me to my destiny. Los Alcazares, the travel agent told us, is a popular winter-break destination.

On the plane I heard a woman's excited, carrying voice call for what the charter company called champagne. She was about twenty rows behind me. She sounded like somebody I knew, but I couldn't place the memory.

Waiting by the luggage carousel in Villanueva's architect-designed airport I saw her dart forward to pull at a big Samsonite suitcase with wheels. A smiling man came to help her. Then I recognised Stella, thinner and looking mature with big silver bracelets and still a neat, bright dress. I had come away to leave my life behind. Contact with Stella, I thought, would materialise the worst of it. I lingered at the back of the exit queue.

Arriving here is easy. It seems as if you get out of the chrysalis before you're ready to fly. The inbound side of the airport is optimistic, calm and orderly. The hall is never more crowded than it was designed to be, unlike the departures side, which starts the morning calmly but looks like a refugee camp by midday, with hundreds of homegoing hedonists sitting wearily on the floor watching the monitors tell them that all the flights have lost their air-traffic slots and won't be boarding for hours.

On the arrivals concourse a few tour guides were checking through their clipboards. People were peeling away from the car-hire desks, keys in hand. The air was hot and smelt dusty. In the little café the waiter was polishing the counter.

'You! It's *you*! I can't believe it, this is extraordinary!' Stella was standing in front of me, holding out both her hands. I realised she had forgotten my name but not who I was. She was alone; the man who had lifted her case was not beside her. She was appealing to me.

'I'm Kim.' I took her hands.

'Kim. It's not you, I'm terrible at names. Stella.'

'I know.'

'This is just so strange.'

'Isn't it?'

'What is it, six years? Seven?'

Curiosity took me over. Because the extraordinary Stella was alone, something had happened to her and I had to know what it was. So a montage of accidents stacked up. We shared a drink.

As she lifted her glass she answered the questions for which I had been trying to find gentle words. 'I was married until last week. He seems to have run off.' Then she drank, the bracelets swinging on her wrist.

'Is he coming back?'

'He didn't say.' Her smile was wide but uncertain. She needed sympathy but wasn't sure how to ask for it.

'Bastard.' This is the password for woman-to-woman bonding, but I didn't know that then.

'Yes. Pity. I thought he was all right. Must have been just a phase he was going through.' She giggled and finished her drink.

Now we were together. Together we went to collect our cars. Mine was no problem but her hirer's desk was closed for the day. Together we set off in my car for the apartment she had rented near the harbour in Playa de los Angeles. At the first sight of the Aloha Hawaii, with the sunshades thatched in pink acetate, she squealed, 'Oh my God and Elvis lives!' I laughed so much I nearly drove into the traffic cop.

Her apartment was created from the same template as the one Matthew and I have now. Never having seen the design before, we thought it was exquisitely clever. We opened all the cupboards, tested both beds and approved the balcony view together. A porter appeared to carry up her case. Then she came with me to the hotel I had chosen. Doing things together was a new adventure.

'This place is mad,' she whispered as the hotel elevator serenaded us upwards. No one has ever understood why an international hotel chain picked the Costa Ubrique on which to build a step pyramid of textured concrete. There were no possibilities in my room, only thick carpets, air-conditioning and a bamboo-patterned comforter on the bed. The balcony overlooked a colossal free-form pool, a fantastical aviary full of bedraggled parakeets and ten tennis courts surfaced in retina-searing green fuzz.

'This is the night of the living dead,' Stella murmured in my ear as we passed other guests on our tour of inspection. The pyramid is never more than one-third occupied and it's true that the guests walk like zombies. 'Watch out, there's Michael Jackson.'

'He's must be looking for Elvis.'

'They're trapped, all of them. They can't escape because their brains have turned to tofu.'

'I've got to get out of here,' I hissed on my cue.

'Sssh, they've got us under surveillance. Act natural. Have a cocktail.'

My cocktail was lavished with fresh coconut milk and a wicked splash of tequila, finished with a spray of paper orchids, a pineapple twist, chocolate curls and a little red plastic monkey hanging off the glass by his prehensile tail. Stella's was seductive with golden rum, rain-forest honey and luxurious Triple Sec, plus two gold tassels on sticks and a blue plastic swordfish with a kumquat stuck on his nose. She twisted up my hair and pinned it with the tasselled sticks, saying "S great. You should always wear it like that.'

A short, fat man heaved himself onto a stool beside me and checked us out. Calling over the barman made his gold watch unmissable. Stella said to me, 'You might as well have "Mug me, I'm worth it," tattooed on your arm.'

'There is very little crime here,' said the fat man, trying to muscle in on us.

'Up to now, you mean,' Stella menaced him.

'They have excellent security. There is nothing to be afraid of inside the hotel area.' He inclined his head, trying to show chivalry by association.

'A good reason for getting out, then.' She was trying not to laugh but the corner of her mouth twitched. My face was out of control by now but I had my back to the man and stopped my shoulders shaking by gripping my glass.

'They have everything you need right here. Fitness centre, beauty salon . . .'

'Do they have a tattoo parlour? We could both go. I'd like, "No Creeps Please" just here,' she tapped a finger along the base of her throat, 'like a necklace.'

'You should be more polite,' complained the fat man, descending from the stool with a beer in his fist and stomping away.

Stella shrugged at me. 'Some people. I said please. I was prepared to be tattooed with please. What more could he want?'

I held the laughter in so hard that my glass broke in my fingers and fell on the carpet. My left hand was cut. The red plastic monkey caught on my thumb and a trickle of blood ran down his body. Because the barman gave us a look that implied disapproval of women who bought their own drinks and laughed at the expense of a fellow male, Stella hopped to her feet and created a scene. A manager apologised, a waitress brought the first-aid kit, I was bandaged, the carpet was mopped and the barman, scowling, had to mix us fresh drinks on the house.

'Have you paid for this?' Stella asked me, before the emergency team was out of earshot.

'My husband has paid for everything,' I told her.

'So has mine, I suppose, in his way. I didn't know you were married.'

'It doesn't matter.' I believed that as I said it. She had lifted the curse.

'Here's to husbands,' she suggested, raising her glass, 'and to making them pay.'

In due time I checked out and we drove back towards Angeles. Coming over the hill we had our

first sight of the bay and the sunset flaming behind
the La Mora mountains. She pulled over so we could
get out and sit on a rock at the roadside to look at it.
That was another gift she has given me: the roadside
joys of life, the miracles eternally on offer which I
had never noticed before.

She is funniest when she is unhappy. Late that
night, after a lot of vodka mixed with scummy long-
life orange juice, she started talking about her
husband again. 'He rang me up in the middle of the
night from Bali. He said he got fired from his job.
So he put his last pay cheque in his pocket and went
to the airport and got on the first long-haul flight
that had room. That's very him, doing that. So I
was miserable for a week and then I thought, hey –
sauce for the goose.' And she threw her head up to
seem brave and sorted, but she had to sniff back
tears. 'And this may not be Bali,' she went on, 'but
we'll have fun. More fun than he'll be having, I bet.
Living well. The best revenge.'

She grinned at me. She has pretty teeth, small,
very white, rounded and slightly spaced like a
child's. 'We're on holiday, we're together and we're
only twenty-four. I'm twenty-four, anyway.'

'Twenty-five.' I tapped my chest with my glass. I
was sitting on the floor. Even that was an adventure.
Wives and mothers sit nicely in chairs. 'Don't feel
twenty-five. Feels like I fast-forwarded from eighteen to forty.'

'Time to rewind.' She flung her arm out at the dark sky in the window, and her arm shook, maybe with distress, maybe with drink. I knew exactly where she was – I had spent years there myself.

The next day we ran around the island being Thelma and Louise. It was about three days later, at night again, when we had made a picnic and taken it up to a place we had picked out above Almonte, looking down on the crazy pothole vineyards in the moonlight, that Stella said, 'Whatever happened with you and that man I took to a party? Irish or something?'

I told her the whole story of Conal. She believed me. No questions, no doubts, none of those looks that said I wasn't telling the whole story. That was a first in seven years. It was a sweet relief.

She cursed Conal but she never pushed me to free myself with a divorce. 'God no, Babes. Men always want what they can't have, don't they? You stay married, take your time, take your pick. And he owes you, for heaven's sake. He has to provide, it's all they're good for. Stupid of any woman not to take it if he's made the offer. He's a banker wanker, for God's sake, at least he can do that. Not like mine.'

Sometimes I wonder how many marriages only hold up because of the wife's best friend. Stella grounded my life for a long time. Husband Number One never came back and that wounded her. The first cut, the deepest. Being single did not suit her and she took as much from me as she gave. Then she met Tom and got the sleekness of deep need satisfied, but Tom never came between us, which means that she never needed him the way I need Matthew.

She calls me Baby, or Babe, or Babes or Babydoll, which makes me feel irresponsible and cared-for. She likes travelling anywhere by any means, but most of all she likes the sea. Our last day of our first trip here was spent sailing on the ferry to Sosiego. I remember her stepping aboard, delicate as a deer in her high shoes, a figure in a fluttering sarong swaying at the rail, looking out over the sparkling sea and the heat-haze.

* * *

15 November. A great number of dead fish were seen floating on the sea off Viera, fish of every species including some which were unknown. By afternoon the sea had carried them as far as Puerto de la Frontera and numbers of people went there to see them with their own eyes. There was great fear in both villages.

Two fishermen whom the people respected came to me at the head of a large crowd saying that they had sailed close to strange areas of disturbance off the coast where the air was foul and the waves churned around violently as if the devil were stirring them with his tail. They begged me to sail

out with them and drive away the diabolical
presence which brought about these events.

Dona Maria is unconscious and thought likely
to die. The sick man is raving and will not drink
water, saying he sees the devil in it. To add to the
fear of the people, the women who washed the
maid's body before the burial said it was
unmarked, which is to say there was no sign of
illness.

Just after darkness on this day the messengers
returned from Guanapay with many remedies from
the anchorite including burning herbs and holy oil.
Your Excellency should know that this man was a
Christian to whom I would myself travel once a
month to take the sacrament. He gathered the
plants growing around his desolate cave and to
discover their properties spent many hours in prayer.

I went straightaway by torchlight to the big
house and gave this unction to the sick. After
midnight, the manservant also died. He had been a
big man but the curse had wasted him so he was as
thin as a boy. No marks were found on his body.

16 **November.** Dona Maria is still living but
can no longer speak or recognise her father. The men
who went to the anchorite had observed goats on the
mountain acting as if possessed, running about in
every direction as if crazy with terror. At this point,
not knowing what more I can do, I have sent a
messenger to Ubrique with an appeal to Fr Domingo,

whose teaching and guidance are always of the greatest help to me in serving Our Lord.

*17 **November.** More reports of animals running mad: In Almonte, three camels broke loose from their hitching line and were found seven miles away. Evidently in a state of terror, they had trampled a field of cactus. The only truly prosperous trade a man can follow on Alcazares is making the red dye from the cochineal beetles which live on the cactus. A dispute has sprung up over payment for the lost crop. Dona Maria is still living.*

*18 **November.** Dona Maria still lives and has opened her eyes. Tomorrow is Sunday and I have resolved to sail out with the fishermen, as is the custom for the annual blessing of the sea, and say Mass on the water. Fr Domingo is detained in Ubrique but sent messages of hope and a promise that he would come the following week.*

*19 **November.** Dona Maria has recovered, all thanks to God. I held a special Mass on the sea with all the fishing fleet gathered around. The day has been completely clear and the sea calm. There were no bizarre manifestations of any kind except that the boy who helped me was sick but recovered on land. People are much relieved and have thanked me for averting their danger. I told them their gratitude belonged to God for I was only his instrument.*

*22 **November**. In the region along the coast at
Jimena, a great many animals have died.
Chickens, goats, mules, dogs, even camels, died all
at once as if killed by the same blow. This happened
last night, so the people woke to find all their
livestock dead in the fields. This is a terrifying
phenomenon, so like the plagues of Egypt that people
begin to ask if a great evil has not been done here.*

After this passage come some entries that appear
only in the old Spanish text. Obviously the German
didn't consider them worth translating. Fr Domingo
arrived. He was the island's senior priest, officiating
at the miniature cathedral which still stands in
Ubrique. Shortly after his arrival, Dona Maria
claimed a vision. At the crisis of her fever, St
Catherine and St Theresa of Avila had appeared in a
cloud of glory above Puerto San Juan, which was
then the island's major port, on the north coast cow-
ering under the cliffs below Ubrique. She claimed to
have heard St Catherine call all the population down
to the port where a ship was waiting to take them to
safety. The girl reported seeing people fighting to
board the ship.

Fr Domingo grilled her in detail about the ship
and it was clear that it was not the apparition that
was supposed to have caused her illness. The Cura
recorded her description of it precisely: a ship like
the big traders built to cross the ocean, with three

masts, one red sail and the rest white. So Fr Domingo interpreted this as an allegory of sin and repentance, and announced that St Catherine was calling the people of Yesto to confess their sins and voyage towards God's forgiveness. He had no trouble convincing the shaken population that the recent episodes of terror were the consequence of their secret evil-doing.

Generously, Fr Domingo stayed over for a week to hear confessions, confident that Yesto would give up its secrets. He was hoping for heresy, as well as the usual tally of adultery, murder and half-wit farm boys buggering their goats. My Cura was worried about this; he wrote with fussy discretion, making it clear that he had never heard anything very major in the confessional during his short appointment. Yesto was scarcely Sodom or Gomorrah. Although he lacked Fr Domingo's intellectual ability, no one had ever questioned his teaching. He thought most of his people, living between the savage sea, the iron earth and the baking sun, were too ground down by their daily fight to survive to have any energy left for sin.

The Cura predicted that the worst offences to be confessed would be connected with the wreckers Don Andreas had sent to be hanged. He said it had been difficult for him to convince his people that wrecking was wrong in the eyes of God when it was only frowned upon, but not specifically forbidden, by the regional government.

Fr Domingo, the tin-pot inquisitor of this miserable crumb of desert, was adamant that some grave sin must have been committed. Nothing else could have incited God to give them the dreadful warnings of the past few weeks.

With prim satisfaction, the Cura noted that after four days of receiving penitents non-stop, Fr Domingo was getting angry at the chicken-feed sins people were admitting. On Sunday he gave the parishioners a roasting from the pulpit and ran through the Ten Commandments to give them some guidance on the dimensions of sins which would enrage God so violently that his anger would boil the sea.

Eventually some terrified child confided to the Cura that two families in Puerto de la Frontera were into stealing in a big way. These were people who had arrived from Sosiego about ten years earlier. Sosiego, being one of the smallest islands in the archipelago, had never really been settled by mainlanders and the people were almost all of the original stock, pure-blooded Guanches. Their ancient but very small community practised a kind of theft which, the Cura tried to explain to his superior, was hardly stealing as the rest of the world understood it, because in tiny little Sosiego everyone knew exactly what belonged to everyone else. So people there had made theft into an art, something the young men did to show they had balls.

These thefts were artistic acts and their aesthetic value lay in matching the crime to the victim, so the thieves might break into a vain man's house to steal his new cloak, or spend days tunnelling into a hard-working rival's barn to take away his plough. They even had a theft festival every year during which everything stolen was returned before sundown. This was held at the Assumption, when, the Sosiegans reasoned, God himself stole the Holy Virgin from mankind.

At this point, Fr Domingo apparently went apeshit. He denounced this custom as heresy and threatened to call in officers of the Inquisition from the mainland. The people, now almost as terrified of Fr Domingo as they were of the ghost ship, energetically blamed the foreigners for all their troubles. They suddenly remembered dozens of incidents in which the Sosiegans had thieved, blasphemed and traduced the holy writ. Every absconding donkey and overlooked hair-ribbon on the island was soon attributed to them. The Cura admitted that the Sosiegans were not regular communicants.

With the help of a posse of Don Andres' men, Fr Domingo arrested two of the lads from Sosiego and rode back to Ubrique, planning to send them to the inquisitors in Cadiz. The Cura, dismayed at the witch-hunt, sadly recorded that the foreigners' aljibes were breached and their crops burned. Rather stupidly, the people also burned the Sosiegan boats, so the last sin of the families who remained was to steal another in which to escape.

Once I got the sense of this section, it reassured me. If this document, of which the original has so conveniently been lost, were a forgery, it would have been more knowing. Eva laughed at me. 'You're happy, look at you. You can believe in your Cura again. I worry about you Kim, I really do. You should get upset when you can't trust your Matthew, not some little dead priest.'

'Do you think I should worry about Matthew?' I asked, hoping it came out lightly.

'A man like him?' She winked at me. 'A woman can't trust herself with a man like that. If he were mine I'd keep him handcuffed in the shower and feed him the best steak and spinach with ginseng.'

'You think it works, ginseng?' Dima shuffled hopefully towards us.

'Haven't you got any work to do?' she demanded.

'Why do you hate men?' he countered.

'Look in the mirror, *cuño*.' When he had gone she turned around to me for some private chat. 'Of course you can trust your Matthew. He's crazy about you, anyone can see it. You can make a little trouble for him, be a little dissatisfied, keep him on his toes. But don't worry. He is OK. I know that.' She squeezed my shoulder.

I went back to work. 'All those animals dying. What was that about?'

Mark spoke. This was so unusual that all the office stopped to listen and Dima came back into our room. 'Gas,' he said.

'What gas?' Eva demanded. 'He says they died "de un golpe", at one blow. What gas does that?'

Mark spoke very fast and blinked at every sentence. 'Gas is my theory about Pompeii. For centuries nobody could figure out why people there were petrified on their beds as if they'd just woken up. Some have even got their mouths open, crying out. Something zapped them, they died in a split second. People said it was an ash fall but nobody could demonstrate that ash would fall fast enough to turn people to stone while they were still screaming. At Herculaneum there are bodies with terrible burns, one hand charred, or half a face seared to the bone. So now the theory is that a cloud of toxic gas engulfed Pompeii, just like he says.'

We were silent, mostly with astonishment at the length of the speech. Eventually Dima growled, 'Thank you for that, Mark. Really. It's good to learn these things.'

Mark blinked faster. 'Cyanide gas would do it. It's a pretty basic molecule. Nitrogen and carbon, building blocks of life. We're saying volcanoes released the essential minerals on to the planet's surface before life began. It's irrational to assume the elements tangled themselves into a huge thing like

DNA and never just joined in a simple bond like dicyanogen. Two of each, that's it.'

'And why should we assume life was always carbon-based?' More surprising still, this was from Suzanne, whose voice was so quiet everyone leaned her way to catch what she was saying. 'Silicon could do the same. Silicon-based life forms could have evolved at the same time as the carbon-based ones. Without photosynthesis, of course.'

She looked as if she were apologising for this personally until Mark said, 'Absolutely. Why not? It's logical. Silicon could have been even more reactive in the surface conditions of that time.'

'Logical? Rational?' Dima shook his head. 'This is life. Life isn't rational.'

Mark and Suzanne blinked at each other. Dima lumbered back to his desk. A call came in for Eva. I closed down early for the day and set off homewards. Then I was afraid that Matthew would not come home for a long time and I would be waiting alone. I turned on the radio and caught a commercial he had recorded for the dive school at Puerto de la Frontera. It's very funny; it usually makes me laugh.

CHAPTER 9

Turn of the Tide

The last fishing boat in Quemada came in on the tide. It's an old boat, hardly more than a dinghy, clinker built, white with a faded stripe of turquoise along the gunwale. The bow rides high because the motor, new, shiny, oversized and black, weighs down the stern.

When she first noticed it, Stella made us laugh, saying, 'Bet he wishes he had a Harley, that fisherman.'

Whenever I saw the boat, with the young man and the older one who take it out, I wondered who they were, if they were father and son, what they caught and who they sold it to and if fishing was their living or something they do the way people in England with gardens have vegetable patches, just to keep a live connection to the food chain.

When I first came here with Matthew, he had the

same thoughts and wanted me to ask. The idea embarrassed me. I am still shy of conversation in Spanish because people speak so fast and I need time to think out my sentences.

'I can't,' I told him, 'Placido doesn't answer questions.' That was true. Placido especially doesn't answer questions from women, but I left that out.

'You can ask one of the boys,' he said reasonably.

So I had to do it. Matthew is full of solutions. I have learned to be careful in choosing the problems I bring him, in case I get a solution I don't want. I'd rather take problems to Stella; she appreciates them as if they were flowers.

The story from Placido's boy was that the two men are not related. The younger one is Placido's wife's sister's son who came for a holiday two years ago and stayed because he liked the life. They take the boat out every day unless there is a storm, and sell the fish to whoever comes to buy it, people from Quemada, people from the little places inland, someone from a big restaurant in Ubrique. And Placido. It's not quite a living; the older man is also a mechanic, he fixes anything – cars, boat engines, washing machines, swimming-pool pumps. The island's fishing fleet is one of the smallest in Spain and Quemada is lucky to have a boat at all. It is permitted because the village is so remote.

The tide rules the work. The two men took the boat in the afternoon when the tide was falling.

When they were well beyond the surf they cut the engine and rowed around in a wide circle, dropping a net overboard. They left the bobbing buoys for an hour or two and dragged an octopus lure around the end of the reef. At the turn of tide, they went back to the net and pulled it in to see what they'd got. Finally they let the running tide take them back to the shore, where the early buyers had been drifting into the bar. The tide runs half an hour later every day. When it's too late for the boat to get back in daylight, they go out in the morning.

The fishermen have a window of about an hour when the water is deep enough to float the boat close to the shore but still low enough for them to see the wreck and sail safely around it. The wreck is out in the surf at the centre of the vista to the east from Placido's. It was once a dredger, and most of what you can see of it now is the two tall arms from which the dredging apparatus was suspended, sticking out of the waves at about sixty degrees to the horizon, Quemada's two fingers to the EU.

A long time ago the island government apparently decided to excavate a new channel out there. Underneath Quemada is the original port for Ubrique, Puerto San Juan, which in the Cura's time was the island's main harbour. The battlements of Ubrique were also the watchtowers for the port. When pirates were sighted, people in the port would pack up their homes and drive their livestock into the caves in the cliff and the people around Ubrique would retreat behind the town walls. When the corsairs found that there was no water, they would sail on, because water was what they needed most. Sir Walter Raleigh put in here on his way to America; I wonder if he made the same mistake. When I have time, I'll find out.

After the eruptions, the whole port was buried in lava and the shoreline changed. The new currents along the coast silted up the bay with sand. Puerto de la Frontera was never more than a tiny harbour so the big ships had to sail around the island and struggle between the reefs into Villanueva.

When they were building the desalination plant, the government tried to reopen a channel at Quemada, probably without surveying the seabed first. Looking at the heaving breakers from the security of Placido's terrace, it was a stupid idea.

So Villanueva got the harbour and at Quemada now there isn't even a jetty for the fishermen. There is a pebbly beach-head with a motorised winch and an area of relatively calm water on the far side of the bar where a boat can find a deep channel next to the rocks.

The fishing boat glided in along the rocks and the young man jumped out with its rope, dayglo orange nylon. He splashed ashore and hooked the rope to the rusty cable of the winch. A man left the bar to start the motor. I caught a whiff of petrol, whipped across Placido's terrace on the wind. The winch snarled, the young man pushed the boat away from the rocks, more helpers ran forward to lay wooden sleepers under the keel and the boat was drawn up to heel over and rest in safety above the tideline.

Briskly, as if they'd already been waiting around too long, the fishermen heaved the plastic baskets of fish out on to the beach. A few cars came down the road and pulled up by the bar sign. For a while there were a dozen people standing over the catch. At the close of their business, the fishermen brought the last basket to Placido's, heaped full, with an octopus hanging glutinous arms over the edge.

I went into the bar for that second beer. Placido was standing the fishermen a few drinks and an argument over the sports page of *El Canarien*. Wishing to appear a proper restaurateur in front of the others, he made me go back out and sit down to be served by one of the boys.

A tentative young English couple came in and sat in the furthest corner away from me. Then a pair of Germans appeared, reserved, older people, wealthy, from their watches, which is almost the only way to tell here where everyone wears T-shirts. I realised that it was a relief to be in a bar where nobody was talking about Tom and Stella.

On the day we expected Tom's body to be flown back, I took another day off and waited at the

Residencias office with Stella for a call from
Margaret Amoore to tell her that the helicopter was
leaving. We had Father Martin standing by. Islewyn
had arranged for the Citroën ambulance from the
international clinic to be on call to transport Tom
back to the cemetery, and Bunny Dagenham was
coming to hold the fort in the office and brief the
people who were going to call in around lunchtime
to get the timetable for the resumed interment.

Stella sat at her desk, desultorily furthering the
ambition of a Dutch security millionaire to own a
villa with coastal frontage anywhere within an hour
of Angeles. I answered the telephone and stuffed
envelopes for a new mailshot. Amoore's call finally
came at half past eleven.

'I see,' Stella said, her voice metallic with tension.
'And when will that be? Well, then. What can I do?
Cancel the burial again? That's all I can do, isn't it?'
She put the receiver back with an angry slam. 'This
is going to be four funerals and a fuck up,' she said
to me. 'They're keeping him in Las Palmas until
the British coroner's authority comes and they can
let him go. Which will be when they decide if
there's going to be an inquest in England or not.
Until they make up their minds, I suppose they all
think poor Tom can rot.' She stood up and pitched
a ball of paper into the wastebasket. 'Fuck,' she said,
suddenly pushing all the paper off her desk. 'Fuck,
fuck, fuck. I hate them. Tom's fucking children.

They're just doing this to hurt me. How old are they? Twenty-five? Thirty? Why don't they just grow up, for God's sake?' Then she sat down, put her arms on the desk and her head in her hands, and started crying.

I went over and put my arms around her. 'They didn't know what they were getting into,' I suggested. 'People don't, do they? They don't know about life out here.'

'That's for sure. Did you look at that son of his? And her, with that Country 'n' Western hair. Don't tell me they're part of the real world.'

In the end I recorded a message for the answering machine announcing that the interment would not be taking place, and led her off to the Macarena, where one by one the usual suspects checked in.

Terry arrived first, on his way back from the airport with some engine part for the boat, which had been air freighted from England. 'No bloody use now, is it,' he complained, taking the chair next to Stella. 'I reckoned I might as well collect it, seeing as I ordered it three months ago and if it stays in the freight bay at the airport it'll be thieved. Bastard guardia wouldn't let me aboard to fit it.' His boat is the only thing that really moves Terry; having it impounded was worse than any psychological torture the guardia could have devised.

Stella gave him the news. Immediately he said, 'They're back here. I saw them here this morning.

Tom's kids. At the airport. Came in on the same island-hopper. What does she look like, with that hair – Dolly Parton? Anyway, you can't miss her, can you?'

Bunny and Fred appeared next, dressed for the ceremony, then Leif, who had seen Tom's son and daughter getting out of a taxi at the Hotel Las Rocas. 'Definitely they were checking in,' he confirmed. 'With a hell of a lot of luggage. A hell of a lot.'

'Why are they doing this?' Stella sighed. She had used up all the tissues in her bag but the tears were still oozing. Delicately, she blotted them at the sides of her eyes with her paper napkin. 'And that lawyer? Was he there too?'

No one had seen the lawyer. 'He'd cost 'em more than the presidential suite at Las Rocas, if you ask me,' was Terry's opinion.

'Why are they *doing* this? They never wanted to come here when Tom was alive. He asked them, you know. He asked them both. He wanted them to see our life here, he wanted them to understand why we love this place. I even said I'd go away while they were here. They didn't want to know, they didn't care then. I don't think they ever cared about him, not as a person. He said the loneliest years of his life began when his son was born and didn't end until he met me.'

Maryse said, 'It's about money, isn't it?'

'There isn't any money,' Stella said at once. 'They've already had it all, those two and his wife. He bought them their cars. He gave her the house, just walked out and let her have it all. Guilt, I suppose.'

'He left a will, didn't he?' Only Maryse would have dared ask that one.

'What's left comes to me.' The opportunity to lay things on the line for us was making Stella calmer. 'But all of nothing isn't a whole lot. There might be a few hundred in the magazine account. That's it.'

'The villa's yours,' Terry added.

'The Residencias owns the villa. It was easier that way, tax and everything. But I own the Residencias, at least, most of it, so yes, the villa's mine. He hadn't got anything, there can't be anything in this for them.'

'So,' pronounced Leif, 'maybe it is about money after all.'

'It's the excitement, isn't it? People never like the truth if it's boring. This is their big thing, Tom's kids. They'd really like it to have been murder just because that's more exciting.' This was from Maryse. Nobody responded.

Stella sat and looked at her napkin, wet and black from her make-up. Terry took it out of her hand and put his own napkin in its place, then called the waiter for more. When the waiter brought the napkins, Terry ordered more wine.

Carole came, late as usual, and during the theatre of ordering her mineral water the telephone behind the bar rang. It was Matthew calling for me, and when I told him what had happened he said, 'So do you need me?'

'Why?'

'I'm at the radio station,' he told me. 'Sam's got to leave. He wants me to fill in on the afternoon shift. He's in a jam, the regular guy's called in sick.' He wanted to do it, there was a lot of urgency in his voice.

'We're OK. Stella's upset, but we're all here with her.'

'You really OK?' he asked. I knew if I said no, he would come, and I wanted him to be with me, but I also wanted to know if he wanted to be with Stella.

So I said, 'Really, we're OK. I'll see you back home tonight.' He accepted that, so I was pleased.

When I got back to the table, plates of tapas appeared. Apart from our sombre clothes, it might have been any island lunch any day. The point of lotus-eating, as Tom himself often observed, is that the flower is supposed to be narcotic.

When I said Matthew wasn't coming, I saw that Stella was hurt. After that she didn't talk much. There was something in the air. Carole babbled up a smokescreen, the story of her plan to organise a world healing meditation. People ate quickly and drank less than usual. They were withdrawing from

Stella; they were picking out their positions. Bunny
Dagenham tilted her head on one side for sympathy,
but she was in control of her husband's silence. Leif
left first, then Father Martin, then the rest, leaving
only Terry with Stella and me.

Terry was still new at our *Casablanca* lifestyle. As
he left, he said, 'That was fun, I really enjoyed that.
Old Tom would have enjoyed it too.'

At the Residencias office, Stella said, 'Back to
business, then,' and started filleting the rest of her
post.

After a few envelopes she stopped. 'I can't,' she
said. 'I must be drunk. Drunk or sad. I can't think.'

By five we were walking slowly down the strip
with a sheaf of documents, heading for the Santander
Bank in the new shopping mall across from the
Aloha.

The mall is an air-conditioned white marble
extravagance of four storeys, contrived within the
planning laws by blasting two floors down into
the rock. Here is as much elegance as we can run to
on Alcazares, our Benetton, our Jil Sander diffu-
sion, our Adolfo Dominguez concession. The
Santander is on the top floor and dignified with
fitted carpet in claret red. Since it became the first
bank on the island to complete transfers of money
from other countries in twenty-four hours or less,
its business with the non-Spanish residents has
boomed.

The Santander may have dignity, but it is not a large office and confidentiality doesn't mean much to anyone there. The interview suites are just areas marked out by angled screens and it's easy to see what's on the monitor at the next desk. What with the gossip industry, there are very few financial secrets in the ex-pat community.

As soon as the automatic doors hissed shut after us, Stella almost bumped into Tom's son, who was sitting with one of the managers, signing papers. His sister reclined in her chair at the far end of the desk, legs crossed in a split skirt gazing at the ceiling to imply that business was for men and her role was to be decorative.

Stella despises professional air-heads. 'Oh, *hello*,' she greeted them at combat volume. The manager immediately looked embarrassed. 'Good to see you. Oh, don't mind me, Joselito,' she said to him, 'No worries, none at all.' Then she turned back to her step-children. 'So you like our island, you're going to stay for a while?'

Because he made no effort to get up or offer her his hand, she patted Tom's son on the shoulder. 'So – welcome. And welcome to Banco Santander S.P.A., Playa de los Angeles branch, sort code 17–16–93. The only decent bank in town.'

They looked at each other, Tom's kids, two over-sized, fair-haired, tired-looking people in fussy clothes, the picture of sweating monolingual Brits abroad. Then they looked back at Stella, bovine in their silence.

'Look,' Stella invited them, 'this is a helluva small place. We'll have to get along if you're going to stay here. We can be grown-ups about this, I'm sure.'

Then the son said, 'That's everything, isn't it? We'd better be going,' and gave the manager his hand to shake as he heaved himself out of his chair.

The girl flounced to her feet and they prepared to steam towards the door without looking at us. The place was too small for a sweeping exit. They came face to face with me, whom they clearly did not recognise, but from loyalty I stood my ground.

In that instant, both Stella and the manager saw that the woman's handbag was still by her seat. Stella got to it first.

'Just a minute,' she cried, emotional with concern, 'you've forgotten something. Won't get far without your handbag, eh?' And she almost skipped towards the girl with her trophy.

The girl snatched it. 'Don't you touch that!' she snarled.

'Oh! Was it a present, or something?' cried Stella. 'Oh yes, of course. I remember it now. Tom gave it to you for your birthday, didn't he? I remember choosing it for you in the bag shop right over there. Behind you. Well, I'm glad you liked it.'

'Let's go,' said the man, pulling his sister by the arm. Her whole face was red; it could have been sorrow or rage. The sun had roasted her brother's temples already. She shook off his hand and squared up to Stella.

'Listen,' she began, but was cut off. Stella had to speak.

'Of course, your claim would be that he never gave you anything, wouldn't it?' The girl recoiled and Stella felt she had her enemy on the run. 'You'd say he spent all his money on me, I suppose. Inconvenient for you, really, having to deal with the facts. I am glad you're here. You'll be able to understand your father better, understand that he chose to live here, with me. He was happy here, you see.'

'Of course this has been a tragedy for all of us,' announced Tom's son. 'You must be very upset, of course. But so are we, especially my sister. If you could be more sensitive . . .' He was trying to keep the two women apart with the overbearing bulk of his body, but the girl wanted to fight and struggled around him, precarious on her city high-heels. Stella was moving too. They circled like flyweights around a large referee.

'A bitch,' the girl hissed, stabbing the air with a finger. 'She can't be sensitive, she's just a bitch. Bitch.' At the third repetition of the word she lurched forward and Stella, thinking she was going to be hit, struck out first with a whip-crack of her arm. The woman screamed, clutching her face, and the recoil scattered us all. Stella ended up in the doorway of the bank.

All around the chilly, claustrophobic room people stayed still and watched. The young manager who had been serving them got to his feet with a face of panic.

'That wasn't necessary,' trumpeted Tom's son. He reminded me of Conal, grabbing at moral superiority with pompous words. 'That was a very silly thing to do. You're a silly woman. Now just get out of our way, please. We don't wish to detain you any further.'

'Pity you don't feel the same about your father,' Stella raged. 'You're quite happy to detain him, aren't you, keeping him in a bag at the morgue like a bloody carcase, instead of letting him be buried in peace like he wanted in the place that he loved.' She was rigid with anger, her clenched hands pressing into her thighs.

'That's nothing to do with us,' the man protested. 'That was the police's decision.'

'And who called them in? And why? You're pathetic, the pair of you. Why don't you own up? This is about money, isn't it? Even though there's nothing, you can't bear that he left it to me, not you. So you'll do anything to hurt me. Well if you knew what he used to say about you, you two . . . God, there's so much you don't know, you can't even begin to imagine . . .'

'We don't need to listen to this,' the man declared, trying again to sweep his sister to the exit. From the glass door to the inner office appeared an older woman, the manager's assistant, who made her way decisively towards the argument.

'You didn't love him,' Stella's face was a mask grooved with sadness. 'Neither of you loved him and he knew it, poor man. I was the only person who really loved him. That's why he's given it all to me. Idle bloodsuckers, that's what he called you . . .'

Firmly, the manager's assistant took Stella by the elbow to move her aside, muttering something soothing in Spanish.

'You bitch,' said the daughter again.

'That's enough,' the manager's assistant told her. 'You should go now. This is a place of business.'

I took my cue and put my arm around Stella. The Banks children scuttled out into the freedom of the foyer where they shook themselves like dogs, before marching away to the escalator.

'I'm sorry,' Stella told the room, now tearful again. Somebody found her a tissue, someone else a chair. 'I'm sorry. I know I shouldn't. I just couldn't help it; I'm so . . . upset.' There was nodding, and sympathy, but people turned back to their business to escape the scene. The junior manager poured Stella a glass of water.

'I'm a fool,' she said sadly, folding over the tissue to dab at her mascara. 'I shouldn't have let him write a new will. I should have stopped him. If he hadn't left me anything, none of this would have happened. It'll be all round the island by tomorrow, won't it?'

'Yes,' I agreed. I was frightened for her. She had never done anything self-destructive before.

Violent feelings were still echoing about the room. 'My friend,' she grabbed my hand, 'trying to keep me out of trouble. You should let me go. I'm a lost cause now.'

CHAPTER 10

Local Customs

Suzanne found a very large glass beaker in our equipment store. Eva gave her permission to wash it out and use it, assuming that she wanted to bring in some of the blind white crabs for observation. Instead she filled it with fresh water and installed two goldfish.

'So,' she whispered, 'what shall we call them?'

'Thulium and Thallium,' said Mark immediately.

'Mulder and Scully,' I suggested.

'Russlan and Ludmilla,' Dima declaimed.

'Ferdinand and Isabella,' Eva retorted.

'Orpheus and Euridice,' proposed Milo.

Multicultural confusion broke out. Between us, we didn't share enough heritage to make an informed choice between Greek mythology, Spanish history, Russian folklore, two obscure chemical elements and *The X Files*. We voted to refer the question back to Suzanne.

'Danish names,' Dima encouraged her.

'Not Danish fish,' she pointed out, squirming with stress.

Eva came up with, 'Rock and Roll?'

We called them Rocky I and Rocky II. Everyone could relate to that.

Since Milo was in a good mood, I asked him, 'What do you think of this journal, really? Do you think it's genuine?'

'Of course. It's a famous document – isn't it mentioned in all the histories of Alcazares?'

Eva looked at him with contempt. 'What histories, Milo? You know there aren't any. What happened here is a footnote to a footnote to the smallest appendix to the least-read history of Spain.'

'It bothers me that we don't have the original,' I said.

Milo was imperially dismissive. 'We assume it was stolen from the Archivo Parroquial in Las Palmas, probably by the German, Von Busch.'

'So why isn't it in his papers in Heidelberg?'

'Perhaps it is and they just don't want to release it. They don't trust us. You know how Germans can be.'

'I e-mailed them again. They were pretty stiff about it, but they're doing another search. And I asked the Archivo Parroquial to have another look. The contact there's quite helpful.'

'Why are you so concerned, Kim? The extracts we have are good enough, aren't they? They give one of the best accounts ever written of a major volcanic event. Even better than the report of Pliny the Younger watching Pompeii.'

'That's it, though, isn't it? They say exactly what we would have wanted them to say. It's all too good.'

'He says nobody was killed,' Eva pointed out. 'Normally, people get killed.'

The word made me smile. I can't believe it was ever this island's destiny to be normal as the term is understood in the rest of the world.

Such histories of Los Alcazares as people have bothered to write usually begin quoting from the Cura's journal at the entry for 1 December:

About five miles from Yesto, close to Tarfaya, between nine and ten at night, a mountain rose up from the breast of the earth.

The earth shook like a gigantic animal in terror. All over the region people were thrown out of their beds and came running by night to Yesto in great fear. The darkness hid everything until the morning, but when the dawn came we were able to see this fearful manifestation, a new presence on our landscape. The mountain is at least as big as the cathedral of St James. From cracks in its sides come clouds of sulphurous vapour mixed with ashes and small stones.

*The fear of the people is indescribable. The foul
smoke and ash covers the sky, blotting out the light
of the sun. To the simple souls of this region, all
sincere Christian believers, this apocalyptic event
appears to be the end of world.*

* * *

When she met Tom, Stella had almost achieved her
goal of being able to work out here full-time. She
had been working towards it for years, perhaps since
the first week we shared here; she won't say so, but
Stella does believe in karma.

Her Spanish was good, she had formed a partnership with the Belgian couple who originally started
the Residencias and they were talking about moving
on and letting her buy them out of the business. By
the time she made the move, she and Tom were married and he had just lost his job. That was two years
ago. A year later, when she called me to her, Stella
had insisted that Matthew should come with me.

'Who is this man?' she had asked, a tinge of
wonder in her voice. Given the eruption he had
caused in my life, it was a reasonable question. 'I
want to meet him. Come out, both of you. You must
come out, Baby. Bring him. Both of you. I should
meet him.' In the beginning, we planned to stay a
week.

They were wary of each other, Matthew and

Stella. They circled each other like Sumo champions, looking for the weakness in the will to win.

When you live here, you don't lie on the beaches unless you're entertaining visitors. The principle of the cobbler's children applies. People like Stella and Terry, and Tom when he was alive, making their living out of sand and sun, have lost their appetite for the product they market so successfully.

The last time we all lay on a beach was around the time Matthew and I started to think about staying on. Stella took us down to Punto Grande, to the tiny crystal bay whose silver sand is scattered with periwinkle shells. The tide was low and the little waves curled on the sand like a baby's hair on its flawless forehead.

'We decided this was it,' she said to Matthew. 'Kim and I, when we first came here. The most beautiful beach in the world. We'd found it.'

'Why were you looking?' he asked her. Matthew has a lot of childlike qualities and one of them is the instinct for those questions that will have you on the mat before you know he's moved.

'Why?' she parried, frowning. 'I don't know why. To enjoy it, I suppose. To get away from everything. My husband had run off. Kim was getting away from Conal. Like she needs to get away now.'

Matthew was sitting on the sand, combing it with his fingers. 'Don't you just bring everything with you?'

'I think you find everything when you get there,' Stella said. 'Everything that matters.'

'That's very deep, darling. Quite philosophical.' Tom fussed over the net bag on a string which was his apparatus for lowering our wine into the water to cool it. A net bag does not look good in a man's hands.

Matthew started picking out little black stones and lobbing them into the sea. 'So it's finding out what matters?'

'Yes. You need to get away to do that. At least, I do.'

'Suppose you find that nothing matters?'

'Ah!' said Tom. 'A nihilist. I knew it, actors are prone to nihilism, I find.'

Matthew didn't like that. He doesn't take offence easily but being classified because of his profession always rattles his cage. He lashed out with charm. 'This is a very beautiful beach,' he proposed. 'Nobody could disagree with that.'

'Nothing *does* matter. You just need to get away to understand that.' Stella directed this at me. Tom wandered off to the water's edge with his clanking net of bottles. His problem was finding the right bit of rock to which to attach the bag. Our beach is cradled in arms of spiky lava and there are only few places near the water where you can tie on a rope. Tom could never find them.

Matthew drifted away in the opposite direction;

he started skimming pebbles into the sea. Already he was so precious to me that I couldn't stop watching him. I had the kind of goofy obsession new mothers have for their babies, a stage of development I'd missed.

Stella watched him. 'Why do men do that? Since I'm so philosophical today. Why do they always have to throw stones into the sea. Or throw stones anyway, wherever they are? What is it with men and throwing stones? They're so destructive, aren't they?'

Matthew got a seven-bounce. He's pretty good at skimming stones. Also at playing pool, backgammon and poker, the games he calls the skills of a wasted life. I didn't answer Stella. I was tired. In that period I was still sleeping a lot. My mind had so much to deal with that it needed to close down half the time.

Towards the end of that afternoon, when the tide had turned and the cliffs were casting a cool shadow on the edge of the beach, Matthew and I swam out to the lip of the bay. The rocks are as sharp as beds of nails. They must have cooled instantaneously, spluttering in the cold sea water, and are too young to have been worn down by the waves. Only out at the points, where the fingers of lava broke off, can you find smooth surfaces to sit on. You can rest there and look out on the ocean and feel fellowship with Columbus looking out for America. Or you can look down in the glassy water and make out the dark backs of the fish.

Matthew said, 'She wants you to deal with what's happened to you in her way.'

'It works for her.'

'Does it?'

'What do you think of her?'

He had his arm around me and I felt him tense at the question. 'She comes with you. She's your best friend. All those years together, all you have shared, that you can share. I'm jealous.'

'She's trying to fight you for me. Our first day, all she said was, "I thought he would be older."'

'That's a fight, is it?'

'Believe me.' True confessions, it would have been nice to be fought over.

He sighed. 'I didn't expect anything. Everything happened so quickly, then here we were. She seems . . . envious. But not for things, for experiences. I think she wants to own things that can't be owned.'

'Meaning me?'

'I'm not fighting her for you.' It was a warning, but his voice was sad. 'Because in my mind, she can't own you.'

'But in my mind, she can?' I was getting wise to him. He has said so many words of make-believe. When something is important he is afraid to say it, so what he leaves unsaid is often what he most wants you to hear. He says he has done the same thing with his feelings, created them to suit his scripts, so he hardly knows what he feels any more. Except, he says, the feeling he has for me.

'You have the choice, don't you? When she's got something, she won't want it any more. Look at Tom.'

'What about Tom? Are you saying she's got him so she doesn't want him any more?'

'They're doing the cha-cha thing,' he told me. 'They both want to dance without getting close. He moves towards her, so she moves away. Then she stops. Then if she moves close, he'll move away. Dah, dee-dah, dee dah-dah dah-dah dah-dah . . .' He camped through a few bars of 'Patricia'. 'Goes on forever.'

'Do you believe that?'

'You can't believe it or you're fucked. It's a kid's game, that's all. Anyway, I was never into Latin-American.'

We'd done the subject for the day. I decided to dive back into the sea then and started swimming in to the beach. Matthew didn't immediately follow me. In the end, I slowed down. He dived in and caught me up only when he saw me pause.

'You always want proof,' he said when he caught up. Lazily, we swam on together, letting the waves carry us in.

'Tom's problem,' he said, while we were still out

of their hearing, 'is that nobody else wants him. If any other woman started prowling, Stella'd be all over him.'

That I could see. Tom, when I first met him, had a bluff, loquacious shine which wore off rapidly when they got out here and he had to grapple with Stella's expansion plans for the Residencias. She wanted to build villas as well as sell them. Tom had no eye for sites, no nerve in negotiation, none of her passion for operating the byzantine bureaucracy of electricity, water and telephone supplies. The magazine he started soon struggled. In a few months Tom had only his height and his old journo stories in his favour. We did like him, even his pedantry could be amusing, but when he talked about the business our smiles started to freeze.

The trouble with Matthew, of course, is that everybody wants him. It is his sickness, he admits it, to need everyone to like him. As well as his pheromones, which give the little kindergarten girls ants in their knickers, he has his good-bloke act which makes every bar on the island wake up as soon as he walks through the door.

He got to the beach before me. As he walked towards Stella she sat up, arching her back, and said something that made him laugh. Maybe it started then.

* * *

'I like Stella,' said Maryse, 'and I know she's your friend and everything, but she's screwing up here. Big time.'

'I know,' I agreed. 'But what can I do? I can't talk to her.'

We were on the terrace of the Dagenhams' place on the south-western fringe of Angeles, celebrating the rite called Beavers. For a while, Fred Dagenham had led the junior Boy Scouts of Los Alcazares in their activities every Thursday night at the flyblown apology for a municipal sports ground across the road from his villa. While the kids tumbled around in the dust, cooked sausages over a camp fire and learned the rules of soccer, Bunny Dagenham entertained the mothers to gin and tonic and cucumber sandwiches. Beavers immediately became the regular girls' night out for all the British women on the island.

There were only five Beaver mothers among them. Stella wasn't a regular. She giggled at the *double entendre* but didn't like the maternal premise of the gathering. Then the boys got too old for camp-fires and Fred couldn't get his mind round graduating them to Cubs and being Akela, but we needed an excuse to throw down gallons of gin and trash our menfolk every Thursday, so Beavers remained a social fixture.

It was the first wedge between Stella and I. When I got here I was still so habituated to motherhood

that I joined Beavers for what you might call sentimental reasons.

'Well, I can't talk to her, that's for sure.' Maryse
has a smoky, mezzo laugh which she breathes out
through the cigarette damage. She shook her head
regretfully, the beads on the ends of her braids clicking. 'It's thanks to Stella the whole island thinks I
was getting it on with Tom. I mean, it's nothing to
me either way. There is an up side – people have
been kind to me since he died. It's nice to know
they feel for me, even for the wrong reason. But I'm
not going to go giving her lessons in appropriate
widowhood after that, am I?'

Truly, I was not going to ask her, but she
answered me anyway.

'No, I was not. Uh *huh*.' She shook her head more
emphatically, making the beads rattle. 'Is that all
you think of me, that I'd run after that poor excuse
for a male?'

'No. Definitely not, Maryse.'

'It was on your mind.' I could see the whites of
her eyes flash in the half-dark. Except about music,
Maryse doesn't get deeply moved. She wafts around in
clouds of dope and scent, half-smiling, half-laughing,
permanently above whatever preoccupations may be
firing up the rest of us. Like a lot of people out here,
Maryse defines herself as creative but came to this
identity late. She backs her claim by viewing the
whole world from the position of an artist. This puts

us non-artists at a lower level of existence. Sometimes this bugs me.

'Don't get mad at me,' I suggested. We were on our fourth gins at least. 'I said I never bought that story. The island's full of talk. I like to get things right. I won't run a theory that nobody's even taken around the block. I'm a scientist, I need proof, either way. You opened the subject.'

'Stella.' Maryse pulled the lime quarter out of her empty glass and licked it. 'She's pulled some strokes, eh? I heard she hit that Banks kid. Tom's daughter. I never even realised he had a family. Is that true? Since we're running all our *theories* around here?'

'Yes, she did that.' I told her what had happened at the Santander Bank two days earlier. Then I got up and refilled our glasses.

'You girls look very serious, talking away down there.' Fred was stiffly balanced on one of the high stools by the pool bar. The Dagenhams, accustomed to spending their lives in their pub, have at least two bars in the villa, indoor and outdoor, as well as the two at The Crown and Anchor. It helps them feel at home.

'They're talking about Stella – aren't you?' This was from Carole. Beavers is a big networking opportunity for her. She hustles me for her meditation circle and arrives early to clip Fred's grizzled mop before the festivities begin. That night she was recruiting for the world healing meditation, urging us to join hands and bathe the globe in golden light. I think I decided to grow my hair long out of an instinctive fear of Carole; her blow-drying is good, but when she isn't hustling, she gossips.

'Isn't everybody talking about Stella?' I parried, fetching more ice.

'You can't blame people for being curious,' whined Carole. 'That CID man's still here, I saw him outside Las Rocas this morning. I heard the insurance company were sending somebody out too. We just want to know what's going on.'

'Nobody knows what's going on.'

'Tom had insurance? He must have done, careful man, family man?'

'I don't know.' I did, but it wasn't their business.

'So if it was suicide, she loses, yeah?'

'I don't know.' We have kept the faith, Stella and I. She's kept my secrets so I had to fight for her against the inquisition. 'I don't know any more than anyone else. Neither does Maryse.'

'I wouldn't be too sure of that, if I were you.' Triumphantly, Carole stuck a cigarette between her scarlet lips and clicked her lighter, stretching out a smirk as she caught Bunny's eye.

The sympathetic look Bunny sneaked in my direction really hit me. I wondered if by now the entire island had seen what I'd seen growing between Stella and Matthew, if as a sideshow to the Stella scandal they were picking over my bones in conversation whenever my back was turned. I said nothing more, and went back to my chair at the end of the terrace.

'What did Carole want?' Maryse demanded. She had been lounging with her feet on the terrace wall, her white tennis shoes glaring against the darkness. 'She didn't have anything good to say, I bet.'

'How long does it take her to do your hair every week?'

'I know, darling, I know. But I don't talk to her. I find an old magazine and I read that the whole time. She just rabbits on over my head. She's s-o-o-o dumb. Now she's *really* down on Stella, Carole is.'

'She's down on everyone, it seems to me. All that spiritual stuff she's into doesn't do her any good.'

'Yeah. But Stella isn't doing herself any favours. Like I said. Someone should talk to her.'

'Like me? We've had a few conversations already. People should just let her be. She's shocked, she's grieving. I think she cared for Tom more than she knew.'

'Aw, come on.' Maryse swallowed down another giggle, 'You've gotta admit, Kim, even you have to admit this, Stella only cares about one person and that's herself. And most of the time we're all just fine with that because she's great. Isn't she? She's so up all the time, high energy, full of zap, ideas, angles. This place would be nothing without her, I mean it. Most people are dead from here up.' And she pulled her closed hand, with her long silver nails, across the base of her throat.

'Yeah, well.' I weighed up my options, gazing out into the soft night. The pool of light from the terrace reached a few feet of coarse scrub beyond the villa walls, then there was nothing but blackness until the lights of Puerto del Ducque a couple of miles away.

There are very few insects here; the wind is too strong for them. So you can sit out at night with candle lanterns or what you will, with no fear of a thousand kamikaze beetles pinging into you.

What kind of fool would I look if I went back to the villa and found a note from Matthew on the kitchen table? I shivered although the air was still warm. But I was tired of all this recreational backbiting by people without a tenth of Stella's loyalty, or energy, or imagination. 'Stella,' I began thoughtfully, 'besides her entertainment value, has been a good friend to me, you know. The best.'

'Well, whatever. I don't know about that . . .'

Gin or instinct, something told me to ride this tiger and find out what Maryse had on her mind. 'Well, I *do* know about it, Maryse. Stella has been a good friend to me, I'm telling you that so you can know it. You're getting the facts from the horse's mouth. She pretty much saved my life when nobody else gave a damn.'

'Hey. Chill, baby . . .'

'Just hear me, OK. There's so much talk on this island, I hear bits of garbage getting to be facts all the time, just because they've been repeated fifty times in a day by people who'd like them to be true. I like proof, I like authentication. I'm a scientist, remember? You want to know anything about my life, you just ask me. Don't sit around assuming what amuses you. It's my life, it happened to me, I'm the one who knows about it. The only one.'

'Hey, Kim, darling – don't get upset.' Maryse was showing a lot of eye-white now, she really was moved. This is what Tom's death has done, it's shaken everybody out of the voluntary coma induced by tropical sun, gin at seventy-five pence a litre and more natural beauty than you could shake David Attenborough at. We are all raw-nerved now, all jumpy in the face of actuality.

'I'm not upset,' I said. 'I didn't mean to make you feel I was, anyway.'

'It's good that you're still on Stella's side,' Maryse went on, picking her fingernails while she organised her thoughts. 'That's true loyalty. I like that. And Matthew's very loyal too, isn't he?'

Here it comes, I thought. This is what I asked for, I'd better take it. 'Is he?'

'Sure he is. Haven't you noticed? Nobody ever tries talking to him about Stella. He's always being there for her, since Tom died. They're together all the time. Jesus and I found them over in Ubrique yesterday. I see them in the Macarena, he cuts out of school early and drives over to the Residencias office. Even the night Tom died, there they were down at the marina.'

'Were they?'

'Didn't you know that? Somebody saw them in the Lumumba just after midnight.'

The Lumumba was intended to be a bar for smart yacht owners and named after the drink they order to warm their blood after a bracing sail-about: rum and hot chocolate in a tall glass. Puerto del Ducque is hardly Cowes – the marina was only opened last year; half of its attractions are still unbuilt and may stay that way quite a while since the financial consortium backing the place fell apart. You rarely find more than six ocean-going craft down there, including Terry's boat; but as everywhere else on the island, traditions take root as determinedly as the lichens on El Mar Negro, and the Lumumba has its regulars.

'Who saw them?' I asked, querying the evidence to play for time while my fearful heart turned over.

'I don't *know*. Somebody saw them. Somebody Leif knows, some Swede or other, I think. Or Danish. Scandinavian, anyway. They all hang together, don't they?'

I knew I was looking at her with scorn. I was angry, as I justified my feeling to myself, that after all we had said about the talk factor she was trying to rattle my cage with another factoid. And for a few moment Maryse glared back at me, and the whole thing was about who was right.

But then she reached over and put her hand on my arm. 'Look,' she said, 'I know it's not coming out right, but I'm telling you this because I think you need to know. I love you, Kim. We all love you. You're not full of shit or moonshine, like half the people here. You're getting your life sorted, people respect that. And they like Matthew, he's good to you and he's really got stuck in here, hasn't he?'

'Yes,' I agreed in a low voice. Sometimes I asked myself what would happen if we split up, whose side the island community would take, because this place is so small it can't accommodate both halves of a broken partnership; one person always has to leave. I reckoned that would be me, that they would side with Matthew if the crunch came.

'So what I'm saying is, we like you,' Maryse was gripping my arm so hard, her fingernails were scratching. 'We want you to come out of this, both of you. So I'm telling you that if I were you, I wouldn't be so strong for Stella at this point. You get me?'

'Yes,' I said. 'I get you. Thank you. I'm glad you told me.'

CHAPTER 11

Night Games

5 December: *On this day, from an abyss which opened in the side of the mountain, a river of fire issued and flowed over Tarfaya, over Almonte and over part of La Negra. This happened from about eleven in the morning in daylight.*

Mercifully, most of the inhabitants were able to run away before the burning river reached their homes. The lava then spread northwards, running as fast as water, then slowing down and becoming sticky like honey.

7 December: *With a terrifying noise like thunder, the earth spat out a great rock near Almonte. This, by its pressure, forced the burning river, which had been continuing to spread northwards, to change its course and run north-west or west-north-west. It reached the villages of Mencia and Santa Carolina, both situated in a valley, and buried them instantly.*

Around Yesto, several hundred people are living in tents. When they abandoned their farms they herded a few goats with them and left the rest of their livestock free to fend for themselves. The animals are utterly terrified and run in every direction, causing much destruction.

Parties of herdsmen have been formed to round them up, and have encountered rustlers who, hearing of the catastrophe, have come down from as far away as Ubrique and Villanueva with the intention of profiting from our misery.

Imagine, Excellency – we are a town without water. We have no streams, no rivers, no lakes. There was never a cool fountain splashing in our market square, or wells at the town gates to refresh travellers. The municipal aljibe is a good size. It was full when the catastrophe began but foul as it is the water is being used rapidly. Violence and disorder are inevitable, with so many desperate people suddenly crowding into the town. The council has posted a decree rationing water to two skins to each household a day.

The council have asked Don Andres to send his eldest son, with two other landowners from our region, to ask help from the junta in Ubrique. They have also sent a party of men to Fuerteventura to negotiate for water, which could be brought over to Alcazares in barrels.

11 **December.** Today the eruption continued with

*greater force and noises like the roaring of the Devil.
The lava advanced beyond Santa Carolina and
destroyed the hamlet of Reales, burning and covering
the entire village where my own mother was born.*

*The lava continued along the shore and great
clouds of steam rose where the sea was boiling. As
the cooling rock forms a cliff, the new flows runs
over the edge like waterfalls.*

18 December. *Today, nothing further
happened. Everything is calm. It seems that the
eruption has finished. In all, nine villages have
been completely destroyed and buried under the
rivers of fire: Mencia, Monte Negro, Almonte,
Santa Carolina, Jimena, San Luis, Molina de
Palmas, Chipiona and Reales. The Chapel of St
John the Baptist at Almonte has also been
destroyed, and another chapel at Reales.*

*Yesto is full of refugees, and their terror is great.
I believe both old people and children will die from
nothing more than continual fear of the awesome
travails of the earth. When the ground shakes,
people scream like souls in hell.*

*Many destitute families came to me for help from
the parish and I used a portion of the relief fund to
buy food from Don Andres' stores. I intervened in a
dispute with fishermen from Fuerteventura, who
arrived with water but charged extortionate prices
to our desperate people. Don Andres sent six men to
stand at my back and we were successful.*

I sent a full report to Fr Domingo and asked him for more money, while assuring him that I had the backing of Don Andres in resisting profiteering. Don Andres posted a man to guard every one of the aljibes on his land, day and night.

25 December. *I learned from Fr Domingo that my reports were to be sent on to the Parochial Council in Las Palmas in the hope that they would vote our parish extraordinary relief. Many people have also fled to Ubrique, and the junta has set up a special committee to deal with the disaster. This committee is also reporting to the regional governor and council. I announced this publicly, and people became calmer, believing that help would come.*

Fr Domingo assures me that my reports were of great value and has ordered me to remain in Yesto as long as possible so that he can be fully informed. He has sent to Tamiza for an account of the condition of the Church lands; although the disaster was far away from them, he had been told of refugees travelling that way. He gave me an account of the volcanic eruption in Italy which had buried two villages there, and which he said he had visited.

Fr Domingo ended his letter by observing that the terrible catastrophe of this month, worse than anything seen in Italy, demonstrated the majestic power of Our Lord, who has shown us how he can tear the earth like a piece of worn linen and call up new mountains as easily as a child can pile up a heap of dust.

20 January. *We despaired when a pillar of fire rose out of cracks in the new rock near Santa Catalina, burning with clouds of very dense smoke which spread over the whole island. Now again great quantities of ash, sand and scree are falling everywhere.*

Bolts of brilliant red and blue lightning shoot through the clouds of smoke, followed by the violent noise of thunder, as if in a great storm. This is utterly terrifying to the inhabitants of this region, because thunder storms are almost unknown here. Some now believe that demons are gathering to drag them down to hell. The majority of the people of Yesto have decided to leave.

The ash and sand have continued to fall for several days. I have seen good fields which are the property of the Church in the region of Tamiza buried to a depth of three hands in black sand.

There is no word in English or Spanish for a volcano groupie, but that is clearly what the Cura became. Even I, the most humble apprentice vulcanologist, can sense that in those few days he was baptised by fire and received into the crazed cult of Pluto, god of the underworld. In these easy times they fly around the world on their obsessive pilgrimages from one live crater to the next.

Mark is one of them. He wears a silver bracelet engraved with his credo: 'To see a live volcano is to lose your innocence about the earth.' Suzanne says he sleeps in a heat-reflecting hammock which he designed himself to hang over the lip of a crater. Out here he has slung it from the pergola shading his balcony.

Frankly, these guys are crazy. They're compulsive, they just want to get as close to the hot stuff as they can. They put on space suits, asbestos boots and anti-thermal visors faced with gold leaf and abseil inside cauldrons of molten lava. They pitch tents on the shores of steaming lakes of sulphuric acid. They use scuba gear to fly Microlites through clouds of scorching gas. We get the best and brightest here, the volcano groupies who have scientific rationales for their adventures, rackety vehicles running on academic funds and lashed together in the name of research and understanding, in which they launch themselves into the fire.

This sect has martyrs. There was a French couple, a man and wife, who met in their early twenties and sealed their love with a pledge never to have children who would certainly be orphaned by the earth. They died young, as they expected, caught out by a pyroclastic flow on a mountainside in Japan.

The pyroclastic flows come before the magma itself. They are torrents of hot gas which pile down the sides of the crater at a thousand miles an hour, belching dead grey ash, carrying along all the junk left over from the last eruption, tumbling along rocks the size of houses.

Nothing can outrun a pyroclastic flow. The French couple knew that, and they knew that, with all the science in the world right now, nobody knows when a crater will blow, or where, or which way the flow will run. We know so much and we don't really know anything. That's what I like about this work. I like the futility; it seems true. It excites me, the way sleeping in a hammock inside the lip of a crater probably excites Mark.

The Cura Rosario saw rivers of fire burn the fields and bury the villages and he was excited. Maybe he searched his soul while he obeyed Fr Domingo and stayed on site to watch the fireworks. It is absolutely evident from his record that he went much too close to things, even going out in a boat to watch the lava spouting into the sea. That must have been a sight.

Milo asked us, 'You've got the old maps of the island, haven't you? When you have time,' he suggested, 'go out and take some rock samples in this area –' he showed us the southwestern region where the Cura had recorded showers of ash and pebbles '– and let me have them for radioactive dating. We'll see what we can find.'

'How?' I asked him. 'What difference will the age of the rock make?'

He shuffled through my papers to find a copy of an old engraving of the plain of Almonte before the eruption. It's crude, like a woodcut, showing a palm tree with a peasant woman and a donkey resting in its shade, corn fields and vineyards in the middle distance and a single mountain peak at the skyline. 'That was La Negra. It was completely buried; it's under here somewhere. You see it was the crater shape, like Mount Fuji, a flat-topped triangle? It was an old crater and when it blew, the first stuff that came out was from the first eruption here. So we should find those rocks and they will be about four million years old. By the time of these rivers of fire they were getting the magma, lava, new rock; we can date it at two hundred years only. Then at La Mora,' he made a wide gesture across the office in the general direction of the southern mountains, 'of course they're much older. They should be the oldest on the island. Scraped up from the sea bed. So we should find fossil shells up there, like there are in the Atlas in Morocco.'

'Hasn't sampling been done already?' Eva always resists extra work.

'Nothing's been done. Nobody ever bothered with this place. That's what's so great about it.'

'If people are going to bother now, it'll be for the tourists, not for science,' I suggested.

'So. Whatever. We should care, as long as we can carry on working.' Milo laughed. His breath smells spicy, as if he lives on cloves and chilli. 'How're you doing Kim? Are the rocks answering you back yet? Are you cooking up a conspiracy theory with them?'

'Maybe.'

'Island life. Nothing ever happens here . . .'

'Something did happen,' Eva corrected him. 'Kim has lost a friend, Milo. Somebody was killed, you don't know about it.'

'Somebody I knew quite well. My best friend's husband,' I told him. 'Car accident. Just a few days ago.'

'I'm sorry,' Milo apologised. 'I had no idea. It must be a shock.'

'Yes.' I decided to accept their sympathy and let Milo take the hint that I was talking out of post-traumatic paranoia. But I know trauma; I'm really quite an expert, and I'm not questioning my documents because of the emotional fall-out from Tom's death. My mind is ravenous for distraction. My work at the Instituto has been the saving of me these past weeks because when I'm involved in it, I can block out the pictures of Matthew and Stella together.

* * *

With my history, I don't like to be the first home. I am afraid to go into an empty house and I can tell if there is no one at home almost from the way my key goes into the lock at the front door, from the way the sound of the lock turning travels into the space inside and meets no human resistance.

From outside the door I can feel the presence of whoever is in the house. Conal used to register like a shadow: bizarre, without a third dimension. Liam felt like a small animal, a mouse or a vole, making tiny movements, curled away in a hole. Matthew is like a low fire, a still glow somewhere at the centre, and every once in a while a log settles and sends up sparks.

Ginned-up as I was when I drove back from Beavers, I knew from the bottom of the unmade road that runs up to our apartment that Matthew was not home. I felt his absence long before I was able to see that his car was not parked where he likes to leave it, alongside the aloes. I opened the door and went inside without turning on the lights because I didn't want to see that the place really was empty.

I went straight through to the bedroom, opened the doors and went out on the terrace. The sky had been overcast for a few days but there was enough moonglow to highlight all the furrows in the fields. Canarian agriculture is also very Zen, especially by night; the fields are small and every plant is set by hand. The young onions are so geometric they don't look real. To catch the dew, the farmers top-dress the earth with the black pumice gravel called *picon*, heaping it up into ridges. The stone walls are wind-breaks; they follow the contours of the hills and in their corners, here and there, grow ancient cacti, all that remains of the old hedges.

From the door the light flowed through the room. After a few minutes standing in the doorway, feeling wretched with jealousy and gin, I saw that the place was untidy. 'Slob,' I said aloud. 'Fucking slob.' And I kicked a pillow that was on the floor, sending it crashing into the kitchen area.

In a few more minutes it came to me that although Matthew is a slob, the mess in the place was a lot more than he had ever achieved before. In the living area all the cushions were off the sofa, all the kitchen drawers had been pulled out, our possessions were scattered all over the floor. I put on the lights and went back unsteadily to the bedroom, where the mattress was askew, the bed frame and the cupboards gaped open.

We had a small safe in the floor of the corridor to the bedroom, hidden by a rug, an old oriental carpet runner we had bought from an African at the Sunday market in Ubrique. I have a key and Matthew had a key. We keep some reserve cash in it, our passports, the deeds to our properties, Matthew's grandfather's watch chain and signet ring. The rug had been tossed aside, exposing the iron lid of the safe.

I knelt down and opened the safe. The passports were gone, and the deeds. The cash was untouched.

I was less drunk than I had been but still burning with the anxieties inflicted by Maryse. Fear crept around me like death itself, turning my toes and fingers cold, squeezing my heart. Only Matthew could have taken these papers. He had taken our passports and our deeds, he had gone to Stella and he had left the cash for me as some kind of insulting recompense for his desertion. He had paid me off.

I was outside the front door. I must have run out there as if I were trying to get away from the fact that he had left me. I was standing out at the front of the apartment, holding on to the wall, shivering. My thoughts had scattered, I could not collect them. In other times of trouble I had been able to run to Stella. Now I had nowhere to go.

A dog started barking somewhere downhill. The islanders keep their dogs tied up on long chains, often on the flat roof of the house. They're meant to be watchdogs and in the days when the island population was three thousand people they were probably very effective. Now that the place is overrun with strangers, the dogs are like car alarms in London: they fire off all the time and nobody takes any notice.

After the barking dog, I heard a car coming up our road. It must have been two A.M. or so. The car was being driven without much urgency. In a few more seconds I saw the headlights on the old wall at the start of our street and heard the tyres crunch on gravel. It was a fat Fiat with spongy springs, bucking over the track. I saw the driver and another man in the back seat.

The car stopped by our door. Matthew got out of the back, jumped up the steps and halted in front of me. 'I was worried about you,' he said. 'I was so worried about you getting back and finding the place like this. Are you OK? Kim?'

I couldn't say anything. He jumped down again to pay the driver, grabbed a plastic bag off the car seat and came back. 'When did you get here?' he asked, touching my face. 'Have they made much mess? They were piling into the place . . .'

'Where's your car?' It was all I could manage to say.

'Still with the guardia.' He moved around me to the door. 'What's this?' Taped to the wall by our post box was something I had not noticed because I had not turned on the terrace light, a page of white printed paper with a signature on it, in a plastic sleeve. I saw the heading GUARDIA CIVIL. 'Some kind of certificate saying the place was searched under warrant. Just in case anyone should wonder. I bet they get a few complaints. Christ, what a mess. Did they lock the door, at least?'

I was able to nod.

'Sadistic,' he went on. 'Wrecking a place like this. If they were serious about searching they'd do it methodically. This way they could miss anything they were looking for, unless it was bigger than a sofa. Stupid.'

I said, 'Where were you?'

'They brought me in for the CID officer. Something else, he is. There was no way I could let you know; they wouldn't let me make any calls.'

'I didn't realise,' I said. 'I didn't see that paper.'

'So what did you think – did you think this was a burglary? You were standing here thinking the place had been turned over?'

Again, I was able to nod. What I could not do was put together any new theory about what had happened. I took the guardia's paper from Matthew and tried to read it but the tiny print blurred under my eyes.

'And you're Beavered, aren't you?' He turned around to look me in the face, a smile twitching his lips. 'You came back here after Beavers, hammered as usual, found the place blitzed and thought we'd been burgled, is that it? Poor Kim, it's too much, isn't it?'

'You opened the safe,' I accused him.

'They made me. They took the passports and the deeds. They're checking back with London, checking us out. They'll give them back when they find out we are who we say we are. Nothing to worry about. You were worried, weren't you?'

'Of course I was fucking worried.' That got him. He reassembled the sofa and made me sit on it. He brought me mineral water and a big mug of decaf. He went to work like a whirlwind, straightening the place out. I wondered if all this was because there was something he didn't want me to find, but tiredness started falling on me like snow, blotting out the world.

After a while he came to get me. He had run a bath and thrown in some of the foaming jasmine gel I never use because it seems too exotically feminine for me. He put something soothing on the stereo, undressed me, took off my make-up with the proper stuff for the job, helped me into the water and gave me *Elle* to read while he finished clearing up. Then he came and washed me all over like a child, washed my hair and rinsed it with the hand-shower.

'This is like *Nine and a Half Weeks*,' I said. I did not go on to make some crack comparing myself unfavourably to Kim Basinger; I was too tired.

'If you think, after what I've been through . . .' I started giggling, silly with fatigue, relief and residual gin. 'Bloody women and their bloody demands. Never know when to stop, that's their trouble. I've taught ten six-year-olds to tell stage-left from stage-right, I've bought your bloody tampons for you, I've been interrogated by the Gestapo, I've done the washing-up, I've made you coffee and now you want hours of kinky sex as well . . .'

'No I don't,' I assured him. 'I'm too tired for kinky sex. Just don't pull my hair.'

'Oh ye of little faith. When have I ever pulled your hair?' He demanded, plugging in the drier. I smiled, but I wasn't really amused. Matthew has a huge repertoire of tricks for raising smiles, from walking on his hands to telling the story of the National Theatre workshop in which he didn't recognise Dustin Hoffman and knocked him over. He saw my blank eyes and gave up on humour. 'Is kinky sex more exhausting than plain?' he asked.

'I'm sure you have pulled my hair, I just can't remember.'

'I have never, ever pulled your hair. I don't do things like that. Are you going to answer the question?'

'What question?'

'About plain sex. Plain as in regular. Regular in the American sense, meaning meat-and-potatoes, not in the Woody Allen sense, like almost never, about three times a week.'

Again and again, his hand was scooping my hair off the nape of my neck. His fingers stroked my scalp. I leaned back against one of his long thighs. The warm air from the drier brushed my shoulders. Sex is still like chocolate to me, it's a total, one-hundred-per-cent, indefensible treat and I can never say no, even when I know I should.

I imagined his hand brushing my shoulders, then my breast. I let the towel fall. He turned off the drier and the night was silent. He turned off the lights. I felt his cheek scrape at the back of my neck, his lips dry on my skin. I imagined my nipple crunching up under the tip of his forefinger. I turned around to kiss him.

We slept after the sex, and four hours later when the morning was already blazing we got up and rushed to get dressed for work.

'There's that cat.' Matthew was sitting on the bed putting on socks and the cat was back on the edge of the terrace, watching him through the glass.

'You've seen it before?'

'It's been hanging around a couple of weeks.'

'You never said.'

He shrugged. 'Haven't you seen it?'

'Yes.'

'Well, you never said either.' He reached for his shoes. 'Shall we give it something?'

'What? There isn't any milk.'

Then he took a deep breath and said what he hadn't been able to say the night before. 'The CID guy. He wants to talk to you today. He said you should call him any time and fix when to go in. I don't think they suspect you of anything.' He gave me a piece of paper with the name and telephone number on it.

I found I was eager to call. After all, I wanted to know the same thing as this detective, the truth about the night Tom died. Would it be worse for me if Matthew were arrested and jailed for helping Stella kill Tom, or worse if Tom's death was officially an accident and Stella and Matthew ran away together? Impossible to compute those questions. 'Do they suspect you?' I asked Matthew.

'Wouldn't you? Wouldn't anybody? Stella couldn't have put him in the car if he was unconscious. I was the only person there strong enough to do that. They can't fix a time of death, or rather they haven't fixed a time of death.'

There it was, the best evidence of my suspicions, slapped down on the table between us. 'What about Stella?'

'She's prime suspect – she must be. She was already there when they brought me in last night. Her voice carries, I could hear it. She didn't sound too good. What she must be going through, on top of losing Tom.'

'She was getting to the end with Tom.'

'That doesn't make it easier, does it? We know that.'

Suddenly he got off the bed and came to hold me again. Matthew does this thing of collapsing just when you think he's a superhero. It's as if he puts everything he's got into getting me through a bad moment and then has nothing left to hold himself together. I could feel his fear. He was crushing me as if he could squeeze strength from me to him. A lot of women – Stella comes to mind – hate it when a man does this. Their universe holds up when the man in it is in one piece. If he cracks, it all falls apart. I'm coming around to this position; I found I did not like Matthew being afraid. With Conal, I never felt that way. The weaker he got, the stronger I grew. His decay let me live; if he had been a whole soul, I might never have got out of my marriage alive, spiritually speaking. Strangely, it used to disturb me more when Liam needed me; my instinct was always telling me to push my son out into the world, to make him independent.

Matthew had cracked on me before. After we had decided to stay here, his confidence evaporated. First of all he clung to me, called the Instituto three times a day and wouldn't leave me alone. So I became very busy. Then he fell in with Sam and spent so long hanging around the radio station that Sam had to pick a fight with him to get him to back off. He even looked different in this period: he went out of focus. Then he started teaching and settled into the new Matthew, the irresistible one. I had ridden all that out but I didn't want to go through the process again. I pushed him back.

'I'm sorry,' he said, throwing up his head. He was looking down at me. I felt he was looking at me without seeing me. 'All this is getting to me, I guess. And this place. Everyone on this fucking island has a theory, don't they?'

'Give me a theory,' I insisted, brave at last. 'I haven't got one yet.'

'I've told you what happened,' he insisted at once. 'Don't you believe me?' I was silent. 'You don't, do you? Now we're getting to it. You think I was . . . well, what *do* you think Kim? Tell me, come on.'

'I can't believe you all,' I kept it reasonable. 'Terry says you took Stella down to the marina. Stella says she went to see Terry by herself. You say she never went anywhere and you left her after Tom had passed out.'

'I did take Stella down to the marina.' He drew a big breath to admit this.

'Why didn't you tell me that?'

'I thought I had told you. That's what I remembered. If you didn't hear me, I must have been wrong.' Irritation was making him snappy.

'How can you not remember something so important?'

'It wasn't important. I didn't think it was important, anyway. Or I'd have remembered telling you, wouldn't I?' He was getting control now; I'd lost my ground.

'Yes, you would,' I offered as a surrender flag. Then I remembered that the cops still had his car. 'Shall I drive you to school?' I suggested, by way of reparation.

'Drive me to Tamiza,' he suggested. 'The school bus stops there. I can ride in with them.'

'I'll see you tonight,' he said as he got out of the car. 'Good luck.' But no kiss.

* * *

When I introduced Stella to Conal she shook his hand with a force that made her little arm muscles stand out and said, 'How very nice to meet you again, Conal. Kim's told me so much about you.' This was as good as kneecapping my enemy. Stella was the only possible witness to the truth of our past, and Conal, I saw immediately by his red face and darting eyes, felt accused by her mere presence. Finally, my friend became the conscience my husband had never had.

A few weeks later Stella was able to perch on the end of our kitchen table and say, 'Isn't it wonderful that Kim wants to finish her degree?'

'Does she?' he temporised, looking at me.

'It's about time,' I observed, in the sweetest voice I could manage.

'Surely it's not necessary now?' he argued.

'It was necessary then,' Stella pointed out. 'You two would never have met if Kim hadn't been a student, would you?'

His size, his loudness, the armour of his stupidity, they were no use to him now. We had planned this and together we could stand against him. 'You can't expect me to throw my whole life away just because I got pregnant,' I announced in a bright voice.

He hissed with exasperation. 'That's so dramatic, Kim . . .'

'It's been six years. It's time for me to do something for myself now.'

'I thought you were happy at home.'

Stella sighed. 'Did you ever ask, Conal?'

'I can't live on antidepressants forever. You wouldn't want me to, would you?' He would, of course, but how could he have said so in front of a witness?

'Why don't you get a little job?' he asked in a phoney nursery voice as to an old woman losing her mind to Alzheimer's. 'Something to get you out of the house, fill up your time in a pleasant kind of way. You're my wife – you don't need to do any studying.'

'I don't want a little job,' I explained. 'I've no training, no skills, no experience – what do you want me to do, be a waitress?'

'You couldn't really introduce your business friends to a waitress,' reasoned Stella wickedly. 'Imagine. You do all those power lunches, don't you? Suppose you went out for lunch to a restaurant where Kim was serving. How would that go down?'

Truly, he looked frightened. I had never seen Conal frightened of anything before. Stella had found the one pathway into his head that was not a dead end. 'There's no need for my friends to be involved . . .' he protested.

'You mean, you want me to be a waitress and lie about it to your friends?' Conal was at that time in a phase of major-bullshit executive lifestyle, which meant that he spent as much time on golf courses as in his office, attended a glittering cycle of international sporting events and went shooting for two weeks every season. Occasionally, I was trotted out as the executive wife. I didn't like the look of any his associates, an ever-changing multinational procession of high rollers whose economic activities were never explained in verifiable detail.

'You're always trying to put me in the wrong, aren't you? That isn't what I meant . . .'

'Of course it wasn't,' Stella soothed her helpless victim.

'You're being most unfair,' he laboured on. 'Nobody wants Kim to lie about anything.'

'Well, that's wonderful!' Stella exclaimed, quite drunk on the irony.

'But we must think about this. You'll be too old, Kim . . .'

'No,' I informed him, waving the college admission papers. Together, Stella and I had explored the backalleys of educational bureaucracy and discovered an earth science course at a humming inner-city college only half an hour from my home. 'When I start I'll be old enough to be a mature student.'

'But you have a *son*.' This was his ultimate victory; he was still announcing it with triumph.

Before Stella, I would have heard those words with despair. Now I bounced back with, 'And I can take the course *part time*.'

'Nobody wants to stop you doing anything you really want to do,' he protested.

'Of course not,' said Stella warmly. 'So that's settled.'

Conal retreated into a ponderous sulk and stayed there for some years. Stella sold the home she had shared with Husband Number One and bought one near us, with pale walls and bookcases. Conal hated her so much he could hardly speak to her.

He banned my books from the entertaining rooms in our house. 'They aren't the kind of books people have in bookcases,' he explained to me. 'Not the kind of books people like to see. And you won't need them, once you've finished this course.'

'You don't know that and anyway, I like them,' I told him and I bought a bookcase and put it in the kitchen, where most families keep a dresser displaying the best plates from which nobody ever eats. Our little family was no more than a biological unit and our home was just a shelter for this unit so our kitchen was never the warm heart of anything, just a place where we kept food. It was also the only place where Conal could not dictate my life.

Perhaps it was to make sure that I would continue to need my books that I decided to become a teacher. Perhaps I wanted a way of staying close to Liam. Perhaps it was just another choice dictated by guilt. Certainly, it was more than the drift of will I saw in some of my new colleagues, the helplessness of minds too timid to believe that a life in art or business was there in their hidden future. Whatever the reason, I felt called to do it and people said I did it well.

All through my years of reclamation, Stella guided and defended me. We behaved like two single women. In my heart, I was a single woman at last. We did the girly things, we shopped, we idled out Saturdays, we chattered in wine bars, we had our sacred holiday each year, we learned salsa dancing, water-colour painting and Spanish. The men – Conal and the catches she landed before Tom – were peevish.

It was the very week I got my teaching diploma that I answered the door to a rather kind, elderly man who did not look at all like my mental picture of a bailiff. With obvious regret and supple avoidance of embarrassment, he broke to me the news that Conal's business had failed and his creditors had made him bankrupt. It was, he told me, very common for men, especially middle-class men, to carry on with their lives as if nothing had happened, unable to tell their wives that they were broke.

Half an hour later a truck almost as big as our house itself drew up outside, blocking out the light from all the windows, and a team of men stripped the house of everything not prescribed by the official list of essential furnishings. These callers, like the guardia, wrecked with enjoyment. They seized Conal's state-of-the-art hi-fi and pompous mahogany dining suite and looked tauntingly at me as if they expected me to howl with anguish. Instead, as they carried out his fake-Regency cheval dressing glass, I wore a Madonna-like smile. As I watched our home being systematically despoiled, I felt lighter and lighter of heart.

Finally the gang stomped out with the last of Conal's framed sporting prints. I saw that they had ignored my books as being valueless, and never noticed the gun case holding his priceless matching Purdeys. I called Stella and laughed until my cheeks cramped.

After that Conal was humbler. We moved to a rented house. He crawled into another corporate job and never argued with me again. Occasionally he had a fit of dog-like gratitude and thanked me for 'everything you do for me'.

'He thinks you'll leave him,' Stella diagnosed.

'I could,' I suggested. 'I've thought about it.'

'Don't leave until there's someone to leave for,' she advised with a bitter drag on her cigarette. 'There's not much out here, believe me. And they always want you more if they think they can't have you. That's my problem, I can see it now.'

After the defeat of Conal, I breathed easier. Liam seemed to thrive; he grew taller than me a few weeks later. I built up my own life and I waited, not knowing, until it was revealed that I was waiting for Matthew.

CHAPTER 12

The Swarm

When I left Conal's car with mud on the seats I knew that he noticed it but he said nothing.

After Matthew went away, I was like a tent with one of its guy-ropes cut. A part of me was flapping crazily in the wind. Automatically I called Stella but when I spoke to her I couldn't find words for anything. 'You're very quiet, Babes,' she prompted me, and all I could answer was, 'Not much to talk about, I guess.'

Conal kept his distance but he was alert now. There was a hole in my armour of decent behaviour and he was looking for his chance to strike through it.

For four, even five days I had felt safe, knowing that Matthew was here and would be at the theatre every night. Then I was pitched into limbo. I had lost him. I went out to a payphone to call him but my call was routed to the voicemail; the message was his own, but in his rich actor's voice. I couldn't speak to it. Then I realised that I had nothing of him except the image I had made for myself.

Hope was a luxury I'd never dared to use before but now I needed it to repair the damage. I hoped the telephone would ring one evening and it would be him. I hoped I would find a letter from him in my pigeonhole in the staff room. I hoped I would open my front door and see him there. I hoped he would be waiting for me at the school gate. Every night when I got on my bus I hoped. When you've never used hope before, you go a bit wild with it.

All this was ridiculous because we had made a date. He was to call me at home at the only safe time, on Friday morning, when I had a late start at school. That morning I went upstairs, away from the telephone, up to Liam's room to collect clothes for washing, planning to take time to reach the phone so that I would be calm before I answered.

Boys leave the worst of themselves behind. Dusty coins and cans of drink long gone flat; torn corners of paper, grimy from life in his pockets, scribbled with redundant numbers; tangles of wiring leading to electrical things that didn't work anymore; that was the residue left by my son to remind me, in a boy's intentionally unintentional style, that my life was not all my own.

I picked up a sock and could not find its partner. I picked up a T-shirt, then another, then put them down, then looked for the first sock again. By the time the telephone rang, my dreams were as shrivelled as neglected fruit.

Matthew's voice was gassy; I imagined it carbonated by a week of talking to people with whom he already had history. At first he was very nice and very tender. Then he started telling me things; the new town had beautiful eighteenth-century buildings, the new theatre was gilded to the tits out front and had rats backstage, the new audiences were good but elderly, and about a third of them were asleep by the time he came to fire his pistols. It was only a matter of time before one of them had a heart attack but the director refused to let the shots be muffled. There was only one dressing room for the three girls to share and the leading actress had refused to play the midweek matinée. They were in a hotel but breakfast by room service meant cold rolls left outside the door in a cardboard box.

I now know that talking total Spam is something Matthew does when he's nervous. Since I go quiet when I'm nervous, this was typical of what used to happen when we were both stressed. Eventually either he would stop or I would speak. This time, he stopped.

There was a terrible silence and then he said, 'God, I can talk crap.'

A laugh bubbled into my mouth. Through it, I said, 'Yes, you can.'

'What I meant to say was I miss you.'

'I know what you mean.'

'Like hell.'

'Never been there but they tell me this is what it's like.'

'I'll be off on Sunday.'

Fear nagged at me. I regretted my message to Conal; it had closed some of my options on his side. 'You're four hours away. We'd only have the afternoon.' His silence said that he would take that afternoon. 'I could get away,' I went on, 'for a couple of hours, maybe.'

'I told you,' he said. 'We can't do this. This isn't for us.'

I was disappointed. I had also hoped he would ask me to leave Conal. 'What else can we do?' I finessed, hoping for the question.

He let out a heavy breath. 'Whatever we do now doesn't matter. I love you and that won't die, we couldn't kill it if we wanted to. We will always love each other. We could never meet again and the love would still be there.'

Then I panicked. I didn't want to hear about never meeting again. All I wanted was to see him. 'I can't deal with this. What are you saying?'

'I'm saying we have love and next to that nothing else is important.'

'Just words. What are we going to do? We can't live like this. Neither of us can live like this. You said it first, you must know what I'm talking about.'

'Oh, I know. Something has to happen. Something will happen.' He sounded tired and sad, as if he would never have the will to make anything happen.

'But what? I've got my son, I can't just turn his life upside down for someone I've known for two weeks.'

'I know what I need to know. This is like a wave, it's just going to happen, we can't stop it.' All these things I had longed to hear him say were coming over more and more quietly, as if the words were taking his life.

'I can't hear you, your voice is fading.'

'Is that better?' I wanted him to persuade me, to beg me, to devise some scheme to rescue me from the tower of my marriage. Instead he was drawing his line in the sand and making me step over it.

'I want to see you,' I said finally. 'When you're home, I'll take a day off.'

That day was like a trip to another planet, where we breathed love like oxygen, and stood on love like a rock, and every ordinary and extraordinary thing we did trailed magic phosphorescence.

I can't remember most of what we did or what we said. We sat in his kitchen. We made love in his bed. I remember that I was surprised at how well he lived, in a big, beautiful flat in a good area. His sheets were linen. The walls were not all pale – he had painted one of them acid yellow. I stroked the polished black stone sculpture which now sits on its own shelf among our books.

'This is beautiful,' I told him.

'I've been lucky,' he agreed. 'With money, anyway. Commercials. When I was younger. It makes a difference, being able to survive. I think I'm paying for it now.'

'Why?'

'I've never got the work I wanted,' he admitted. 'People think of you a certain way, then it's all they can see you doing. I'm a nice boy in jeans who needs aftershave and a car. That's it, that's me. I can't be a schizo in a gulag or the Duke of Clarence. Unless I prove it. At least I can afford to do theatre and get myself seen.' He tried to smile at me as if he were fine with all of this, but it failed. He had to fill in the rest of it. 'So I've done a lot of good stuff and the right people have seen it and they've said the right things and – nothing. It could be I've made my run and I didn't get there.'

'You're doing more than survive,' I proposed.

'I had good advice; I took it. I'll be OK if I don't screw up. Scarey, huh?' He looked at me with a bitter tenderness. Here was no invitation to starve in a bohemian attic. I could bring Liam to a nice room at a good home with real art in the living room. It could be done. Nestling at the back of my mind had been the possibility that Matthew was poor and would have the grace to realise that the two of us could not live on my teaching salary. So an option closed on the other side.

You will think me bizarre, but I remember that day as the most tragic I have ever lived through. The impossibility of love seems more cruel to me than the death of a person. We were one immediately, we became the unity which has kept us safe for so long, but Matthew refused to take control. He asked me for nothing. All he did was he let me feel how life would be unless I chose to make it different. All the way home the decision was a pain in my head.

In the train I painted on a flawless face and let the cold night air finish the job and freeze my senses as I walked back to our house. He had gone to bed when I got in. We had agreed on a bedroom compromise, twin beds bolted together, so in effect we slept apart and never needed to touch each other. Even so, Conal sensed another spirit with me. The threat to him was something his maimed mind registered at once.

The morning was Sunday, that day which for an unhappy family is always too long. To protect myself, I kept a pile of work for Sunday. Conal circled me, not declaring himself until Liam had gone out with his friends in the early evening. Then he came to stand over my desk and said: 'I was wondering if you would like me to sleep in another room.'

'We haven't got another room. Until your debts are paid, this is all we are allowed.'

'I could sleep on the landing.'

He stood there, swaying from foot to foot. Conal never had the humility to beg when he ought to have done. This was his final pathetic grab at me, at someone to whom he had never had any right, whom he had imprisoned by luck and kept only because I had nowhere else to go. He should have begged. Instead, he loomed at my side with a phoney brightness on his face, as if he were proposing a picnic, not clutching at a straw. My anger gave me strength.

'I'm in love,' I told him.

'Uh-huh,' he said, hypocritically reasonable. 'I thought something of the kind. And so – what do you want?'

'I want to leave.'

Then he said with despicable craftiness, 'You can't. What about Liam?'

'I haven't talked to him about it. Liam will be fine, it'll be good for him if I'm happy.'

'I don't think so.' Now he was in his mode of illogical insistence. 'He loves you, he's your son . . .'

'He'll be an adult in a few months. Don't argue with me, Conal. You've had more than you deserve of me, far more. You knew this day would come. I want my life, that's all. You've no more right to keep me now than you had to take me in the first place. The very first place.'

'You'll never forget, will you?' He actually accused me.

'Believe me, if I could forget I'd be the happiest woman in the world. I'd be the happy woman I was meant to be. How can I forget? You're here, you have taken my life. So don't talk to me as if you'd never done me wrong, as if it ought to be down to me to rewrite our history. And don't use Liam to make me wrong. It's over, you can't do that any more. You've had your pound of flesh. I can go now.'

He fell back while I was speaking, the only time, apart from the day the bailiffs came, that I ever made Conal back down. If there was something else I could have seen then, I missed it. The force of my true feelings spoken out loud blew me about like a leaf. From that moment, I was free.

* * *

'*Mierda*,' said Eva, her eyes fixed to her screen. She said it with such passion that the whole office heard and was spooked.

'What?' I asked.

'What?' demanded Dima, who was skulking at the edge of the room with another bag of washing.

'Something happening?' Mark pulled his nose out of his laptop. Suzanne looked up but at him, not us. There had been some chemistry stirring there for a few days.

It was around eleven, the time Eva would normally start bullying one of the boys to go over to the bar to get us our *amorza*, the plate of rolls she had decreed we required for our coffee break.

'I don't believe this,' Eva backtracked, re-entering commands. 'It can't be right. It's a mistake.'

I got up and went around to look over her shoulder. She had the readings from the underground monitors on her screen. I'm not great with figures; it was taking me a few seconds to understand what I was seeing. Eva entered her commands a third time and all that happened was that the screen flickered. 'No, that's right. Madonna. Now what do we do? Fuck off, *cuno*, eating onions in the morning.' That was to Dima who had crept up and was exhaling his stinking breath over our heads.

Eva made a few passes with her mouse and put the figures up as a nice blue graph with a yellow line. Then we saw what had moved her. Instead of a flat-line, the seismograph was registering little mountain ranges at regular intervals.

'I know I'm stupid, but what does it mean?' I asked her.

'She means, does it mean what we think it means?' Dima added helpfully.

'Of course it does. Something's happening, that's all. You can see that. I don't know what it means.' She shook her head as if the trace were oscillating just to rile her.

'Things are hotting up down there,' Dima suggested with relish. 'Maybe there'll be a crisis.' And he mouthed 'Boom!', rolling his eyes.

'Oh, go away. I can't think with you crashing about here like a pig. Just go away.'

Dima would have left, but he was now in the middle of a small crowd. Everyone in the building was standing looking at Eva's screen. As we watched the line moved on and within a minute had registered another peak.

'Hello! Come in!' giggled Dima.

'Can it,' Eva advised him.

'Cyclic activity,' said Mark with satisfaction. 'It's going to be a regular swarm.'

'It's like having a baby,' Dima suggested. 'Isn't that exactly how it looks on the monitor when you have a baby?'

I didn't respond. At the Instituto, I am just Kim, from England, living with Matthew. Nobody knew that I was the only person in the room who had given birth and I had buried those memories.

'It's very small,' Eva confirmed, clicking back into the tables for confirmation. 'We can't feel it. Can we?' For a few moments we paused in silence, wondering if we could feel the earth shaking. We looked at the

fish tank, hoping for ripples. People had been bringing in nice pebbles to furnish their habitat and Rocky
I and Rocky II were cruising near the bottom inspecting them for uneaten food. The surface was calm.

'Nothing. We're feeling nothing. But it's there all
right.'

'We should check this,' I suggested. 'I can go out
to the surface stations.'

'OK, you do that.' Eva agreed readily, eager to
take some action. Like Dima, we all heard this signal
from the centre of the earth like a knock on the door,
and when the earth itself calls you, it does seem rude
not to respond. 'Do all the observations, check everything. But call in and tell me what you get. I'll
check here. I'm going to send this over to Milo in
Tenerife. If he comes on while I'm away, tell him
Kim's verifying the reading, yeah?'

I ran out to my car and streaked away on the
weekly circuit. About twenty tourist buses were
parked on the tarmac in front of the Panorama Bar,
and another four or five were off already, snaking
nose-to-tail along the road around the most fantastic
craters. The usual ugly figures in shorts and sunhats
were milling in and out of the lavatories with no
idea that under their feet the earth was waking up
and snarling. I had a momentary image of the grill
crater itself exploding, hurling rocks and chicken
wings over the buses then spouting a fountain of
red lava.

It was another scorching day. The air was as clear as vodka and the sky such a flawless, uniform, cerulean blue it could have been air-brushed. One of the many bizarre features of the National Park is that, unless you count the tourists, there is no animal life here at all. With nothing but lichen and rocks, you don't see lizards basking on the hot stones, or hear invisible crickets churring at dusk, or find birds nesting under the eaves of the buildings. We've never even seen a fly.

There is a legend that a hermit lived in this magnificent desolation, surviving with only a camel, trusting God to send him food and water. I don't believe this; the landscape is so barren that you can't imagine that even a camel could live here. With no living things to react to it, our weather always seems unreal. As do many other things.

I decided to go south first, before the midday rush crowded the road. The nib of the seismograph was drawing its line dead-centre around the drum. 'We've got a flatline from the south,' I called in to Eva. Up on the ridge the tilt meters had moved. It was really quite neat. The lowest showed the most movement, nearly two units. The highest had moved, but hardly enough to measure. The one in between was showing just less than one unit. Tiny movements, fractions of a millimetre, but after months of looking at nothing at all it was quite a thrill.

'It's on the tilt meters,' I called into the phone.

'Don't yell at me,' she yelled back. 'How much?'

'The most showing is two units. Did you get through to Milo?'

'He's at sea this morning. He's switched his phone off, I can't get a connection. I've e-mailed him – he'll call in this afternoon. The big one checked out. I ran it again, it's really happening.'

I got back in the car and rattled over an un-metalled track to the northern station. Nothing on the tilt meters. The gas samples were deranged but Mother Earth's digestion didn't seem any worse than usual. The northern seismograph had registered something. Not much: the movement was not more than a tiny square on the graph paper at the most, but the cyclical pattern was there.

Actually, Dima was right but I wasn't going to agree with him because he is a jerk. Seismic activity expressed as a graph looks just like childbirth. I was watching the earth having contractions.

'Milo is coming tomorrow,' Eva told me when I got back to the Instituto. 'Actually, I think he's quite excited.'

'I should hope he is.'

'And he says I should remind you our work is confidential.'

'Right. All the Brits are still obsessing about the accident anyway. Even if I wanted to say anything, I don't suppose I'd get a word in.'

'I mean it – don't even think it. You can imagine what a scare would do to this place.'

'Trust me.' I had a flash vision of Los Alcazares minus its million tourists a year: the deserted apartment blocks, the untended pools, the ghostly dark bars, discarded timeshare leaflets blowing along the empty strip at Angeles, the neon extinguished, the beer souring in the pumps, the airport silent, the banks shut and eighty thousand people ruined, while a ship-load of volcano groupies cruised off shore waiting to see action.

All the same, we were excited. Actually, we were a little combat crazy. We got silly over lunch and the earnest pleadings of Cura Rosario bored me. All of a sudden I had a cosmic sense of purpose. For the first time since I had left England I had a good reason to get to tomorrow.

It was not until mid-afternoon that I thought about Matthew, which led me to remember his message from the CID and call the police station.

'Oh yes,' responded one of those throttled-back British voices that suggested a man with a tie knotted tight round a flaccid collar, 'I was hoping you'd be able to drop by.'

'Maybe in an hour,' I promised. I wasn't going to get any work done anyway; everyone was too high on crisis.

It was worse than the voice had suggested. He had a Hitler-Jügend haircut, a short-sleeved shirt, sweatmarked in the normal places, and the tie was patterned with Yves St Laurent logos. I wondered what Stella had made of him; she won't even look at a man who wears a self-evident designer tie.

'This is a very tight little community you have here,' he began. 'I've been out trying to get a feel for the place, in the short time I've been here. Quite a lifestyle people have. Fun in the sun – that's what it's all about, I suppose.'

The Banks kids had called down upon us an irony-free dork who probably went into the police for the discounted mortgage and the pension. I didn't say anything.

'I'd like to go over the events of the night that Mr Banks died.' He was running a tape recorder but there was nothing else on the desk in front of him. Knowing our local guardia, no one had translated my first statement for him anyway.

'I met Stella in the bar opposite her office. She was there with Tom, and Maryse St Clair and her partner. My partner, who you saw yesterday, joined us. We had a couple of drinks, drove to a restaurant in Tamiza for dinner, broke up about midnight. Tom had drunk a lot, so Matthew drove him back to their house. Then he came home to me.'

'What time would that have been?'

'Half past two. I missed him. I was watching the clock.'

'Mrs Banks does not drive?'

'Yes of course she drives. She drove her car and Matthew drove the other one.'

'This would be the Peugeot? Why did they take both cars?'

'Tom's car. We're dependent on cars here. There is no public transport except the tourist buses. Tom would have needed his the next day, and Stella would have needed hers. She was going to drive Matthew back to his car later.'

The man was frowning as if I were describing some bizarre primitive ritual. 'Actually, we laughed about it. We said it was like that reasoning problem about the dog, the cat and the mouse who have to cross the river and none of them can swim and there's only one boat.' And you couldn't send the cat over with Matthew in case she ate him.

My man was looking grievously perplexed. He spent a full hour putting me on the spot about every detail of the evening: what we wore, what we ate, when we did what, who said what to whom and how much we drank. 'This is a pretty relaxed lifestyle here, isn't it? People tend to drink a lot,' he pushed me. I could see no reason to disagree. I did not pass on Maryse's claim that Matthew and Stella had been seen at the Lumumba. I've watched enough American TV to know that hearsay is inadmissible.

The light through the dirty window started to fade. The temperature in the interview room finally began to drop. I guessed it was about seven when we started on my history, a topic he opened by stating, 'Disaster seems to follow you around, Mrs McEverdy.'

'Was that an expression of sympathy?'

'There was no intention to cause offence.'

'You didn't quite achieve your objective.' I was still trying to keep it light.

'I don't follow you,' he complained.

'No.'

'This isn't helping.'

'It isn't helping me either. It was only a year ago. I can't say I feel ready to respond to humour yet.'

'This is a misunderstanding, Mrs McEverdy. No humour was intended.'

'I'm sure it wasn't.' And he swallowed that reassurance whole. I found I detested him deeply.

'I'd be comfortable if you called me Kim,' I said, trying move things on to neutral ground. 'And I've gone back to my maiden name.' I spelled it for him. Then he opened up the big hypothesis.

'What relationship did *Matthew*, your *partner*, have with Mrs Banks?'

'The sort of relationship your *partner* usually has with your best friend. I don't think she thought he was good enough for me.' Another of Stella's early shots had been, 'Pity he's an actor. You deserve a man who'll give you all his attention.'

'People out here don't seem to go in for getting married,' was the next observation.

'Stella and Tom were married. The Dagenhams.' I decided to leave Terry unmentioned.

'But none of their friends were. So what does Matthew think of her?'

'Of Stella? You've talked to him, didn't he tell you?'

'I'd like you to tell me what he told you.'

'He likes her,' I said. 'She's spunky, dynamic, fun – most people like her.'

'More than you like her, would you say?'

'I find that a strange way to put it. Stella's my best friend. We go back a long way; we've supported each other through everything that's happened to us and, like you say, we haven't had quiet lives.'

He took off his spectacles; they had Armani frames. I thought of him questioning some teenage London crackhead with logos on every limb, and coming on with the brand-name superiority. 'Her first husband. What happened to him?'

'When we met, he had already left her. I never knew him.'

'And she and Mr Banks decided to live out here – when?'

'Two years ago. We met here, you see, and she'd loved this place ever since. Stella was in the property business. She wasn't happy with her life at home. She was working towards coming when she met

Tom, selling holiday homes, retirement homes, that kind of thing.'

'Suppose I said I thought Matthew and your best friend were having an affair?'

I weighed up my options. If I agreed with his theory, he might give me the information I didn't want to have. If I negated it, he still might tell me what he knew. If I said nothing, he might suspect me also of being involved in the murder of Tom. A thin blade of fear flickered around my stomach. I was afraid for myself, I was afraid for Matthew. I found that I wanted to protect him from this meat-head. I found I didn't want to know whatever facts there might be about Matthew and Stella. I decided to keep the faith with Matthew.

I said, 'I haven't had much experience of love. I don't know how someone like you would evaluate what's between Matthew and me. But I don't think either of us could have an affair in the sense I think you mean.'

He made a grimace of cynicism. 'Aren't you being naïve, Kim?'

'I'm trusting. There is a difference. I trust my partner.'

'Too trusting, a lot of people would say.'

'People would say anything. Stella's very attractive. So is Matthew. People gossip here; they've got time on their hands and it's a small place.'

'So you'd say I was wrong?'

'I'd say I don't suspect Matthew of having an affair with Stella,' I told him, amazed that the words could ring so true.

'So your relationship with Matthew lately has been . . . what?'

OK, I thought, you want to play therapist, I believe I can give you the proper chat. 'We've all been turned over by Tom's death. Matthew's been very sensitive, very supportive of me. I've needed to lean on him a lot.' I took a fresh gulp of sincerity and went on, 'Maybe this has opened up things for me that I haven't been able to express before. I can get in touch with feelings that were still too much to deal with a few weeks ago.'

He took that as an invitation to start picking over the whole of my history. Very soon I let myself start crying. It did the trick. He stood up, acting irritated, as if I were weeping to offend him, and went out of the room.

When I was alone some internal barrier came down. I started sobbing out of control, so badly my whole chest hurt. After a very long time he came back with a box of tissues, nearly empty, dusty and discoloured by the sun. Presumably it had been a long time since a suspect had broken down at the police station in Angeles.

'You're upset,' he observed.

'I think I'm entitled. Like you said, disaster follows me around.'

'Someone's waiting for you,' he told me. 'You're free to go.'

'I've been free to go since I got here,' I reminded him.

After a few hours in the public area of a police building everyone begins to look as if they're guilty of something. The environment is intended to make you feel disadvantaged, powerless, frightened and unable to resist when they want to herd you all together as underclass, fit for elimination. My tears started again when I saw Matthew sitting on the bench, crouched over the open book in his hands without a breath of confidence in his body.

'Eva told me you were here,' he explained. Then he put his arms around me. 'Little prick. I told them you didn't know anything.'

'Let's go,' I said. I couldn't say anything more. Specifically, I couldn't tell him that I had passed an hour resisting the idea that he was a liar and a cheat. All the lies of omission I'd used in my marriage were like toxic residue in my heart. He threw his book into the back of the car and I noticed that it was a play script.

We ended up in the Lumumba. Terry was there, and Islewyn the naturopath, and Stella, for some reason as noisy and excited as a parrot, although she had plenty of sympathy for me. 'Isn't he just a slime-ball, Babe?' This was of the CID officer. 'I kept thinking, where did they find him? They must have searched for months to find a creature with absolutely *no* style.'

'D'you think he'll give me my passport back?' Terry asked, looking moodily at his glass. Terry wasn't a big drinker but tonight he had a serious brandy in front of him.

'Terry's wife's ill again. He wants to fly to London,' Stella explained.

'Sorry to hear that,' said Matthew.

'Yeah. Thanks.' Terry shifted on his stool. 'Serious. Came on suddenly. Looks like this could be the big one.'

'Compassionate, it'll be compassionate grounds, or something,' Stella assured him. 'They're bound to let you go. They can't keep you, not if your wife's dying.'

'I'd want to be there,' he protested to us all. 'I never expected this, never. She's been stable for years.'

'I'm sure they'll do it,' Islewyn announced, tugging at his beard. 'They let people out of jail for that kind of thing. Get the doctor to send a fax, confirming the prognosis.'

'Right,' Stella pounced on the suggestion. 'We can do that, he can fax from my office.'

I sat back and tuned out. Terry's expedient feelings for his wife seemed very small to me. For months he'd been talking about his escape from home with the jittery jubilation of a weak man who thinks he's defeated a strong woman. Now he was trying to delete that and look like a caring husband, with Stella buzzing about him issuing bulletins on his right to our approval.

I was tired, very tired. I was thinking of the underground seismograph, working in the hot vault below the empty Instituto building, filing the rhythmic data from the centre of the earth.

* * *

13 February. No more ash has fallen. All is quiet.
2 March. Another flow appeared and ran south-west, arriving at Chupadero, which very quickly was no more than a great inferno of fire. This flow spread all over the plain of Yesto, burying our good fields. Then it changed direction and ran at incredible speed towards the seashore. It arrived at the water's edge on 7 March and formed a small island in the middle of the ocean, around which were found many dead fish.

I was very happy when Milo pointed out that my Cura was wrong about that island. It's a fantastic extrusion of yellow rock named El Caracol because it looks like a snail, and it is only half a kilometre from La Quemada and a short swim offshore. People tell little children that a dragon lives over there.

According to Milo, El Caracol could not possibly have been formed by a lava flow from the mainland.

His theory is that it was created by magma forced up through a new crack in the sea bed. Just to be sure, he brought one of his diving team over to go down and photograph the sea floor. Despite the layers of sand that have washed up since, you can see that the island bursts up vertically through the water and is of a different kind of material from the small-bore black basalt around it.

'And what he didn't understand is that the lava was really bubbling down there. The magma chamber must have been five miles across. It was bursting out of the ground wherever it could find a weak point. The process had been building for months. All the sounds he thought were gunfire and the steaming seas which frightened the fishermen were caused by earlier eruptions from old craters on the sea-bed. This whole area was just boiling over.'

'Maybe he was going mad?' Maybe I've been too close to mad people. You can't say 'mad', of course. It's not a clinical term. The grief counsellor was kind enough to set me straight on that. Another reason I was happy to leave. 'You can see him with his cassock all dirty with ash, climbing the church tower to watch the rivers of fire pouring towards him. And saying mass by himself in his empty church with ash on all the statues of his saints and his crucifix.'

'It's like face powder, the ash, you know,' Eva wasn't really listening any more, she just picked up the word. 'Only it's dead grey-white, the colour for Morticia Addams.'

I had to push myself through the next four months of the Cura's isolation. Week after week he recorded new craters, new flows, more destruction, mountains building themselves up and then collapsing in with the noise of a thousand thunderbolts. To read, it's dull. To experience – well, I too wondered how he lived in a hallucination and stayed sane. This section of the journals never mentions any other living thing. Perhaps the discipline of recording each day's apocalypse held his mind together.

20 July. A messenger has come from Ubrique. They had seen no more clouds there for a month. He is surprised to find me still alive. Fr Domingo, having had no news from the new bishop in Las Palmas, asked me, supposing I had survived, to give a full account of the continuing catastrophe for the parochial council. The messenger brought two mules with him to carry me and my belongings. I have decided to travel to Ubrique to tell Fr Domingo of the marvels which I have seen this year.

CHAPTER 13

Last Exit

I came into the restaurant near the airport and saw Matthew and Stella together in the far corner. Matthew looked up and saw me, and said something to Stella, who turned around and called, '*Hi*, Babes.' The gloss came off my new trust when I saw the set of his shoulders and heard the tone of her voice.

I went through the motions. I never know what else to do. While my mind is writhing, I just walk on and try to act natural. So I ignored the furtive rearrangement of limbs that went on under the table. I kissed them both and to Matthew I said, 'I thought you were at school today? Couldn't take the time out.'

He turned a transparent face to me and said, 'I can't stay long. But I wanted to say goodbye to Terry.' Did he look at me for too long? I thought so.

Saying goodbye to Terry was the business of the

day. Surprisingly, The Meathead had released his passport and so we gathered again, as on many happier Thursdays, with a departure as the excuse for a lunch. The form was to meet at a restaurant near the airport, buy the departer his or her favourite meal with excessive wine and generous slugs of brandy, then drive to the airport with five minutes' grace before check-in, breezing past the queues of tourists who were already weary and unaware – because for some reason the monitors on land side of the departure building don't show the delays – that they were in for hours of waiting on the air side.

'So – here we are again.' Terry took the seat opposite me. I thought of him arriving in London that evening, standing swaying among the pale-faced, dark-clothed commuters on the train to his suburban home, with his salt-bleached clothes, his walnut hide and his sea-blue eyes trained to focus on a far horizon.

'I hate flying,' he was saying. 'Unnatural. Like being in a bloody sardine can.'

'You couldn't have sailed back in less than a week, even if they had released your boat. Have a drink, sweetheart.' Stella filled his glass and called the waiter for another bottle. 'Then you won't feel a thing. Happy landings.' She raised her glass and they clinked. We all clinked with Terry.

'You should try the tetrahedron meditation,' Carole urged him. 'Completely cleans out any fear.

Connects you with the energy of the universe. Based on that drawing by that artist? Wossisname? The one with the man and the arms and legs and things?'

'Leonardo da Vinci,' said Matthew. He smiled like the shark, with pearly teeth.

'That's him. What you do,' she came to sit by Terry to get her message through, 'you visualise this great golden shape, right, tetrahedron, five sides, like this . . .' She sketched in the air around his head. Terry leaned patiently on an elbow. 'No, no, you sit up, spine vertical, feet on the ground, so the energy can flow through you . . .' She took his hands and rearranged him like an Egyptian pharaoh, hands on knees.

'How am I supposed to keep my feet on the ground in a plane?' he argued.

'Doesn't matter. You visualise this great golden tetrahedron and then you put your fears into it, whatever you're afraid of you put it in there, in the middle, and then you visualise the golden light all around it and the tetrahedron floating away, up, up, away, like a balloon . . .' She waved her arms, causing our waiter to dodge before she hit him. 'All your fears, floating away, and then you ask for peace and you see it like a silver thread, a thick silver thread . . .'

'Coming up my arse. I know. Thanks Carole, I'll give it a try.' Terry returned to his wine. 'No, I will, I promise.' Leaving makes people mellow.

'Darling, we will all be thinking of you.' Maryse wafted in, followed by Islewyn, who gave him a white paper pharmacist's bag and said, 'These may help with – ah – things at home. Goldenseal, fever-few, hypericum. And I made up a homoeopathic formula, based on what you told me. Ease her symptoms, anyway. Lift her mood a little. Don't worry about declaring them, they aren't prescription. And there's something in there for you, for the flight. Ginger and vetiver. Acts on the motion centre of the brain, calming effect. Better than booze, anyway.' And he frowned at the glass in Terry's hand.

'You know, I've got a good feeling about this,' Carole was back in her own seat, eyes bright. 'I know it's sad and everything, but at least you got your passport back, Terry. It's positive, I can feel the energy moving. Things have been blocked, haven't they? Since the accident. But it's happening now, things are rolling again.'

'Freedom,' Isleywn intoned. 'That's what it is. We're not people who like to feel shut in, are we?'

I watched Matthew. Matthew watched Stella. Stella was watching Terry, and Terry watched the long, low waves running in and out all along the beach at Las Pocholas. We were in another of those self-effacing places, this time tucked into the end of a cul-de-sac between the apartment buildings which ended at the shore.

'Come back to us,' Maryse gurgled to him. 'Terry! Are you hearing me?'

'I'm hearing you,' he confirmed, but he did not turn to face the group. Today Terry looked uncomfortable in his skin.

'You got a lot on your mind, darling, we know.' Maryse was picking through the olives for the little green ones she liked.

'Leave him alone,' put in Stella.

'You want to know what's on my mind?' Terry challenged her.

'If you want to tell us, darling.'

'It's no big deal. I'm thinking the guys who put the playa in Angeles must be bloody proud of themselves, because none of it ever ends up here. Not like Costa Ubrique, where the whole bloody beach washes up five miles north every winter. That's what I'm thinking, if you want to know.'

He was talking about the golden sands of Playa de los Angeles which had been imported from Morocco to top-dress the natural but unsatisfactory beach when the resort was first built. At the same time the place's original name, Tiñosa, which means fleabitten, was erased and it was rechristened with the most glamorous title the tourist board could invent. The fake beach stays where it was put, now within the protective embrace of a promenade with municipal hibiscus plantings, which twinkles with fake Victorian lanterns for night-time strollers. This successful sand is studded with umbrellas and sun loungers. It is raked clean of flotsam at dawn every day, of cigarette butts and Fanta cans instead of seaweed and driftwood. The colour has faded with passing time. Already it looks natural compared to the fake beach at the Costa Ubrique, which is a raw yellow close to the colour of builder's sand. Every year, when the currents change in the autumn, this beach washes away and clogs the redundant but picturesque little fishing harbours along the coast. Every year, new sand is imported and dumped on the Costa Ubrique.

At Los Angeles the natural beach was probably like the one at Las Pocholas, wet, pewter-coloured, muddy here and there, patches of flat rock, strips of grey shingle, not nearly opulent enough for international luxury tourism. Being close to the airport, Las Pocholas never appealed to international development consortia and so it keeps its natural beach.

'You're so practical,' Stella marvelled at Terry. 'I'd be shipwrecked with you on a desert island any day. I mean it.'

'Do you?' Terry looked at her very directly. Then he picked out an olive, stabbed it with a toothpick and twirled it before he said, 'Do you really?'

'Just try me, sweetheart. The Bible and Shakespeare and a nice practical man. What more could a girl ask for?'

'Plenty,' rasped Maryse.

'You could say that we were on a desert island already,' proposed Islewyn. 'Could hardly be more like the desert, could it?'

Terry chomped his olive and palmed the pit discreetly. 'That's what I can't get on with. Too bare. Too many rocks. Barbados, now, they've got flowers the size of soup plates and avocados as big as footballs all growing wild in the jungle and hanging down over the sea. That's what I want.'

'You'll get there,' Stella promised him. Matthew didn't say much and at three, when we had only just started eating, he left. He has been more and more silent these last few days.

* * *

22 October. Fr Domingo celebrated the nuptial Mass at our Cathedral for the marriage of Señor Alfonso José, son of Don Jaimé Ducque Munoz our governor, to Dona Maria Caterina, daughter of Don Andres Joaquin Achimence Jablillo, Regional Governor of Yaiza. There was some rain today, which is considered a good omen by the islanders. Dona Maria appeared in a new gown of Chinese silk. On this day there was complete accord between all the people in Ubrique, who seem no longer ruled by fear and truly believe that their troubles are over. Fr Domingo spoke to me of his plans for a further service of thanksgiving for our deliverance.

25 October. On this day the eruptions resumed and it seems that there will now be no end to the suffering of the people. Imagine our despair, Excellency, when three new cones appeared at the same time around Tarfaya, larger than any of the mountains which had yet risen up, thrusting through the lava already solidified and pouring rivers of new rock over it.

This was accompanied by the most violent tremors to be experienced in the whole period of the eruptions. Even in Ubrique itself the shaking of the earth was enough to dislodge roof tiles. Hellish noises again resound over the whole island and the people have fallen into a new depth of terror.

From the city wall we saw the three cones quickly merge into one, and lava again running from a single mouth down to the sea. This eruption covered everything which had previously appeared.

After this, yet another new cone rose up, at about the place where Almonte had been buried. A crater opened on the side of this cone and threw out more ash and lightning. From yet another new peak at Rota came a cloud of white gas, which was a phenomenon not seen before.

A special meeting of the junta convened at once and it was resolved that as many people as possible should be taken to other islands without delay. It was also decided that Señor Alfonso and his new bride should sail immediately to Las Palmas to

*impress on the authorities the danger of the
situation, taking with them money to induce ships
to come to the aid of the people here, as there are
now not enough boats remaining on the island to
carry the whole population.*

*The governor also did me the honour of insisting
that Señor Alfonso should take with him the
original text of this journal, and for this purpose,
to be able to continue writing and keep a complete
record of the events, I have made a copy of
everything I had written up to this date, which was
parcelled together with a letter from Fr Domingo to
the new Bishop.*

'Bless him,' I said to Eva. 'He's so picky. Now I
know why this reads the way it does: he copied it all
out for the Bishop.'

'*He's* so picky,' Eva protested. 'You're so picky,
always worrying if you've got the real thing. What
does it matter?'

'For the sake of science . . .' I began.

'Science. Look, Kim, don't worry about it. Milo
wants us to try from condensate gas samples for
tomorrow. Can you give me this afternoon? All this
stuff was two hundred and fifty years ago. For the
sake of science now what really matters is that we
get the money to extend the sea-bed programme.'

'Condensate samples?'

'You cool the steam. I'll show you. There's enough

water vapour coming out to do it. That's a big deal, you know, steam. Steam is what really drives the lava up. If we can find enough steam in the gas samples . . .'

I considered the way she had said 'we'. 'Are you having an affair with Milo?' I asked her. I wanted to know, and I wanted practice with the question. Call me too English, but it seemed like a big thing to ask.

'Maybe,' Eva tossed her head. She was pleased about something. 'Maybe love is in the air.' She inclined her head towards Mark and Suzanne. 'At least I don't have to worry about who'll get our rock samples now. They came over and volunteered this morning. All they want is permission for her to test for her silicon-based life forms as well. So, why not?'

'As long as we don't have to do it.' I agreed. I saw for the first time that Suzanne had moved her desk round so she and Mark were working side by side. A big change; it should have struck me as soon as I came into the room. That day I started forgetting things as well. Stupid things I really knew, like the phone number for the Residencias. Something was stirring under my mind's surface, building up the pressure to break through.

At the end of the afternoon I got an e-mail from the Archivo Parroquial. The search for additional documents had been successful. They had discovered what appeared to be the original journal of the

Cura Rosario, and other files that would be of interest to me. I mailed them back to ask how much there was.

* * *

A fax had come in for Matthew. It was from his agent. It was short and sarcastic, and suggested that they had already talked about the subject at length. She wanted to know what she should tell someone who had called about a date in two weeks' time.

I left it on the machine and went into the bedroom. As usual, there were plenty of clothes on the chair and the floor and the cupboard doors, some begging to be washed while others could get by with being put away. I can't get my head straight about Matthew's dirty clothes; in principle, they should be washed. They look better clean. But I like the smell of him on them. I could sleep with one of his T-shirts if I had to sleep without him.

Somewhere I read of a couple who fell in love and locked themselves into a hotel room together for two months to find out everything they needed to know about each other. That's pretty much the route that Matthew and I chose when we decided to try living here. We went for the big break, we didn't even go back home to rearrange our lives. It was a good game, doing everything long-distance by technology.

He rented his flat by fax and placated his agent by phone. We left behind the tax offices and lawyers, who were still dawdling through the official formalities of my freedom. Out here we furnished our new life together. We bought new clothes when we needed them. We took over the Suzuki from a friend of the Dagenhams and Matthew's Seat from a dealer Sam knew. We asked friends to pack up the things we decided we needed and until the crate arrived at the docks in Villanueva, we had only the landlord's furniture in the apartment. We spent whole days in bed; we were euphoric. All the same, my tragedy was standing over our life like the mountain outside our apartment.

The cat was on the terrace, daring to drink from a saucer. Milk. Very quietly, in order not to scare it, I backed out of the bedroom and went into the kitchen. The carton was in the fridge. Matthew had bought milk for the cat.

I heard his car and went out to meet him. 'You're here,' he said, then felt stupid.

'I know, I'm never here. Don't make a noise. The cat's drinking your milk.'

'I couldn't hold out any longer. It was always out there looking at me.'

'Your agent's faxed you again.'

He went and read the page, running his hand through his hair. He was thinner: in the last weeks he had lost so much weight I could see his ribs through his T-shirt when he lifted his arm. His shoulders were not as brave as they had been, and I noticed lines at the edges of his eyes. Did he drag Tom out to his car and send him down the hillside to his death? I was ashamed of myself for having the thought.

We had some wine. I found it, opened a bottle and gave him a glass. 'What's this?' he asked.

'Glass of wine, what does it look like? It means, can we stay in tonight?'

'Stella . . .'

'I don't want to see Stella. Someone else can be on Stella duty.'

'Fair enough.' He drifted into the bedroom, then drifted back with that wary face all men put on when they think a woman is plotting something. 'Cat's still out there,' he told me.

'If we feed it, it'll try to move in.'

Luxuriously, he sprawled across a corner of the sofa. 'You want it to try to move in,' I suggested.

'It's cute. It's got a silly face. I like it. And it's trying hard, it's been out there a month.'

'You identify with it,' I teased him.

'I do. That cat deserves a break.' This came over in a general sense; he wasn't asking me for anything. All the same, I wanted to give.

'What's your agent on about?'

He let out a breath so deep it was nearly a groan

and let his arm fall over his face. 'Usual crap. She made a pile out of me, she wants her golden goose back.'

'No, I'm not buying that. What's it all about?'

'Look, there's no point. It's a film, right? I've got no passport so I'm not going anywhere. I've told her. Fuck-all I can do. She doesn't understand.'

'You could ask. They gave Terry his passport.'

'Dying wife. Haven't got one of those.'

His voice was soft, because he didn't like what he was talking about, and bitter. So bitter that he didn't want me to see his face, he still had his arm over his eyes, the back of his hand to his face. I decided to ask for access. I said, 'I'm sorry.'

'Nothing to do with you.'

'Except without me you wouldn't be here.'

'The mess I'm in isn't your fault.'

His world – his real world, not this interlude with me – was strange to me. I wasn't sure of the right way to ask. It seemed amateurish but all I could say was, 'What film is it?'

'Just a film.'

'Come on, don't do this. Tell me what's happening.'

'It's good, it's a big part, I'm the first choice, I've worked with the director before . . . OK?'

'So, you want it. You must want it, Matthew. It's what you've wanted for years.'

'Yeah, well. Timing's everything, isn't it?'

'I'd be OK, you know. If you got your passport. I don't want you to think I'll go to pieces if you have to be away for a while.' Was I saying that because I believed it, or because I wanted to get him away from Stella? I was sick of having those thoughts, angry at my weak faith and the damage it had done him. This wasn't the same man who led me into my own life. He had taking a beating here and it wasn't deserved.

'Leave it alone, Kim. They won't give me my passport.'

'Have you asked?'

'What's the point?'

'You don't ask, you don't get.' I remembered him asking for me, the bravest thing I'd ever seen, in Conal's vulgar car in the rain. He was losing his magic, as Stella had lost hers. I could make him angry if I pushed him now. It was worth the risk. 'Ask them,' I insisted. 'Ask for your passport. For me. If you don't get it, you won't be worse off.'

He took his arm away from his face and looked at me. 'Dominating bitch,' he suggested, softly amused.

'So, obey me. Stop lying around whining and get moving. You'll need a proper letter from your agent, make her send it first thing.'

'Yes, miss.'

'Mistress to you.'

I took a shower while he wrote out a reply to her,

his big splashy writing covering a page in three sentences, and sent it over. When I came back, the air was crackling. I pushed him down on the sofa and started ripping off his clothes. This is another thing I need to practise, but between us we got the job done.

The sofa wasn't wide enough, the floor was too cold and standing up doesn't work for us because he's too tall. So we ended up in bed again.

When he was asleep, I saw the cat sitting in its Egyptian pose close to the glass door. I had never kept a cat. To me, a cat meant a home, and a home meant something permanent, and this apartment was not permanent – our lease would end in a few weeks. On the other hand, while I was lying beside my lover, it seemed that we had something to offer the animal. Matthew must have thought so – he had bought the milk. I got up and went to open the door. Quite possibly the cat had wheedled its way into people's homes before. It squeaked some basic thanks and slithered inside. In the morning, it was asleep on Matthew's shirt on the sofa.

CHAPTER 14

Key in the Door

I got off the bus at Green Lanes and walked home through the yellow haze of the street lights. It was the usual time, just coming up to six. It was the day after I told Conal I wanted to leave him. Spring was just detectable, a quickening in the dank air. Or maybe it was spring for me and I imagined the rest.

The lights were on. Lights from any house shining into the street always give the illusion of beaming out warmth and love from within. No more illusions now. We were going to a new home, one where there was real warmth for me, and for Liam.

My key was in my hand. I'd got it ready while I was still on the bus. My bag of books was heavy; I let go if it while I put the key in the lock. The noise of the latch was large, and that was really when I knew, but I mistrusted the knowledge and went in as I always did.

The house was silent. Breathing easily in solitude, I went to the kitchen and poured myself some juice from the fridge. As I drank, I saw Liam's trainers under the kitchen table, and a half-eaten piece of pizza on the table top. He was always hungry when he came in from college, so hungry that he'd grab the first food he saw and sit down to eat it without plate or knife. He would also kick off his trainers while he was eating and forget them. Then he would change his clothes and go out to find his friends. I let him do whatever made him happy. He was my debt which would never be paid, and after all, I knew how it felt to need freedom.

I threw the gnawed pizza crust in the bin, picked up the shoes and started up the stairs with them. On the landing there was a whisper of something sweet in the air. As I don't smoke, my sense of smell is sharp.

The door of his room was ajar. There was resistance as I pushed it open, presumably clothes he had thrown on the floor. At first I thought he had crashed out on the bed, and I thought he had opened jam or ketchup carelessly and splashed it up the walls, even over his football posters. He was lying on his back on the bed with the quilt over his head. Another opened beer can was the source of the smell lingering above the blanket aroma of unwashed boy and furtive cigarettes.

I went forward to wake him. There was a second body behind the door; its limp arm, outstretched, had been what had made the door difficult to open. So next I assumed that my son had been sitting around with a friend, drinking beer and messing the place up. I was annoyed and I kicked at his unprotected foot. The ankle moved too freely.

The stains spread over most of the low ceiling, splattering the underside of the sloping roof. The second body was very large. I recognised Conal. He was lying with his face pressed sideways into the floor, and under the mess of Liam's stuff on the carpet I saw the blood which had spread from his cheek. There were more stains on his collar and all over the front of his chest. Looking closer, his face had settled unnaturally into the carpet, not resting on its cheek but nestled into the surface. The reason for this proved later to be that half Conal's face had been blown away.

Then I understood that the stuff splattered on the ceiling was blood. I pulled back Liam's quilt and the cover stuck to his shirt. His face was unmarked and his eyes were closed. I touched his neck. The skin was cool. He wasn't there any more.

Conal was dead and Liam was dead. For a time I stood in the centre of the room, looking around me, trying to get the fact into my head. Like my pregnancy, it was something too big to fit into my mind. I tried out explanations. Someone had shot them.

Each had killed himself. One of them had killed both. My reasoning was like a rusted lock: it would not turn.

There was a cause. The gun was over in the far corner of the room, lying innocently like another discarded toy beside the golf clubs and shin pads. One of Conal's prized pair, one of those the bailiffs had missed. Later, it was agreed that the gun was thrown there by a spasm of Conal's arm as he shot himself. He had used one of the golf clubs to lever the trigger. The coroner also proposed that Conal had fired his first barrel at Liam while they were both standing, causing the blood stains on the ceiling, and then picked up Liam's body and arranged it on his bed with the quilt over the head.

When I was teaching I used to feel bad sometimes because I sat there with my children, purporting to open their minds to an understanding of their world and claiming to be preparing them for their adult lives, when I knew that all I could teach them was irrelevant. We can't understand the world. Nothing prepares you for life; there is no way of making ready for this journey, nothing you can take in case you need it.

Downstairs in the house I had to stop moving for a while. Like a child in a fairy tale, I was rooted to the spot, turned to stone in the middle of the kitchen. All my mind was trying to understand and there was no capacity left in it to make me do anything.

Feelings I could have had were just hazy shapes in my peripheral vision; I could make out loss, regret, remorse and guilt, but relief was hovering with them. I was frightened to even acknowledge relief.

The telephone rang. At first it seemed so far off I thought I was hearing the phone in the house next door. Then I understood that it was my telephone, and I found the strength to pick up the handset.

'Is this a good time?' It was Matthew, his voice charged with longing, reciting from the vocabulary of forbidden love, a language we weren't going to need again.

I said. 'Yes and no.'

'What's happened?'

'Is this really you?' Since my faculty of believing things was so stretched, nothing seemed possible at all, especially not things I would have hoped for if I had been able to find any hope at that moment.

'Yes, it's really me,' he confirmed. 'What's happened, Kim? You're different. Where are you? Is anyone with you?'

'There's no one else here.' I lost control of my voice as I said it. I was afraid I was going to lose control of everything, wet my knickers, throw up or pass out. There was a chair near enough for me to get to while my legs were still working.

'Kim? Are you sitting down? Can you tell me what's happened?'

He coaxed the words out of me. He called the

police for me. He made me give him telephone numbers, repeating what he wanted over and over again until my control came back and I could get my organiser out of my bag and make it work. He called the couple who lived next door, who were ringing our bell within a minute. He made me tell him Stella's number and called her. He called my parents. He told me to stay in the house with my neighbours, that the police were on their way, and that he was coming to get me.

When Stella called from the island we had one of those lines with an echo, about as intimate as semaphore. First, she said, 'Babes, why didn't you tell me?'

'I don't know.' Panic was hovering now. I had betrayed her, my truest, strongest, only friend. 'He killed Liam,' I tried to make her understand. 'He thought he was God, he could give and take away. He had no right.'

'He was mad.' she answered. 'Mad. I was always scared for you with him. Babes, I've got to see you. I want to be with you.'

'Matthew will be here soon.'

'Is that the man who rang me? Who is he?'

'He's . . .'

'Were you having an affair, Babes? He sounds material.'

'Material. Yes, he is that. You could say we were having an affair.'

'Good. OK, I get it now. Be strong, Baby. I know you are. You'll be OK. Get away from it. Come out here. At least you're free now.'

Hours later, when I was still in the kitchen and there were police all over the house, Matthew arrived. He took me away and I never went back. When the time came, he went to get Liam's things for me, packed them all in boxes with enormous care and brought them to me. They are stored at his old place. I have never been able to open the boxes. And of course I am not free and never will be.

CHAPTER 15

Vital Signs

Dark, soft clouds had gathered and the sun was about to sink behind them. Over the height of the heavens, puffs of cirrus swirled around to the west. It looked as if the clouds were being drawn across the sky by the sinking sun. I can't come up with an explanation for this effect.

When I was teaching I used to draw pictures of the solar system and show the children that sunset happened because the earth turned, not because the sun moved. At the moment, winds in the stratosphere are blowing the clouds westwards at the same time as the sun appears to us to be sinking. There's no reason for this, it's just an accident.

The sky above the horizon was radiant and almost colourless. Below the cirrus some veils of smoky vapour were forming, the forerunners of darkness. There was a boat in the mouth of the bay, a yacht. I was tired of naming clouds. It seemed better just to look at them.

Another guest had taken a table, a lean, tall man with round tortoiseshell-framed spectacles. He looked about thirty. I liked his expression: something surprised in the eyes and his lips were thin but naturally set in a half-smile. He had a book, but it was unopened on the table by his glass of Tres Reyes.

We had chosen the same drink, we had that in common. Matthew and I both drink black coffee; I could have argued that I had as much connection to him as I did to the man with the book. Maybe I was closer to the man with the book. We had both found our way here. That argued some kind of fellowship: we believe that the same things are important. Perhaps if that man had been on the bus in England that evening, I would have waited at Placido's for him. Chance is scripting my life and art-directing the sunset.

Last night I dreamed that a new volcano appeared in the north, near Aranda. Instead of spewing out lava, this new mountain pushed up under the whole island and tilted it like a tray. The houses, little white cubes, tumbled over each other as they spilled down the inclined landscape. Palm trees were uprooted. In Angeles the apartment blocks cracked into pieces and tipped over onto the beach.

This dream wasn't frightening. I found I was enjoying it. There I was, driving to the Instituto to check the instruments, hurtling down a road that was getting steeper and steeper, and all around me other cars rolled over and over like marbles. It felt exhilarating, like a roller-coaster ride. Liam was with me, at about eight years old; he was screaming with joy and hanging on to my arm. His eyes were enormous and his hair had been blown flat to his head. Our car, for some reason, began to slide, skidding down the precipitous tarmac at ever greater speed until it left the road and plunged over the first peak of the La Mora range and fell free into space, where it swooped away into the stars under its own power.

Milo came the day after Eva told him about the seismograph reading. She stood over him with one hand on her hip and demanded: 'So what's going on?' as if five kilometres down in the guts of the earth a thousand tons of molten rock were fooling around like a crowd of naughty children.

'Activity,' he said, switching from one screen to another.

'Yes,' Eva prompted him. 'So? What? Is that all?' She was flirting with him and he was talking around her to the rest of the team and trying to ignore her. Everyone was switched on this morning, hyped with the excitement of a real event after working with theory for most of our lives. I was probably the calmest, but I still felt as if my pulse were running higher.

'Is the door shut?' Milo asked Eva. There was a pause. Nobody wanted to miss out on anything for the sake of security. In the end, I went over to close the outer door and lock it.

Milo was standing by Eva's terminal, one of his heavy hands moving the mouse. Everyone at the Instituto had gathered around her desk. There were a few strangers too. I recognised the mayor of Yesto, an inconspicuous man of about thirty-five, in his usual checked shirt and black jeans. His shoes were worn and dusty, half-sandal things which made him shuffle slightly as he walked. He came in with two other men, a little older, and Milo did a lot of manly handclasping, as if he were delighted to see them.

'Yes,' he said, 'that's all. There is activity down there, it's registered. It's very typical, a trace like this, a pulse effect. Cyclical, repetitive disturbance.'

'What does it mean, then? What's causing it?' Maybe Eva was being provocative to help lighten the atmosphere. Nobody was smiling at this point.

'It probably doesn't mean anything. We can't say with a tremor as mild as this what's causing it. It's within the normal seismicity of a volcano. If it were stronger, we could say we should expect a series of tectonic earthquakes. Just little shakes.' He sounded like the dentist with his hypodermic, promising, 'Just a little pin-prick . . .'

'Then what?' Dima was standing where Eva could

not avoid seeing him, again mouthing 'Boom!' and
rolling his eyes.

'No one can say. It's true that eruptions are typically preceded by activity like this, but it's just as
typical for seismic incidents to stop before the eruptive phase and for nothing to happen at all. For
hundreds, maybe thousands, millions of years. This
may have happened before. We've only been monitoring this site for a few months; we are still in the
process of finding out what's typical here.'

The mayor was frowning. Dima stopped fooling
and decided to impress the audience. 'Do you think
the activity we're seeing is magmatic or phreatic?'
His wet lips spluttered over the words.

'He's asking if the movement that's registering is
caused by magma or by steam and gas,' Milo
enlarged, grateful for the cue. 'And again, it's
impossible to say. What we're seeing is evidence of
movement deep in the earth, several kilometres
down. Steam, of course, makes itself evident as it
gets close to the surface by escaping through small
weaknesses in the crust. We can see here that the
gas samples are not indicating a rise in water
vapour. That would be some indication of magma
rising near the surface, because it is actually superheated water vapour that agitates the molten rock.
But there is, actually, no way to tell if magma is
involved in an eruption until a short time before
you see it.'

'What do you mean?' This was from one of the men who had come in with the mayor. The three in that party were starting to jostle. They had the look of Western bad guys squaring up for a gunfight.

Milo came back quickly. 'This data doesn't suggest an eruptive episode soon. Or at all, actually. Typically, if there is to be a crisis, activity builds to a much higher level than this for several months at least. Nothing is going to happen in the near future, I can promise that. We will know if the situation develops.'

'Typically? Is that a word you can really use?' the mayor was asking. Yesto might appear to be less than a one-horse town, but its region includes both national parks, the beaches at Punto Grande and the resort and ferry port at Puerto de la Frontera, making it the second most important region on the island. The local politicos may dress like truck drivers, but they're no fools.

'Vulcanism is a new science,' said Milo splendidly. 'Eruptions are rare; we have only been studying them for thirty years or so. We are only just developing equipment to tell us what goes on in the inside of the earth. That's why the Alcazares site, and the eye-witness account which is part of your heritage, is so important. Our understanding of "typical" is limited at this point.'

'What are you seeing over in Tenerife? I heard there was activity registering there.' This was from

Mark. The mayor shifted in his sloppy shoes, folding his arms.

'Yes. We've been getting evidence of quite big gas movements below Teide and doing some work computer modelling the developments.'

The mayor frowned and said nothing. His silence prompted Milo to expand. 'The increased activity we're seeing here may be a local phenomenon but my opinion is that it is part of a global picture. Volcanoes are waking up all over the world.' This was the cue for the mayor and his supporters to step away from the main group and for Milo to sign off with us and join them. They went into the only place they could talk in private, the geothermal team's office, which left Dima drifting about to annoy us while his colleagues decided to make for the bar.

'Cost, that's what this is about,' Mark said, sitting on the edge of Eva's desk while Suzanne drifted towards him. 'Carrying the science forward means money. Unless there's a risk you can demonstrate, nobody sees the need.'

'I didn't know Teide was active,' I said to Eva.

'It isn't,' she told me, still with that cat's-got-the-cream look. 'It's dormant, just like all the craters in Tarfaya.'

'Why do they bother calling these things dormant?'

'It's not a scientific word,' she shrugged.

'It means they don't know.' Dima had taken Eva's swivel chair and was twisting to and fro. 'It means, who can say? You know what they can do in Japan? With underground seismographs and the most sensitive monitors ever invented? You know how deep they can hear what's going on in the earth?'

'Get off my chair,' Eva ordered him. 'It'll stink of you all day, *cuño*.'

Dima wasn't obeying this morning. 'Two kilometres.' He held up two fingers. 'Two kilometres, max. Where the crust is ten kilometres thick. Not so good.'

'What do you know? Have you been to Japan?'

'I go to international conferences, I've heard them give their papers. They can tell when a volcano is going to blow, yes they can. The last one, they could give a warning so people could get away. Guess how long?'

'Get off my chair, Dima. I won't tell you again.'

'Twenty minutes. *Twenty minutes* before the explosion. That's the best we've got.' He got up, pretended to dust the chair seat and waved Eva towards it with a courtly bow. 'Your chair, *madame*. I don't know for how much longer, but you'll be OK here for another twenty minutes.'

* * *

Only two or three pages of the Cura's journal remained. The job had been sticking to my fingers for weeks; I didn't want to finish. When I finished, my purpose at the Instituto would also end. Milo had agreed to let me go to Las Palmas, which might spin things out a while longer. Anything to stay. I discovered that I liked my life.

The last pages were the most tragic, another reason they stuck to my fingers. It was too sad to read for long.

30 October. On this day Don Guillermo Zurdo de Tortosa, the special emissary of His Highness King Philip V, arrived in Ubrique. He has travelled overland from Villanueva.

The lava had continued to flow for twelve days, the violent explosions causing tidal waves. No vessels now dared enter or leave the port of San Juan.

When the captain of the ship bringing Don Guillermo and his party to us saw the wall of smoke and steam rising a thousand leagues high from the coast in the area of Jimena, and having been further terrified by the great waves which had threatened to overturn the ship, he had decided to sail around the island and navigate the southern reefs to make landfall near Villanueva. From there the party had found a way through the smoking hills to Ubrique.

Don Guillermo de Tortosa brought the new decree from our government, which was received by our leaders in Ubrique and the remaining people in

*the town as the worst possible news. The order
forbids the inhabitants of the island to leave on
pain of death. It also announced that those who
had already arrived at Las Palmas would be sent
back as soon as a ship could be found to take them.*

*Don Guillermo, having seen what danger we
face, has advised that a special mission should be
sent to Las Palmas as soon as possible. He himself
will return to describe to the regional government
the catastrophe which threatens this island.*

*Don Andreas and Don Jaimé, fearing that if
either one of them leaves the island fresh disorder
will break out among their people, have resolved
that their children, Don Alfonso and Dona
Maria, the very flower of our people, shall go with
him to plead for the order to be revoked. In this way
they hope to secure the lives of their children.*

*2 November. When the eruptions had subsided
somewhat and the sea was calm, the biggest ship
remaining in San Juan was made ready as fast as
possible. Fr Domingo, seeing that Dona Maria was
now in extreme fear of the voyage, reminded her of
the divine protection implied by her vision of St
Catherine. In spite of his arguments, advanced
forcefully with all of his great authority and
learning, the young woman seemed half dead with
terror.*

*The only ship of any size remaining was an old
two-masted trader. At Fr Domingo's order a red sail*

was rigged as Dona Maria had seen in her vision, so that she might take heart. A vigil was held at the cathedral to pray for the safety and success of the voyage. Fr Domingo said a special Mass, choosing the gospel reading from St Matthew and giving an address which affirmed Our Lord's promise that a mountain could be moved by a speck of faith as small as a mustard seed. Don Alfonso and Dona Maria embarked at midday, accompanied by Don Guillermo and his followers who, it seemed to me, were anxious to escape as fast as possible.

Then occurred the most terrible and most cruel event in the many catastrophes which we have endured on Los Alcazares. I myself was among the crowd of people who watched from the town walls as the ship gained the open sea.

We saw first a great mass of steam rise from the surface of the sea. The ship immediately changed course away from these emissions, but from the waves directly in its path, there then rose up a huge pillar of fire, accompanied by the most violent explosions, which threw fountains of water many hundreds of metres into the air.

The ship was instantly hurled towards the sky and was seen to break in two parts across the keel, spilling people into the ocean like beans from a pod. The timbers themselves burst into flames in mid-air from the incredible heat of the fiery pillar and the burning fragments were extinguished in the water.

A silence fell upon the people as they witnessed this disaster. Don Jaimé and Don Andres, who were standing side by side when their children were lost, could say nothing and were as if turned to stone. It seemed that even the dogs in the streets were stilled and the only noise to be heard was the terrible roaring of the flames which continued to burn several hours into the night.

3 November. *On this morning were washed ashore some pitiful remains of the lost ship and it was reported that these were nothing but scorched pieces of timber, none more than a foot in length, indicating the terrible force by which the ship had been destroyed.*

Despair has taken hold of the population, seeing that all hope is lost and no supplies will reach us. Fr Domingo has withdrawn to the smallest room in his house, appearing as stricken with grief as the two fathers who mourn the loss of their children. It is true that he had valued Dona Maria exceptionally among women because of her visionary powers.

4 November. *On this morning I was woken before dawn by the sounds of Fr Domingo leaving the house. Being concerned, I got up and followed him as he left the town and took the road which led towards San Juan. He carried a lantern and appeared to be praying as he walked.*

Before the road descends to the port it is joined by

*a path which leads to the caves in the high cliffs.
Fr Domingo took this path and passed the caves,
where some of our people from Yesto were sleeping.
At a point just beyond them where the path ends, he
halted. He was praying but still standing, with
his back to the cliff, because the path is extremely
narrow there. This path is so high that the noise of
the sea can hardly be heard from it.*

*Fr Domingo was not aware that I had followed
him and, believing that his intention was to pray
for those lost with the ship, I did not call out to
him. After some time, when there was enough light
for me to see clearly what took place, he put out his
lantern and leaned sideways to rest it on a ledge.*

*He then stood up straight and extended his arms
in the pose of Christ crucified. Fr Domingo then
fell forward to his death on the rocky shore below.
All this took place without warning and in an
instant, giving me no opportunity to call out to him
or to intervene.*

*I regret, Excellency, that it is not possible for me
to say whether Fr Domingo fell from the path
deliberately or not. He did not appear to me to lose
his footing but the place from which he fell is
narrow and the strong wind prevailing on the
north coast could easily take a man off balance.*

*Some of my people recovered his body from the sea
a few hours later. It is horribly broken by the rocks
but otherwise of normal appearance.*

5 November. Being then the only priest in Ubrique, I said a burial Mass for Fr Domingo and gave instructions for him to be interred in the crypt below the cathedral. The junta then convened and agreed that I should be sent to Las Palmas to put the case for relief. This is done in the belief that the government will not execute a priest. Furthermore, I had witnessed and recorded all the events to that date and can give a good and full account of the ever-renewing disasters which afflict us.

With Don Guillermo's captain and two of the fishermen from my region who came forward as volunteers, we will take the largest boat left at San Juan and sail east. If it is the will of Our Lord, we shall escape further catastrophe and reach Las Palmas to make a final appeal to the mercy of our government. I therefore conclude this, my only journal, and if this account is ever read again, it will give evidence that I have served the will of God, who has so far preserved me in the midst of all the infernal disasters with which He has been pleased to reveal his glory and omnipotence.

To which I, Don Jaimé Ducque Munoz, Governor of Los Alcazares, set my seal this 5th day of November 1794.

(The gubernatorial seal appeared here)

* * *

With Terry gone the island seemed a little vacant. People went on with their lives. The Bankses' son flew back to England, but his sister was still conspicuous, tripping in and out of her hotel. Islewyn, who saw much from his clinic on the strip, reported that the man from the CID had got into the habit of having lunch every day in the Wok-Wok-Wok. The sun reddened his arms, his left more than the right because he drove around in his little rented Seat with the window open and his elbow on the sill.

One day there was a woman with him, a black-haired, grey-suited, white-faced British woman of about my age who carried one of those boxy leather bags lawyers use for documents.

'Fuckbitch loss adjuster,' Stella observed witheringly. 'Isn't it great? She's going to want to prove Tom topped himself so she doesn't have to pay out. The CID wants to prove I killed him, so he can get a result. If either one of them wins, I lose. Brilliant, don't you think?'

The loss adjuster called us all the next morning, a truculent voice on the telephone. She drove out to the Instituto to interview me, stomping into the building like an angry pig on her short legs. She snapped her business card down on my desk and tried the girls-together, common-pool-of-oestrogen approach.

'All these rumours about your partner and Mrs Banks don't surprise me,' she confided. 'OK, so I come from a very boring world, insurance, but to me he seems . . . exotic, really.'

'Does he?' I tried not to react. Then I decided to correct her. Matthew had asked for his passport and was waiting for the answer. He had no more laughter, he was tired of his good-bloke act. He was fading out and still losing weight. Making love, his collar bones cut across my throat and the points of his pelvis dug into my hips. His face was hollowed like an El Greco saint. 'My partner,' I told her, enjoying my claim on him, 'has been looking almost ill to me. All this is just official bullying. I wish you'd all leave us alone.'

'But before . . . all this, as you call it . . .'

'What's your point, exactly?'

'Just that I can empathise, you know, with your situation. Especially after all you've been through yourself.'

'I don't think anyone can empathise with my situation unless they've been there. Is the death of your only child something you have experienced?'

She refused to take the hint. 'Do you feel you haven't really had the time you need to grieve?'

'Would you mind just asking me what you need to ask me?'

She was cut up by that. She had planned that we would be friends. She tried again.

'The pressure on your partner will be lifted once the coroner's report is completed. Unless, of course, he is implicated in any way. But from the point of view of my enquiries, it's the state of Mr Banks's mind that I need to focus on.'

'Tom was drunk,' I reiterated wearily. 'But not depressed. He wasn't even in a bad mood.'

'I've heard that there were troubles in the marriage.'

'I think everybody knew that but Tom. Don't they say the husband is always the last to know?'

'Coffee break!' This was from Eva, sweeping past with an enquiring face. 'Almond pastries today. What can I get you? And your guest? Hello.' She extended her hand to my pugnacious visitor and sent out a blinding flash of Andalucian charm. I loved her for this interruption. Eva's so full of life, you feel you can warm yourself around her like a fire. Or the devil's barbecue or the seismograph pit.

'Look,' I said to my third inquisitor, 'I can't help you. If you want to talk about emotional intelligence, Tom didn't have any. I don't believe he ever noticed Stella had fallen out of love with him. He was too self-important to be jealous of Matthew, or anyone else, as far as I knew. And his hobby was self-medication, he always popping pills for something. The night he died he was drunk. Matthew came home to me at two thirty-two. That's all I know.'

Eva went for the coffee herself and used it as an excuse to break up our interview. When the woman had gone, I thanked her.

'*De nada*. She was a bitch. I could tell. You don't need people like that in your life.'

'No,' I agreed.

'What did you say, about losing your child?' She said this carefully, not wanting to open a wound.

I remembered that nobody at the Instituto knows my story. They were all strangers when I had arrived, and I didn't want to be notorious. So I never told them. I'd even forgotten that. Rapidly, I sorted out the essential information and gave it to her.

'All this time you never said anything,' she marvelled. 'Some woman, you are.'

'I didn't want to. What could I do, anyway? Come in, say, "Hello, my name is Kim and by the way my husband just killed my son?"'

'I should have felt it.' She put her hand on my shoulder, straight-armed, the gesture that belongs to men, to fathers and sons, sergeants and privates. 'You forgive me, yes?'

'Nothing to forgive. You should forgive me.'

'No!' She flounced with outrage. 'But when you are ready, show me a picture. If you have one.'

'I've got one. You can see it.' The photograph I chose to bring is between some books on the shelves at home, where I can't see it by accident. It's in a folder. I haven't been able to look at it myself yet.

The almond pastry was moist and luscious. In this multinational Utopia, racial dominance can't be denied. Each nationality gets the job it's good at: the

Swiss run the best clinics, the Spanish own the best restaurants, the Chinese set up the most profitable duty-free bazaar and the Scots operate the bakery. Up in Santesteban, three bristle-headed gays from Morningside get up in the small hours of the morning to stuff their ovens with a polyglot succession of baguettes, bagels, pumpernickel, Danish pastries, filo pies, organic sourdough rolls and cotton-wool sandwich loaves.

There were two pastries left on the plate. I thought of Matthew's concave cheeks. 'Can I take these home? He's not eating enough, my old man.'

'Sure, have them,' Eva agreed, with the horsey toss of her head which indicates her very positive approval. It seemed to both of us quite correct to make plans for feeding my man in a time of crisis. 'They'll be nice for breakfast tomorrow. You're worried about him, aren't you? I heard you tell that woman. You're lucky, you've got a good man to worry about. Better than worrying about the other sort, anyway.'

Disclosure was in the air. I decided to push my luck some more. 'What worries me is that he and my friend were the last people who saw her husband before he died. I don't know what to believe about either of them.'

Eva shrugged. 'Believe the best. If you're wrong, accept the worst. That's what my mother says.'

* * *

'I'd like to go to Las Palmas,' I told Matthew. 'I ought to go. If there's more of the journal, it would be great to read it. The eruptions went on for seven years. What I've got only covers the first year, before people left. I'd be surprised if he stayed away all that time. Seven years is unprecedented, as far as history goes anyway. Most eruptive episodes only last a few weeks.'

'How long will you be away?' He seemed to have expected something like this.

'I don't know. They say there are a lot of documents but I don't know what they mean. I might be back in a day.'

We were at home on a Saturday, with nothing planned except a rendezvous with Stella in the evening. It was a moody day, but you can always sit outside here, so we were wandering aimlessly onto the terrace and inside again, to the annoyance of the cat, who wanted us to settle so he could pick a spot to sleep.

'You don't want me to go,' I suggested.

'We've never been apart since we've been together,' he said.

'That's very Irish.' I was amused and touched and irritated at the same time.

'Do you want to be on your own?' he asked.

'This isn't about us,' I answered, but discovered that I was lying. Once more I was looking forward to a hotel room. I wanted that space quite suicidally.

If it pushed him into Stella's arms, I didn't care. All I wanted was to be in a place where I didn't have to think about things like that. I took one of his hands. 'Let me go, love. I need some air. Just a couple of days. I can spin my job out a few weeks longer if I find enough. But it's not just the work, you're right. You're always right, rot you.'

'OK,' he agreed. He looked very tired. 'I suppose it's been tough for you too.' Annoyance flared but I decided to keep quiet. Perhaps I was too accustomed to being the focus of sympathy. I revived the pastries in the oven and made our coffee. 'Bribery,' he accused me.

'You're getting crumbs everywhere.' I pushed his plate towards him. 'And don't talk with your mouth full,' I said. It was the sort of thing I hadn't said for a year. I went over and put my arms around his neck.

CHAPTER 16

The Trial of the Cura Rosario

Gran Canaria is big compared to Los Alcazares. It's the large-scale nightmare of what our island could have become, if the mayors and the artists hadn't taken control. The tourist areas are high-rise rat-mazes several miles from the capital. The capital itself is a weary town, like a tattered guru who has seen too many hopeful travellers to give away his wisdom lightly.

From a distance the museum has a grand Hispanic façade. Close up, the peach-coloured walls are blistered and the decoration is crumbling. It has the embarrassed atmosphere of a place of learning neglected in the midst of a cheap resort.

A timid young man led me to the papers, which were waiting for me in archive boxes in the document room. Twenty-four boxes. They filled a long library table. I called Matthew and Eva to say I would be more than a couple of days.

Soon after I opened the first box, an elderly cleaner appeared and began to dust the boxes. The museum authorities had not quite believed I would be interested until I proved it to them. I soon saw why. From Milo's viewpoint, this trove of documentation was a waste of time.

The first box held the Inquisition Register, written in Latin in a book the size of a paving slab. Its covers were bound in leather, embossed with the episcopal seal. The colour was dark red, unevenly faded; maybe Alcazarean cochineal had been used to dye it. The clerks had covered both sides of the pages, copying and translating from the original drafts in Spanish, which I found on loose parchment pages, very dirty, tied in bundles with fragile black ribbon. I hardly know any Latin; conjugating the present tense of *amo*, I love, is about as far as I can go. At the front of the box was another Spanish translation, maybe fifty years old, done on crackly, thin quarto paper with a smudgy typewriter. That was easy.

The papers recorded the examination of the Cura Rosario by an episcopal tribunal. The bishop and his staff firstly noted that the devastation of his disregarded homeland, and the loss of the Church holding and income, had been caused by extraordinary natural disaster. This, they conceded in the preamble, was a tragic and terrible event but nevertheless the will of God. Was it blasphemous to seek

to understand the pattern of divine purpose in the
Cura's story of exploding mountains and fountains of
fire? They referred to a body of Papal philosophising
and left their question unanswered.

In grand language they ruled out an investigation
of the purpose of human life as outrageous sacrilege.
They sought only to establish the facts of the death
of Fr Domingo and the circumstances of the loss of
the Church lands at Tamiza.

My man had been afraid of this. I turned over
grimy sheets and remembered in his journal the
notes angled at the suspicions of his superiors. It
was for their benefit that he had expanded on the
beliefs of wreckers and stressed that he took the
sacrament to the hermit of Guanapay every month.
He had lived in doubt and fear just as I had done
with Matthew. Perhaps he had written too much.

*Inquiry: Was the Cura aware of any fact which would
have indicated an improper relationship between
Fr Domingo and the flower of Yesto, Dona Maria?*

*Response: Having diligently searched his memory, the
Cura could recall nothing. His belief was that their
relations had been conducted in an entirely proper
way.*

*Inquiry: Was the Cura aware of any time which
Fr Domingo had spent alone with Dona Maria?*

*Response: Only on the occasions when he heard her con-
fession.*

Inquiry: Were Dona Maria's confessions heard in private or in the cathedral?

Response: In private, at the house of her father or her father-in-law.

Inquiry: Was the Cura present in these houses when Dona Maria confessed herself?

Response: Yes.

Inquiry: On every occasion?

Response: The Cura was unable to recall with certainty.

Inquiry: So it was possible that the priest and the young woman had been alone together?

Response: It was possible.

In the beginning, I skimmed the pages, trying to figure out how things had gone for my man. Being honest to the point of stupidity, he had also noted in his journal that he had been unable to say whether Fr Domingo fell or threw himself to his death. He was examined over eight days repetitively, one inquisitor after another, all asking the same questions. The questioners were diabolically tenacious. They followed the smallest discrepancies in his accounts with hysteria, excited to madness like hounds on a scent. They reminded me of myself, obsessing over Matthew and Stella. At a safe distance now, I felt ashamed that I had given in to fear, then and before.

On my second evening away, I was invited to dinner by Margaret Amoore. She took me to a pompous, white-tableclothed restaurant where she looked worn and dusty beside the resplendent waiters. Oddly, I could see Stella becoming like her in another decade or so, belonging to the species of British diplomatic tabby, a finger of misplaced post-imperial authority scratching energetically in foreign soils.

'Mr Race's wife has been lucky,' she observed as our main courses arrived.

'Terry?'

'You saw him after he came back to the island?'

'I didn't know he was back.'

'Oh yes. He left London about five days ago. She recovered, his wife. Out of hospital before he got there.'

'He always said she got better and worse and better again, all those years. I think they were married twenty years, you know.'

'I thought he would be back by now, but passport control at Villanueva's very casual.' She poured me more wine. I realised that this was the business of the evening: she wanted information and was trying to get me drunk. The idea made me smile. A year of island lunches prepared you for something, anyway. I took her for two bottles and a vintage brandy, and said a lot about what Stella's friendship had meant to me.

The dust on the archive papers irritated my hands. I used after-sun cream to protect them and worked on. Over and over the same ground the inquisitors went, sifting through external details to get into the tortured mind of the dead priest. The Cura was made to quote again and again from Fr Domingo's address on the topic of faith, to list the volumes in the church library at Ubrique, to recall the texts the priest had consulted, to rehearse their conversations.

My man eventually learned cunning. He manoeuvred the inquisitors into the decision that saved his people.

Inquiry: *When Fr Domingo examined the people of Yesto, was he satisfied that no heresy had taken hold among them?*

Response: *The Cura could not say. Fr Domingo had come to no final conclusion on that point.*

Inquiry: *Was the Cura himself aware of any heretical practice or belief among the people of Yesto?*

Response: *The Cura considered that his own learning was insufficient to determine such a matter. He was aware that isolated communities were very likely to fall into errors of thought. He had done his utmost to make the word of Our Lord known to his parish but being young and lacking education himself he had struggled with many things. Simple people were still able to have complex difficulties with dogma.*

Inquiry: *Had the Cura observed or heard of any heretical practices in the region?*

Response: *Certainly, all manner of curious superstitions were held by those people.*

Thus he hinted at raging heresy among the *conejeros*, which Fr Domingo had discovered, but concealed from him. And what, he asked his persecutors, could a young and ignorant man like himself hope to achieve alone when hundreds of people conspired against him? If the tribunal decided to get to the root of the matter, the survivors of the inferno should be examined by men with experience, learning and subtle intelligence.

The inquisitors saw their place in ecclesiastical history and leapt at it. At the conclusion of the Cura's ordeal, three ships were immediately sent to Los Alcazares and all the remaining people brought to Gran Canaria. With them came the parish records from Ubrique, Yesto and Aranda.

The rest of the boxes were stuffed with loose parchment sheets tied with ribbon, records of the examination of every single adult saved from the inferno of Los Alcazares. The process went on for years, that was clear from the dates on the pages. The occupations given were touchingly repetitive: fisherman, herdsman, labourer, woman of the hearth. I found drafts in the island dialect, signed with marks, or with whole-hand prints. The priests grilled the peasants on every article of their faith, every detail of their lives. The questions were far beyond their understanding.

I sifted through these papers for four days, almost laughing with pride in my Cura. He had played the sophistication of the episcopalian council against itself and brought his people to safety.

A separate tribunal was set up to pronounce on the death of Fr Domingo and concluded that he had died with ample cause for despair but leaving no positive sign of his state of mind or proof of his intentions; it could not be proved that the priest had lost his faith.

The Cura asked to return to Los Alcazares as soon as it was safe to do so and the bishop, in agreeing, added a commendation of the young man's courage which even at this distance of more than two centuries implied clearly that the kid was deranged. Pinned into the register at the back was a separate page in a less educated hand. The eruptions on the island of Los Alcazares had continued for six further years. When no manifestations had taken place for two years after that, an expedition had been sent to survey the island. They had discovered the Cura still alive, inhabiting a hut close to the spot where his mother's birthplace had been buried. He had lived off fish, cactus flowers and the milk of a single camel which had survived the inferno. He appeared lucid and content with his life, perpetually giving thanks to God for his preservation.

CHAPTER 17

Strangers on the Shore

'You must come back,' said Matthew after I had been away four days.

'There's a mass of stuff here.' I had worked out that sorting through the peasants' testimonies would take at least two weeks.

'Please,' he said. 'You must come back. I miss you. I want to see you.'

This cut me; it didn't sound right. But I had made a pact with myself. I would not be my own inquisitor. I had resolved to be like the Cura and trust the process. God or whatever. Belief was new to me, but I felt I had enough experience of new things to accept it.

'We've got to talk,' he offered in desperation. I was about to challenge him when an e-mail popped up on my screen. It was from Eva and it said, 'Milo wants you back for tomorrow. Big event, you must be here.' So I told Matthew I'd come back and we decided to meet at Placido's.

I went straight from the airport to the Instituto and from there to the dockside at Puerto de la Frontera where Milo had staged a ceremony for the benefit of our local media. The harbour has never been so busy. The expedition ship from the Canarian Oceanographic Institute was moored at the quay and outside the sea wall a jaunty old wherry was riding the swell. This, they told me, housed a meteorological team on their way to check out the gate in the stratosphere over the equator. They would be sharing the Instituto's facilities for a few days. A harbourmaster had been found to tell them to lay offshore while the ferry came and went.

Milo and the mayor of Yesto were photographed for *El Canarien* standing either side of a device that looked like a white fibreglass egg-timer about ten feet high.

Eva distributed our press release which explained, in Spanish and English, that this was the latest thing in vulcanology, a digital sea-bed monitor. A string of them would be dropped into the trench a few kilometres offshore. They would rest on the ocean floor and measure not only the volume of water above but also any changes in the magnetic field of the rock below.

With this device, the smallest change in the sea

level could be recorded. The store of human knowledge would be increased; the boundaries of science would be advanced. Eva's original draft had also suggested that the future of Los Alcazares and all its inhabitants would be safeguarded 'as far as possible'. Milo had deleted all this, demanding, 'Are you mad? Do you want to sabotage everything?'

A team photograph was then arranged, with all of us gathered around the monitor as if we were pagan worshippers and it was our idol. Eva told the reporters how much more accurate the new monitors would be than the old device out on the cliffs by Jimena. She did not mention that the sea level is now only part of the picture, because if Tarfaya is getting ready to blow again the land may be rising relative to the sea, pushed up like a pie crust by the hot stuff underneath.

Milo made a speech. There was a decent crowd to address; I could see some of the geothermal boys and the senior students from the new Puerto de la Frontera school. We had been introduced to a team of technicians from the instrument manufacturer. A posse of the mayor's faction, uneasy in the company, kept an authoritative distance at the side of the gathering. Passing tourists stopped to see what was happening.

Milo started with thanks to the mayor and praise for his understanding and foresight. 'He means they're paying half from the municipal budget,' Eva whispered to me. 'They fixed it up while you were away.'

Smiling kindly at the children, Milo explained that the earth's crust is thinnest at the depths of the oceans, so, if you want to listen to Mother Earth's heartbeat, that's the place to do it. Then he proclaimed that this project was as important to the world as the volcanic monitoring schemes of Hawaii and Japan. All the great questions about our planet, why the dinosaurs died out, why the Ice Ages began, why the weather changes, how life itself was created, all these could be answered by the study of volcanoes. The children looked at the mayor with admiration. 'He's grown about ten centimetres already,' Eva commented. 'If Milo puffs him up much longer he'll explode.'

Next came some sober stuff about the laws of geophysics and the potential role of computer science in olinometry, gravimetry and magnetometry. Soon, Milo promised, a giant necklace of monitors would be strung along the ocean trench right across the junction of the African and Eurasian tectonic plates, linked by fibre-optic cables to his central computer in Tenerife. Then he read some poetry, made a bow and stepped down.

About twenty of us made up the selected party who boarded the explorer ship to watch the monitor being lowered to rest on the pulse-point of the planet. A pair of divers went down to guide it underwater. Eva waved to them, the wind whipping her long hair as she leaned over the rail.

'He didn't say anything about the seismograph. There is a seismograph in that thing, isn't there?'

'Of course. And of course he's not going to talk about earthquakes in front of half the tourists in Puerto. Nor are we.'

'Or global warming, rising sea levels, surging volcanic activity all over the world . . .'

'No. We don't talk about that stuff. We talk about the advancement of science and finding out why the dinosaurs died. Little boys love dinosaurs, all over the world.' Eva nudged me and pointed towards the stern, where Mark and Suzanne were standing close together. She seemed radiantly pleased about something.

I realised I felt good. I am like a baby now, when it finds its toes and fingers, fascinated by features of myself I've never seen before. A potential global catastrophe was a good-enough excuse for a day out. Maybe Stella was right; boats are magic, and there was something primevally soothing about being rocked in the bosom of the ocean. And I was missing Dima.

'Where's Dima? I didn't see him on the quay. Did he go on a trip?'

'You could say that,' she said gaily, twisting her hair to keep the wind from tangling it.

'Where'd he go?'

Eva shrugged, bright-eyed. 'Who knows? Back to Moscow, maybe.'

'He went home?'

'Maybe he went home. Milo got rid of him. He was such an asshole. Aren't you glad? No more stinking underpants around the place.'

'He got rid of Dima because he annoyed you?'

'And he was a security problem, you know. He was going to get drunk and tell every bar that hadn't already banned him that Tarfaya was going up. And, yes, I asked him.'

Milo came lurching across the deck and put his arms around our shoulders. 'A great day. For the project, for the science, and for us. All down to you two. Have I thanked you properly?'

'You will,' Eva promised him.

'I will. Count on it, I will. You must come to Tenerife soon. Come and listen to Teide for a change. See if you can get the old man going, eh?'

'Promises, promises.'

'They want a full report in Madrid. An event-probability tree, computer modelling the data we're getting. Something to wake them up in Brussels. Kim, you're not thinking of leaving us, are you?'

'Uh . . .' With my CV, I'm not in the habit of thinking specifically about the future. It was alarming suddenly to be asked to declare my intentions towards my life. 'Well – is that thing going to make me redundant?'

'No, no!' He seemed genuinely dismayed. 'I'm relying on you, really. Vital to have a proper technical translation. Talk to Eva, work out whatever you want. I want to knock their socks off in Brussels. There's a move to set up a European commission, but they're so slow. Damn Italians. Brussels has to make some decisions. I need a budget.' His arms were still around our shoulders, his hands were squeezing as he spoke, but Milo wasn't really with us. He was already rehearsing his pitch to Madrid. But as I moved away, he dropped his arm to Eva's waist, an interrogative movement, and after the proper moment of hesitation, she let him pull her closer.

* * *

Placido was standing in the middle of the bar talking to people I couldn't see, throwing his hand about. He was agitated. I had never seen anything get to Placido like that. He was facing seawards and the red of the sun was glowing on the tiled wall. The door was open. He was looking out on the bay.

The yacht had left the solitude of the sea. It was slipping past the wreck, coming our way. I turned away from the sun to watch it. A strange boat hasn't landed here for years.

It was a very average little yacht. There are hundreds like it in the islands, a standardised charter fleet which moors in rows in the big marinas. Next year we'll probably have twenty yachts like this one outside the Lumumba. They have engines, but it was gliding in under its jib.

A trick of this bar is to make you feel almost as cut off from the rest of the world as if you are in a cinema. If you try, you can hear cars draw up outside, but your ears are never tuned in that direction. So when I sensed a presence at my table and took my eyes away from the sea, I saw Stella and was stunned. Then my stomach froze over.

'God,' she said, sitting down, 'You know you've gone white?'

'I was waiting for Matthew,' I defended myself, in terror of what she would say next. She looked different, disarranged. Half her hair was dragged up in a band on top of her head and the shorts weren't made for her kind of legs.

She reached over the table and took my hand. 'I know. He'll be along. Forgive me, Baby. I couldn't call you, I'm sure they're listening in on the phones.' I must have looked dopey because she spelled it out for me. 'He called you because I asked him. I wanted to see you and it had to be here. I'm off, Baby. I can't hack this any more. All this pressure. I just had to see you, I couldn't leave without saying goodbye.'

'Where . . .'

'Well, Barbados, I suppose.' In lighting a cigarette, she nodded towards the sea and flashed me a

smile. 'A girl's gotta do what a girl's gotta do, eh?'
The yacht was sliding alongside the rocks, its sail
folding itself obediently as it ran down. I saw a man
in a blue shirt come forward and lean over the bow
to throw a light anchor plumb into a crevice.

'Terry?'

'We couldn't tell you, Baby, you do understand?'

'That you were leaving?'

'What happened. We decided we just couldn't lay
that on you. I know you asked. I nearly told you; you
saw it, I know you did. But Matthew was right.
You're carrying too much already, you didn't need
any more from me.'

'You and Matthew . . .' I tried to catch a few
images from my memories of the days since Tom's
death, which were reconfiguring in a blur.

'We had time to work it out, before the guardia
piled in.' The cigarette had burned down to the tip.
She pulled a face as she crushed the butt, then lit up
another, the lighter flame flicking in her cupped
hand like a lizard's tongue. 'Broad shoulders, he's
got. I must say, I didn't expect that. I never liked
him, you know. It's quite mutual so I guess that's
fair enough. I thought we covered up pretty well.
He's done this for me but really he only did it for
you.'

'Done what, exactly? I thought you were . . .'

She giggled, shaking her head as if I'd said something incredibly stupid. 'You told me what you

thought, remember? Now you can believe me. It was nothing.'

'Look,' she folded her arms the way she does from habit. She started to do this when her star began to wane, a trick to squeeze up her breasts to look their best.

'Matthew drove Tom back to the villa, right? I followed them. Tom was out of his head, violent, I couldn't be alone with him, he didn't know what he was doing. Matthew was worrying about you, saying he had to go . . .' She exhaled and pulled her jaw down in a grimace.

I saw that she envied me, impure and simple. The tendons in her neck were like wires. For the first time I noticed that she was looking older.

'So Terry came back with me that night and Matthew pissed off. Which started another almighty argument. So I told him to get out, Tom, I told Tom. I told him it was over. God, he was so stupid. I honestly think he'd never noticed there was anything wrong. All those months he'd been making me wretched, he hadn't caught on. He just stood there like an animal, a fucking great cow or something. Then he just staggered out and got into his car and passed out. We thought he was just drunk, of course. He must have taken the pills already, stupid man.'

'So how did he end up halfway down the hill?'

She shrugged. 'Don't ask me. Terry and I had

better things to do than hang around watching him snoring away all night.'

'You and Terry?'

'As of then, yes. Baby, I was lonely. I mean really lonely, lonely like falling down on the road and starving to death. You know what I mean. In a bad marriage, you think you're going to die of loneliness.' There were tears standing in her eyes.

Had Terry helped her heave Tom into his car, let off the brake and shove it down the hill to kill him? I was high on belief now; I let the question go easily. 'Bad marriage.' I felt her pain, and thought of all the years when she had felt mine. 'I had you, that's how I survived.'

'Well, I had Terry.' She dragged deep and blew out the smoke. 'And you had Matthew. So there we were, all sorted.'

'Do you mean if I'd been there for you it would have been different?'

'No.' Again, she reached her free hand over to squeeze one of mine. 'It would have been nice, but it didn't happen, so that's all right. So, Terry and I got out of bed just in time to hear that fool start the car up. Couldn't exactly go out and stop him, could we? We didn't hear the crash. Then it was next morning. He was dead, and it wasn't looking too good for Terry. He's an innocent really, he hasn't been out in the world like us.'

'You thought that . . .'

'I can't remember whose idea it was. But you do see, it was going to be a nuisance for Terry. For both of us, if anyone knew he'd been there with me. And Matthew had you for an alibi. So we decided if there was any trouble we'd just . . . muddy the water. But you do see . . .'

'Yes,' I assured her, mostly for the sake of peace to think. 'I see. And Terry's wife?'

'That? Well, that was a gift of the gods. Oh, he did see her. She did relapse, whatever it's called, but only for a week or two. He did go home, he wanted to, before we set off. She's just the same, apparently. And she's on his passport but she won't be travelling anywhere, so it's all quite convenient. He's gutted to leave his own boat, of course, but it could be months before they decide on an inquest and we can't wait around. I'm going crazy here with all this. Be pleased, Babe. If I clear off, they'll take the heat off Matthew.'

I saw one of her bags, a holdall stuffed to splitting, resting by the wall. She could have been any of the barelegged *Rough Guide* hopefuls who get off the ferry. Estelle Mahoney, and her neat little dresses, had left me and I hadn't even noticed.

Terry was standing in the stern now, looking alternately at the sinking sun, the waves on the rocks and the pennant at his masthead. 'He's fussing about the tide,' she said, and it was almost fond. 'Such an old woman, sometimes.'

I thought of Matthew, his frayed spirits and cutting bones, the affection I could have given him so much earlier if I had understood. 'Matthew's been falling apart. I've been wondering what the hell was wrong with him.'

'Oh, he'll be OK, Baby Doll. You'll be OK.' She was talking with distracted assurance, watching Terry scanning the shoreline, enjoying the fact that he was looking for her. 'You can have the Residencias, if you like,' she said suddenly, as if the realisation that she hurt us had finally hit and she wanted to offer compensation. 'Look, I'll give you the keys now. Matthew can run it, if he wants a proper job. I'll do all the papers when we get somewhere. I'll write something now, if you like. It's not a bad little business . . .' She put down her cigarette to reach into one of the holdall's pockets and brought out her key-ring.

'You let Matthew be suspected of murder . . . you let us all be suspected . . . that's just – wrong.'

'I told you, he agreed. Baby, what is the matter with you? You could see it that way, I suppose, if you wanted to be judgmental. I was just thinking of keeping Terry out of trouble, that's all. Maybe I didn't do the right thing.'

'They wrecked our apartment. All these weeks we've been interviewed and questioned over and over . . .'

'They had to send that bitch out, the insurance,

they have to try to cheat you, but I know they'll have to pay in the end. The policy's quite clear and he assigned it to me. That'll be my fuck-you money.'

'. . . And you set up this whole conspiracy and you dragged Matthew into it and you lied to me . . .' This was a new anger, clean and clear. Just for once my feelings had managed to line up with my morals. It was quite a buzz.

'What about me?' she rejoined aggressively. 'Spare a thought for me, if you can. I've had more hassle than any of you. It was a bad accident, there was nothing else to do. Bad things happen sometimes. I shouldn't have to tell you that.'

Awkwardly, she put out the cigarette so it snapped at the filter and carried on smouldering. She stood up. 'I suppose I knew when you came out here with Matthew it would end up being him or me,' she said. 'Good thing I'm leaving, eh?'

'Don't say that.'

'It wasn't a conspiracy, as you call it. It was just the way things happened.' Terry had seen her and was waving with impatience. Already, even at this distance, he seemed less carefree. 'Look at him,' she said with routine fondness. 'Can't keep him waiting any longer, got to go.' She bent down and kissed me on both cheeks. 'It's been magic. Stay in touch, yeah?'

She took off her sandals and carried them by their heels in one hand, then picked up her bag with the other. 'Goodbye,' was all I managed as she stepped out on the rocks and began to pick her way towards the water's edge. One of the boys ran out from the bar to help her. Terry had the boat's ladder over the side and between them they handed her aboard. She still stepped as delicately as a deer. Her blouse fluttered in the wind. I probed around my heart for signs of my old enchantment, but it wasn't there.

I saw them kiss, then disappear at the stern. Over the purr of the evening sea the motor droned, then Terry appeared again, going forward to give the rope a couple of twitches to dislodge his anchor. Turning in the narrow channel with the swelling tide was difficult but he did it; after all, it wasn't his boat.

When they had passed the wreck he started getting the sails up. In the failing light it was soon impossible to see any more than the two triangles and the pale hull rising and falling on the swell.

Placido's terrace is on the sea side of the bar, so the building screens it from the road and you can't see people coming until they appear in the doorway. All the same, I knew that Matthew was there, out on the road, and I took my eyes away from the sinking sun and the vanishing yacht to watch for him.

He came out of the doorway. I remembered the day Liam ran out of school. Matthew was a new soul now, I could see him for himself. He looked older and he was moving stiffly, as if recovering from a great adventure.

'Has she gone?' He took the same chair as Stella, dragging it diagonally over the gravel as if he hardly felt he had the right to it. I didn't get my kiss. He was scared of me but I felt I could put that right.

'That's their boat.' The yacht was a small, pale triangle at the edge of the bay, heeling over as it caught the strong wind from the open sea.

Matthew wasn't impressed. 'I thought nothing would ever come between Terry and his own boat. That's what makes me think it is possible, that they killed Tom.'

'Yes, it's possible.' I set out my new theory. 'Anything's possible. We have to choose. I'll choose not to know, for the time being.'

He didn't understand, but it didn't bother me. He went back to clearing up the ground between us, saying, 'She decided it was going to be easier to get Terry away from his boat than to take me away from you.'

'So she did try.' I wasn't quite ready to start living without proof.

'Oh yes, she tried. You were right.'

'So you knew I knew?'

He couldn't resist saying, 'I thought you knew I knew you knew,' in his Cary Grant voice. We laughed, then he moved to the chair beside me and I got my kiss.

'My head was messed up, I couldn't work out what to do. She was your friend, she was in trouble . . .'

'Well,' I said, 'she was in trouble, anyway.'

'Yeah.' That sound was warm, like the noises he makes in foreplay. I felt he wanted to put his arm around my shoulders, so I picked up his hand and settled it in the right place. Another reason lovers don't come to Placido's is that they're so into each other they break up everyone's concentration.

I still wanted his story. 'Was it an accident? Or do you think they . . .'

'No. Not Terry. She hadn't reeled him in then; he'd never have been up for it. Tom was too far gone to do anything sensible. I think it was an accident. They do happen.'

'Good and bad.' I let my cheek lie against his arm. His skin smelt sharp like lemon. I wanted to smell it forever.

'I could never get that about Stella. Why she always had to move on. She's got to keep moving on now, hasn't she?'

'What shall we do?' I asked. I didn't want to talk about Stella any more, not for a long time, maybe not ever again. 'What do you want to do? Stay here? Go back? Take that job?'

He couldn't say anything; I could feel his conscience gagging him. I knew the feeling. 'You want to take that job,' I told him. 'Have you got your passport?'

'Uh-huh.'

'Well, go. I order you.'

'What about you?'

'I'll be OK. I'll stay, we'll work it out. Milo wants to keep me, there's work here and I like it. We can renew the lease on the apartment . . .'

'I've always fancied one of the houses in Ubrique,' he said suddenly. 'With the courtyard in the middle. You could have a telescope on top and look at the stars.'

'You never said . . .'

'I didn't know how things were going to work out.'

I settled back against his body and for a while we watched the show. The yacht had disappeared but the trace of its wake could still be seen on the surface of the water even though the waves were rising. In the sky, the colour flooded up suddenly as the sun dipped into the horizon, underlighting all the little clouds with pink. All the people in Placido's murmured.

Matthew said, 'What are they called, those clouds? Cumulo-nimbus or strato-something?'

'Shut up,' I advised him. 'You don't want to know and I don't want to remember. Just shut up and let it happen.'

GETTING HOME

Celia Brayfield

**THERE IS ONLY ONE RULE IN A SUBURB –
NEVER TRUST YOUR NEIGHBOURS**

Westwick, the ultimate suburb. Nothing ever happens in
Westwick; that's why people live there. Nice people, like
Stephanie Sands. Loving husband, adorable son, dream
job and a beautiful garden – life is just about perfect for
Stephanie until the day her husband is kidnapped.

Big mistake, losing your husband in the suburbs. The
neighbours turn nasty. The TV totty sees Stephanie as a
media victim and the totty's husband sees Stephanie as
'lonely' – codeword for desperate. Stephanie discovers that
she isn't the kind of woman to take this lying down.
Suddenly it's a jungle out there – adultery, blackmail,
sleaze in high places and lust on the lawns, until Westwick
scrambles the helicopters and takes to the streets with an
army of eco-warriors in the hilarious live-TV climax.

Getting Home has outraged upholders of Volvo culture
everywhere. It's the funniest and wickedest novel yet from
one of our most gifted modern storytellers.

'Deliciously comic – lightning flashes of wit and scalpel-
sharp observation'
Daily Mail

'With a sharp wit and snappy dialogue Brayfield has
produced a very funny, cleverly plotted novel that displays
Fay Weldon's understanding of the pleasure to be derived
from seeing the bad get their just desserts'
Daily Telegraph

<u>HARVEST</u>

Celia Brayfield

'Cunningly plotted, extremely well-written and
compulsively readable'
Beryl Bainbridge

The lover, Grace, clever and passionate, ran away to find
new happiness, but can't escape her guilt. The wife, Jane,
loves her children, her brilliant career and her French
farmhouse, but wakes up crying and alone. The daughter,
Imogen, is beautiful and talented, but is also a wild child
hungry for revenge.

Three women who all made the same mistake – loving
Michael Knight: a TV star, a public figure but also in
private, a serial adulterer driven to destroy the women
whose love he craves.

Now, as friends and family gather to celebrate his birthday,
Michael reaps what he has sown.

'A great black comedy'
Daily Express

'The fierceness with which she manipulates her characters
and plot and traces the psychology of revenge and female
dependence grabs the attention'
Sunday Times

'A cool thriller, cleverly overlaid with issues of power and
deception as it heads to its shattering conclusion'
Woman's Journal

Other bestselling Warner titles available by mail:

☐ Getting Home	Celia Brayfield	£5.99
☐ Harvest	Celia Brayfield	£5.99
☐ Pearls	Celia Brayfield	£5.99
☐ Heat	Sally Emerson	£5.99
☐ Friends Like These	Victoria Routledge	£5.99
☐ All That She Wants	Maeve Haran	£5.99
☐ Soft Touch	Maeve Haran	£5.99

The prices shown above are correct at time of going to press. However, the publishers reserve the right to increase prices on covers from those previously advertised without prior notice.

WARNER BOOKS

WARNER BOOKS
Cash Sales Department, P.O. Box 11, Falmouth, Cornwall, TR10 9EN
Tel: +44 (0) 1326 569777. Fax: +44 (0) 1326 569555
Email: books@barni.avel.co.uk

POST AND PACKING:
Payments can be made as follows: cheque, postal order (payable to Warner Books) or by credit cards. Do not send cash or currency.

All U.K. Orders   **FREE OF CHARGE**
E.E.C. & Overseas   25% of order value

Name (Block Letters) _____

Address_____

_____

Post/zip code:_____

☐ Please keep me in touch with future Warner publications

☐ I enclose my remittance £_____

☐ I wish to pay by Visa/Access/Mastercard/Eurocard

Card Expiry Date

_____